SEA

of

DOUBT

CAN YOU EVER ESCAPE YOUR SECRETS

P.L. JONAS

Black Rose Writing | Texas

ISBN: 978-1-68513-494-5
LIBRARY OF CONGRESS CONTROL NUMBER:
PUBLISHED BY BLACK ROSE WRITING
www.blackrosewriting.com

Printed in the United States of America
Suggested Retail Price (SRP) $20.95

Sea of Doubt is printed in EB Garamond

*As a planet-friendly publisher, Black Rose Writing does its best to eliminate unnecessary waste to reduce paper usage and energy costs, while never compromising the reading experience. As a result, the final word count vs. page count may not meet common expectations.

To my siblings, Karen and Mike, who have supported me
through all my creative endeavors.

ACKNOWLEDGEMENTS

This book came as a surprise to me, since I'd been telling people I don't write series. And here I am with the second book completed. I don't think it would ever have happened without my family, friends, and readers who had been supporting me since I started writing novels. With special thanks to Linda C. and Pam M. for their undying support. You have stuck with me reading all of my books in early and later drafts and giving me valuable feedback, not to mention listening to me as I talked endlessly about my stories and lifting me out of moments of self-doubt. As always, I thank all of my alpha/beta readers and reviewers for their time and effort in making this book possible. I deeply appreciated their thoughtful input.

SEA
of
DOUBT

CHAPTER ONE
ELLEN

August 1960, Starlight Bay, California

The dreaded first day of high school was two days away. I intended to enjoy what was left of the summer break and spend as much time possible on my daily beach outings. As I went out the sliding glass doors, I found Mom leaning against the terrace railing facing the ocean.

"I'm off for my walk," I said.

She turned around and smiled at me. Her shoulder-length, dark blonde hair swirled about in the breeze. "That new two-piece bathing suit looks smart on you, Ellen. The pale green color brings out the golden specks in your brown eyes."

"Thank you."

I had pleaded for the new bikini, but she claimed I was too young, though I would turn thirteen in two weeks. She said Sandra Dee hadn't worn a bikini in her movies and she was older. I adored the actress and even had my curly blonde hair cut into the same short bob.

"Want to join me?"

"Not now, honey. You enjoy yourself. Be back in time to dress for dinner."

"I will."

Each day I asked, and she always had a different excuse. I wondered if she was unhappy too. With my beach bag over my shoulder and my straw hat securely tied under my chin, I headed down the wooden steps that led to the beach. I stopped and turned to wave at her.

"Do you have your inhaler with you?" Mom shouted.

"Yes." I pointed to my bag, then jumped from the next-to-last step onto the planked walkway and skipped to the point the high tide reached each night. In the wet sand, my feet left footprints until the waves washed them away. Standing with my back to the ocean, I stared at our new house jutting out from the hillside.

Mom had gone inside and my body relaxed. I longed for more freedom. Since we moved here, she watched my every move. Was she seeking a sign I was happy? If she had asked me, I would have given her a resounding, "No." Just like Dad didn't ask if I wanted to move three thousand miles away from our home in Massachusetts. He'd said we would all be happier living on the California coast.

I was already happy. I'd always been happy, until Dad announced he was selling the only home I'd ever known, Rothmorton Hall. Granted, the enormous mansion had cold unfeeling marble floors and rooms so big our voices echoed throughout. The private school had caring teachers and all my friends attended. It made no sense to be uprooted and dragged across the country.

I missed everyone. Ben, the chauffeur who made me laugh. The housemaids who giggled and whispered in the halls. The French chef, and his staff who prepared feasts for us every day, and the gardeners who gave me flowers. We ate breakfast and lunch together like a family. I never felt alone. Daddy would come home from work each day, or he worked from home.

Here, it's just Mom and Mrs. Chambers, our housekeeper who I've known for as long as I could remember. I called her Mrs. C. She moved with us and cooks now with my mom's help. Her late husband was a master chef in the old days before she worked at Rothmorton Hall. The food's good. But not like our former chef's.

And Dad? That's the saddest part of moving here. He hasn't spent much time with me. Always busy working on his new business. Maybe he was going through that mid-life crisis I'd heard about. Trying to find himself by starting his own company, instead of the old family business he'd inherited a year after I was born.

My mom had been my tutor. I used to call her Miss Danes. When she married Dad, she adopted me. She's the only mother I'd ever known and a beautiful, kind, and loving person. Turned out, she was also an orphan, so we had something in common to connect us.

Before they were married, I called Dad, Uncle Hugh. They explained it all when I was six years old, but it confused me. Now, it no longer matters. They've been wonderful parents and I would always love them.

Aunt Sylvi had also been my nurse for a while. I haven't seen her in a few months. She was my real mom's sister. That was another confusing story of how she had become my nurse that I'd put out of my mind.

Walking along the sand watching the tide going out exhilarated me. The warmth from the morning sun comforted me as I dragged my toes along the water's edge. A shiny iridescent seashell peeked up from the sand. I dug it out and rolled it over, making sure it was empty. Its inhabitant had long since vacated, so it could become a part of my growing collection. I cleaned and dried it on my beach towel and shoved it into the bag.

We moved here in July, and none of my closest friends in Plymouth had responded to my letters. I feared I'd end up completely friendless.

Finally, out of eyesight of the house, a curly-haired dog with its long ears flapping, came bounding down the sandy slope toward me.

"Well, hello there, little doggy. Where did you come from?"

Running behind the dog was a girl about my age. She whistled. "Bentley!"

Bentley ignored his mistress calling and sniffed all around my feet and legs, wagging his tail. He let me pet him, then he licked my hand, making it all slimy.

"He's not bothering me." I wiped my hand on the towel in my bag.

The girl stopped short about ten feet and clapped her hands. Bentley turned around, his tongue hanging from his mouth, but didn't move an inch.

"I'm sorry," the girl said, "he's always interested in new people. I'm Dana. Didn't you just move into that new house on the beach?" Dana tucked her chin-length straight brown hair behind an ear, despite the wind blowing it every which way. Even her uneven bangs.

She wore stained white shorts and a short-sleeved, blue and white striped shirt, and those rubber thongs I'd seen at the local convenience store. Mom would never allow me to wear anything that cheap.

"How do you do? I'm El-Ellie. Yes, we moved here last month." I don't know why I said my name that way. Maybe because I'd always wanted a nickname, so I gave myself one.

Bentley finally went over to Dana and she clipped a leash to his collar while talking to him low. "You know you aren't supposed to run out of the apartment without your leash." She looked at me. "I've been hunting him down for an hour. Almost two miles from home!" She let out an exasperated breath.

"He must like the beach."

"Yeah. Too much. So, where'd you move from?"

"The East Coast. What kind of dog is Bentley? I've always wanted a dog."

"He's a golden cocker spaniel. We're from upstate New York. Moved out here last year. So, where on the East Coast?"

"Near Boston."

"Oh, is that why you speak different?"

"Different?"

"You know, sort of formal."

"I went to private schools." I'd never thought about my speech sounding different. The school didn't allow slang, and I'd been taught to enunciate words clearly. Maybe that's what she meant.

"No kidding. Well, stick with me. I'll show ya the ropes. You wouldn't want people to think you were stuck up."

"Uh, no, I wouldn't want that." I hoped she was wrong.

"You wanna dog?"

"I'd love to have a dog?"

"Well, we got two dogs, Bentley, and his wife, Dotty. She had a litter of pups. We already promised most of them to buyers, but still have a couple left."

"They're for sale? Do they all look like Bentley?"

"Mom sells them for extra money. The puppies are different colors. Dotty is black and white."

"I would need to ask my parents. I couldn't have a pet because of my asthma. My condition is much better here. So maybe."

"Asthma? Don't know much about that. Ask them, okay?" She narrowed her greenish eyes.

"I will. Are you in high school?" I shaded my eyes from the sun.

"Freshman at Starlight Bay High. You?"

"Me too. This is the first I'll be attending a public school." I tried to hide my excitement that I'd met someone from school.

"Cool. What's your first class in the morning?"

"English."

"I'll save you a seat if I get there first. Gotta get home now. We got a long way back. Nice meeting ya. Come on Bentley." The dog wagged his tail and looked over at Ellen.

"See you at school." I waved.

Dana waved before heading uphill with her dog towards the road into town.

I dilly dallied a while longer, walking farther down the beach, found a place on the sand and opened my notebook. I wrote about my day, meeting Dana and her dog Bentley, and started a new poem. Dinnertime beckoned when my stomach rumbled. I picked up my things and headed back to the house.

Once on the terrace, I wiped the sand from my feet before entering, carried my sandals, and tiptoed down the hall.

My new bedroom faced the ocean with floor to ceiling glass windows. Sometimes I would sit by the window and get lost in the rolling waves and the seagulls flying by. The room was large enough. Not the grand size of my bedroom back east, which had an adjacent study room that had been my playroom when I was little.

The decorator for this new bedroom chose soft pastels of pink and aqua walls and bedding. She hired an artist who painted a mural of a fantasy woodland scene, like something from a fairytale with fairies flying in the mist. It mirrored a little of the pine-laden hills that rose from behind the nearby town of Starlight Bay. Although no one consulted me on what I wanted on my wall, it brought me some joy.

From my beach bag, I retrieved the new shell and placed it on the bookshelf among the myriad of other shells I'd found since moving here. The new shell dwarfed the others. With a smile, I twirled around the room on my way to take a shower. Having met a classmate, my mood had improved, and I was less nervous about my first day at school.

Wrapped in a luxurious Turkish towel, I entered the spacious closet where my clothes hung on double rows of padded silk hangars. The closet was a vast improvement over the antique wardrobes at Rothmorton Hall, with plenty of vacant space to fill with future shopping sprees. I sat on the stool in front of the vanity table against the farthest wall. Peering into the large mirror surrounded by small lights, I frowned at the red patches on my face.

"Oh dear, I still got sunburned wearing that dumb hat."

I turned around to contemplate the new dresses Mom bought in Boston before we moved. My hand lingered on the pink silk shantung with a wide satin sash and full skirt. Would I ever have a reason to wear it here? I sighed and chose the yellow cotton pique sundress, which matched my hair. It had a full skirt over a petticoat layered with ruffles.

As I towel-dried my curls, my mind went to the girl from the beach, Dana, hoping she would become a friend. What did she wear to her dinners at home? I sensed that Dana's family was in a lower financial class than us. But then, most people seemed to be in a lower financial class. Dad was very wealthy and he and Mom had always been selective of who I socialized with. What would they think of Dana? All clean and dressed, I headed for the dining room where Mom and Mrs. C waited for me.

"I love that dress on you." Mom smiled while filling my plate with sauteed fish and fragrant rice.

"Thanks." I lifted the plate and sniffed. "Hmm, isn't the smell of basil and rosemary divine?"

"It is, and you look nice, dearie," Mrs. C said. I loved her lilting Irish accent. When we lived in the mansion, she was in charge of the whole place.

Now she just managed this house. Mom says she's like family. But Dad still pays her salary.

"Thanks Mrs. C." I turned to Mom. "When is Dad coming home?"

Mom pursed her mouth. "Not sure, honey. Sylvi is due tomorrow. Won't that be nice? We haven't seen her for months."

I ignored how she hadn't actually answered my question about Dad. "Finally! I've missed Aunt Sylvi. Oh, and I met someone today. A girl. She's a freshman too."

"How nice. Where does she live?"

"I don't know, in the town somewhere. Does it matter?" I sighed at the question.

"Of course not. I mean, I don't care, but you know your father always asks."

"Right. Anyway, she has the most beautiful dog. His name is Bentley. Just like our old car."

"What kind of dog?"

"A cocker spaniel. One of those golden ones. The female dog had a litter. They have two puppies available. I want one."

"You haven't seen them yet, have you?"

Mrs. C offered me dinner rolls from a silver basket. I took two.

"No. I've wanted a pet for the longest. My asthma has been under control since we arrived here. Have you noticed?"

Mom stopped eating and looked up. "I guess I haven't. That's an excellent sign. We might need to check with your doctor first."

"I don't have a doctor here."

"I mean, I'll call your doctor back in Plymouth to find out. Yes, we need to find you a local physician."

I squirmed with excitement. "Oh goody. I sure hope he says I can."

"Don't get your hopes up too much. We'll ask Sylvi when she gets here. The dog would have to be properly house-trained. Your father wouldn't want this newly decorated house damaged by a puppy."

How could I not be hopeful about the prospect of having my first dog? I remembered the gray and white cat I used to feed outside the kitchen door years back. She'd disappeared, and they never found her. I cried for days.

Still, I missed the mansion and all the servants and my big birthday party each year that hundreds of people attended. That wouldn't happen this year. I stuck my lower lip out.

"What's that look for?" Mom narrowed her eyes.

"Nothing, just thinking about my birthday coming up." I pushed the rice around on my plate.

"Oh sweetheart, I know it will be different this year. But we just moved here and don't know anyone yet. And your father—"

"I know. He's never home."

"He will be here on your birthday. He promised."

"Right. Not that he keeps his promises."

Mom didn't reply to that. What could she say? He hadn't. He's changed.

CHAPTER TWO
DEE

The warm ocean breeze washed over me with my arms stretched out wide as I took in a deep breath and gazed over the terrace railing. It hadn't taken me long to appreciate our new California beach house. It overlooked the long stretch of sandy beach below, with the roar of the ocean waves filling the air. The full skirt of my sundress whipped against my legs and my ponytail flapped against my neck.

Ellen dashed off for her morning beach walk with barely a greeting. She'd been sleeping in practically every day and missing breakfast. Almost as tall as me, I couldn't believe she would be a teenager in two weeks.

My life as Mrs. Hugh Roth and mother to Ellen, who I adopted after our marriage six years ago, had been a full one. Social and charitable activities demanded more of me than I could stomach, and the fear of losing my true self haunted me. What happened to the farm girl who lived in awe of everything? Living in luxury, waited on by servants, wearing designer fashions and being chauffeured in fancy automobiles, had changed me. When I looked in the mirror, I saw a carefully coiffed and elegantly clothed clone of my former self.

I had continued to tutor Ellen for another two years until the invention of a portable asthma inhaler. She could attend school with other children without her nurse present. Although Sylvi still lived with us and served as both aunt and nurse, I convinced Hugh to put Ellen in a private school nearby. Ellen thrived at connecting with the world after she'd been a virtual captive at home. She made friends with ease and gained popularity with her peers.

I enjoyed living at Rothmorton Hall, with all the amenities and servants at my beck and call. However, it lacked the homey environment I thought necessary for raising a child. Due to the terrible events during my first winter as Ellen's tutor, Hugh and I considered moving. But four more years passed before Hugh was ready to make major changes to our lives.

Hugh opened the West Coast office of his own company, Roth Enterprises, in San Francisco two years ago. Sylvi and Jack Clayton had moved right away. Jack helped to set up the company, and Sylvi worked as a part-time nurse in a hospital.

We rushed to put Rothmorton Hall on the market. Who knew it would take two years to find a buyer for the mansion? Hugh had been flying back and forth until this summer. Just as well, for Ellen had graduated eighth grade and it would be a better transition for her to start school here.

The excitement and adventure of moving to California still made me lightheaded. I hoped we'd made the right decision. In a few short weeks of arriving, Ellen and I had settled into our new surroundings despite her resistance. Of course, it helped that we convinced Mrs. Chambers to come with us.

It worried me that Ellen might have trouble adapting to a new environment and attending public school. The closest private school for girls was too far for daily commutes, even if we kept Ben as our chauffeur. I refused to board her because she would have felt abandoned.

Since moving to the beach house, Ellen showed her unhappiness by sleeping in, moping about all day, or taking long walks on the beach. She missed her friends. Some days, she would watch television in her room for hours. I didn't complain because she needed time to adapt.

Hugh had promised the move would bring us closer together since he wouldn't be flying back and forth from San Francisco to Plymouth. But so far, he'd only been home four nights.

He insisted we start fresh with everything new. First, he hired the famous architect Frank Lloyd Wright to design the beach house. Next, a decorator to help me once they built it. But the decorator did most of the work. I made a special trip here to review and approved her expert choices. By the time Ellen, Mrs. Chambers and I moved here, the house was ready. What did I know about decorating in a style Hugh would be comfortable in?

"Mrs. Roth?" Mrs. Chambers' voice startled me out of my thoughts. She refused to call me Dee. Old conditioning, I guess. "Sylvi is here. Shall I bring her out here or do you want the tea and coffee served indoors?"

"Oh, I didn't hear you. Serve us out here. And, no need to be so formal. Just send her out."

"Of course." Mrs. Chambers left.

"Dee!" Sylvi swooshed through the open door and pulled me into a big hug. She smelled of lavender and roses. "The house . . . your decorator did a fantastic job. Forgive me for taking so long to come down. I was working too many shifts at the hospital and exhausted. I can stay a few days, if you'll have me."

"You can stay as long as Jack will let you. You have a permanent room here."

"Jack knows not to tell me what to do." She laughed, leaning on the rail next to me. "Wow! This is some view. It's gorgeous. Our flat is lovely, with a narrow view of the San Francisco Bay. Nothing like this. The air smells fresher here than in the city. Does the terrace go around the entire house?"

"Just along the beach side. Hugh wanted the terrace large enough to accommodate entertaining. A small band would fit over there." I pointed to the V-shaped area of the terrace that jutted outward. "And dancing could be here and downstairs."

"There's a lower level?" Sylvi leaned over the rail.

"Careful. The terrace provides cover. There's a patio area and on the inside is a gaming room with men's and women's bathrooms and showers, like a small locker room for swim parties. I rarely go down there. We'll go later."

"I definitely want to see it. Is it a private beach?" Sylvi's short, straight black hair ruffled in the wind. She took the scarf around her neck and tied it over her head.

"Sort of. There are signs on either side of our property, but people can walk along the beach if they want. Just not loiter, sunbathe, or picnic." I laughed. "It's lovely sitting out here. I don't know why exactly, but this ocean differs from the one we left in Plymouth. You cut your hair off. It's cute. I should do something new with my hair, too."

"Thanks. I like yours long. You have natural waves."

Mrs. Chambers brought out a tray of coffee and pastries, which were covered to protect them from the gusts of wind. I motioned her not to serve us. "Thank you, Mrs. Chambers." I poured the coffee.

"Just let me know if you need anything. It's wonderful to see you again, Sylvi," Mrs. Chambers said.

"Yes, it's nice to see another familiar face here," Silvi smiled.

After Mrs. Chambers went inside, I leaned close to Sylvi when she sat next to me on the loveseat. "I don't get it. She calls you Sylvi, but insists on calling me Mrs. Roth."

"It's a sign of respect, I suppose. You and Hugh being her employer. I see she still wears her black uniform with the white collar."

"She insists on wearing that, too. We think of her like family. Yet, she does everything, unless I do something before she gets to it."

"What a gem. You're lucky she's here."

"Don't I know it. I'm still recovering from the move. I thought there wouldn't be much to unpack, since we brought virtually nothing with us. But it is surprising how much stuff I've accumulated over the past several years."

"I can imagine. By the way, I like the intimate seating arrangement. The stuffed armchairs and sofa in front of the TV remind of the library at Rothmorton Hall. We sure had a lot of evening chats there." Sylvi uncovered the pastries and took one.

"Yes, I missed it, so I asked the decorator to come up with something with a similar feel yet still modern, to satisfy Hugh."

"It works. I noticed the family portrait of the three of you is over the fireplace."

"That, I made sure, wasn't included it in the auction. It was a sad day, though, seeing Hugh's family heirlooms and priceless artwork sold to the highest bidder. It's what he wanted."

"I wondered about that. Did he go back for it?"

"Uh, no. I coordinated with the auction house and the movers and packers. Hugh told me what to keep and store on this property. It was part of our deal." I added cream and sugar to my coffee and took a sip.

"What happened to Ben? Where did he go?" Sylvi popped the last piece of pastry in her mouth and selected a cheese Danish. I eyed her, wondering where her appetite came from, and still stayed so thin.

"He took a job at a local auto repair place where he is content getting his hands dirty. He sent a postcard just this week. Ben was a good friend to me during those confusing and dark times."

"Yes, he was. So, what will you do when Ellen starts school on Wednesday?"

"While you are here, we will enjoy our time together. Eventually, I'll need something to do with all my empty hours."

Having Sylvi here would help with my feelings of loneliness in between Hugh's visits. That was a situation I hoped would be remedied soon.

Ellen returned from her walk and threw herself on Sylvi.

"Aunt Sylvi!

The two hugged and kissed each other. Delight showed on their faces.

"You've grown more . . . and filled out." She winked.

Ellen matured once she turned twelve, filling out her figure. She was becoming a young woman faster than I wanted. However, I was grateful she wouldn't stand out as a freshman in high school and be the brunt of nasty remarks by mean girls. Something I knew about from my own experiences.

Ellen turned sharply to me. "Did you ask her yet?"

"Ask me what?" Sylvi let go of Ellen and poured another cup of coffee.

I shook my head at Ellen, aware she was referring to the dog.

"There's a puppy I want." Ellen took the chair next to Sylvi and grabbed a donut. "Mom is worried a dog would be a trigger for my asthma. But I've hardly had any incidents."

Sylvi's brow knitted together. "I don't know, Ellen. I haven't been around you much the last two years to observe firsthand. You carry the inhaler with you all the time?"

"Faithfully." Ellen's eyes went back and forth between us.

"My main worry is not the asthma, but rather the carpeting in this house compared to the mansion. Wouldn't all that dog hair cause a problem? It's Hugh that would have final say."

Ellen pouted, then took a big bite of the donut.

"Now, none of that. You are too old for childish pouting." I turned back to Sylvi. "There is also walking the dog and extra cleaning. I just don't know Ellen. If Sylvi thinks it's not a problem health-wise, then you can ask your father."

"Okay." Ellen brushed crumbs from her lap.

"I'll talk to Hugh," Sylvi said.

"Maybe tomorrow you could go with us into the city. Ellen needs more appropriate clothes for a public school. I thought afterwards we would meet Hugh and Jack for an early dinner."

"Great idea," Sylvi said. "I'd love to help you shop for Ellen. Don't you think?" She said to Ellen.

"Oh yes, Aunt Sylvi, it should be fun."

The next day, I asked Sylvi if she didn't mind driving into the city. "We could go in my car. I'm not comfortable driving in that confusing city with all those steep hills and one-way streets."

"Sure. I'd love to drive your new car."

I relaxed while Sylvi took over. Ellen chattered about the clothes she wanted.

We started at I. Magnin because of its closeness to Hugh's office and we could all meet there. We soon realized the clothes for Ellen might seem overly ostentatious for high school and we ended up going to the Emporium, where we found a wide variety of styles and shoes, too.

"Mom," Ellen whined, "I don't want to wear saddle shoes anymore."

"You don't," I asked, "then what?"

"I like those penny loafers you put a shiny new penny in." She hurried down the aisle to the shoe department, searching for the shoe she desired and waved her hand to get our attention. Sylvi and I followed. We both agreed they would be perfect for her classes.

After shopping for several hours, I found a pay phone and called Hugh, letting him know we'd meet him at 5 p.m., at the Fisherman's Grotto Restaurant at the Wharf.

Ever since Hugh started his new business, he'd become chronically late.

"You'll be there on time?" I said.

"Of course, darling." He made a kiss sound and hung up.

I crossed my fingers.

CHAPTER THREE
HUGH

Hugh Roth stood holding a lowball of his favorite Scotch while staring out the window of his office overlooking San Francisco. The sun was setting with brilliant orange, pink, and red radiating across the sky, scattered with streaks of stratus clouds.

The offices of Roth Enterprises took up a small square footage in the tallest building in Union Square, the financial district. He and Jack and a couple of clerical assistants made-up the skeleton staff the first year. After two years, the staff had grown little.

He was so sure of his decision to step down as chairman of the board of Rothmorton Insurance to start his own company on the West Coast. He'd been doubting his decision was a smart one.

His grandfather's business ruled the cargo shipping industry on the East Coast. His father before him carried on the tradition. Hugh had always struggled to maintain traditions, wanting something he could call his own.

He knew insurance, so when he started Roth Enterprises, his goal was to break into travel insurance for cruising passengers. But it was slow going. Sure, he was still a major stock owner of Rothmorton Insurance, but just this side of success in his new company. Cash flow was an issue. Although the sale of Rothmorton Hall generated a significant sum of money, Hugh had already invested funds for the startup. He wanted new business to prove his success, not just pad it with more of his own money. He sighed and took another sip when Jack entered.

"Beautiful sight, isn't it?" Jack stood next to Hugh.

They'd become fast friends when Jack and Sylvi moved into the mansion seven years ago, to be close to Ellen. Hugh found Jack a high-level position at Rothmorton Insurance, using his skills as an accountant. He learned about the shipping insurance business at breakneck speed. But the offer to help start Hugh's new business forged an even stronger bond between them. Jack had worked for a casualty insurance company in New York, so that helped.

"Yep. You've been holed up in your office with the door shut for days. I figured you'd come up for air, eventually." Hugh tipped his glass toward Jack. "Can I get you one?"

"Sure. I have a proposal to make to you." Jack casually leaned against the wall with one hand in his pants pocket.

Hugh's brow shot up as he poured Jack a lowball. "You?"

"Don't look so surprised." He took the glass Hugh offered.

"Tell me about it." Hugh sat on one end of the long cordovan leather sofa, similar to one that used to be in the library in the manse.

Jack sipped his drink and paced. "Well . . . for the past couple of months, I've been playing racquetball at the club with some executives over at Bauer Cargo Limited. They know Rothmorton Insurance well. But they want a West Coast company to replace their current insurer, whose service has been inadequate and charge high premiums."

"Now, Jack, you know I promised not to take any business away from them." Hugh leaned forward with his elbows resting on his knees.

"Just listen. I was thinking maybe Rothmorton would underwrite the first policy, which will be a big one and Roth Enterprises would manage the account as an agent. It would help significantly with our cash flow issues."

"Not sure Rothmorton would be willing. Have you talked to anyone over there?"

"I mentioned it to the CEO, and he said he'd talk to people. But the big thing with Bauer is that they are planning to start a cruise line subsidiary next year." Jack sat next to Hugh. "It's a foot in the door."

"Now I would really like to get a contract for insuring cruise lines. With so many going out of business in the past few years, I figured that was a dead end. This sounds promising. Great job!" He gave Jack a pat on his back.

Jack puffed with pride and drank the last of his scotch. "How's Dee and Ellen handling the move?"

Hugh grimaced. "I don't think Ellen is happy about it. Dee tries to be positive. She doesn't know anyone yet."

"She will once she gets involved in the club. Which one did you buy into?"

"The closest one to our place is the Burlingame Country Club. It has all the usual amenities but a thirty-minute drive. I'm hoping she will find something to do in Starlight Bay."

Jack nodded.

"They're in the city today, shopping for new clothes. Ellen starts high school tomorrow. I'm meeting them at Fisherman's Wharf for an early dinner. You and Sylvi want to join us?"

"Sylvi called me last night to tell me. You and I are meeting them together. She emphasized us being on time, but I'm pretty sure she meant you." He chuckled. "I'm glad I don't have to wait until Ellen's birthday to see her. It's been ages."

"Great! How much time do we have? You know how I love taking every opportunity to ride the cable cars."

"A taxi would be faster, Hugh." Jack looked dubiously at him.

"We can make it."

"Okay, I love riding them, too. It's only eighteen minutes from here. By the way, is Dee still giving you grief over the apartment here?"

"That's been a sore point between us for the last two years, and especially since they moved here in July. Dee's been nagging me about overworking and spending too many nights in the city. She wants me to give up the apartment. I should, but the apartment is convenient."

"When Sylvi was working as Ellen's nurse back then, things were pretty tense between us. I hated being apart. You'll work it through. You and Dee have a great marriage."

"I think so."

"But—something has been off about Sylvi lately." Jack frowned. "I can't put my finger on it. When I ask her, it's like she's dodging the question. Not like her at all."

"Women," Hugh said, "you know that old saying . . . can't live with 'em, can't live without 'em."

They both laughed.

Hugh and Jack stood on the sidewalk waiting for the next trolley to Fisherman's Wharf. Hugh checked his watch.

"I better not be late or I won't hear the end of it from Dee." Hugh hated when he made Dee sad, ruining her gorgeous Bette Davis eyes.

"That goes for me too, from Sylvi!" Jack said.

As the trolley approached, people crowded around them. Hugh took a step forward first and right before the trolley stopped, Hugh grabbed the side rail, lifting himself onto the platform. Jack followed suit and took hold of the side rails at the steps.

Hugh grinned at Jack. Despite his agility, he wanted more physical activity. Sitting at a desk for twelve to fourteen hours a day was making his body weak. He missed working on the grounds of Rothmorton Hall. The labor had always made him feel resilient. He'd heard of the fitness guy, Jack LaLanne, who ran a men's gym in Oakland and planned to join.

Hugh sighed in relief as the trolley arrived on time, giving them ample minutes to locate Dee, Ellen, and Sylvi. He inhaled the strong smells from the fish market.

"Don't you just love that aroma?"

"If you mean the odor from the old fish, not particularly." Jack kept up as Hugh's steps increased with speed, when he saw Sylvi parking Dee's new car in the parking lot. "I see them," Jack said.

They arrived just as Dee and Ellen got out of the car. Hugh snuck up behind Dee and hugged her about the waist.

Dee let out a yelp, and Ellen laughed. "It's Daddy!"

Hugh grinned at her. Ellen hadn't called him daddy since she turned twelve. She said it sounded childish.

Dee turned around and gave Hugh a swift peck on the lips. "You're here."

"Of course. I wouldn't miss a dinner date with my two best girls. Now, would I?" He held his breath for their response, because he had missed a few dinners this past year, though not at a restaurant. Being late was another thing.

Jack embraced Sylvi. "Long time no see," Sylvi said.

Arm in arm, they strolled to the Fisherman's Grotto restaurant. The maître d' seated them right away at a table next to the large window overlooking the marina, crowded with sailboats and other types of vessels. Hugh's eyes lingered on a yacht docked at the end of the pier.

"I see that look, Hugh," Dee said. "You miss the yacht."

"Me too," Ellen piped in.

"It was best to sell it. I'll find something else when the time is right." He tore his eyes away and gazed at his wife and daughter. "Tell me all about your shopping day."

While Dee and Sylvi chatted about the day, Ellen interrupted.

"Daddy, I want a dog. Mom and Aunt Sylvi said you were the one to decide yes, or no."

Dee and Sylvi both raised their brows. "Ellen," Dee said. "We told you we'd discuss it with your father."

"What's wrong with right now?"

Hugh found it amusing. "How did this come up?" he asked Ellen.

"I met this girl on the beach. Her dog, Dotty, had a litter of Cocker Spaniels and there are two left that haven't been promised to anyone. They are too young now, so it would probably be a while till they can leave their mother." Ellen took a breath.

"Sweetheart, I won't make a snap decision on a dog right now. The house isn't designed for a dog. The contractor needs to build the perimeter wall and security gate. Until then, we will just have to wait."

"I hadn't even thought of that," Dee said. "Sylvi and I were more concerned with Ellen's asthma." She turned to Ellen. "Your father is right about the timing. You'll need to be patient. Maybe there will be other puppies later, by that time."

"Oh," Ellen's shoulders slumped. "I didn't think of where the dog would be outside, except for running along the beach with me."

"I need to remind the contractor to start the wall project. Things seem to move a lot slower in Starlight Bay. Or am I imagining it?" Hugh rubbed his chin.

"Could be the small town," Jack said.

Hugh dodged a big one. Having a dog in his brand-new house was not a top priority.

After a leisurely meal and the sun had set, they piled into the car and dropped Hugh and Jack off at their office building.

"I'll see both of you on the weekend." Hugh kissed Dee before getting out of the car.

Jack kissed Sylvi at her car window. "I'll see you in a couple of days, right?"

"Right," Sylvi said with a smile.

"You better be home. Pinkies promise?" Ellen asked Hugh.

"Pinkies promise," Hugh said and shut the door. The look on his girls' faces revealed a level of doubt. "I'll be there."

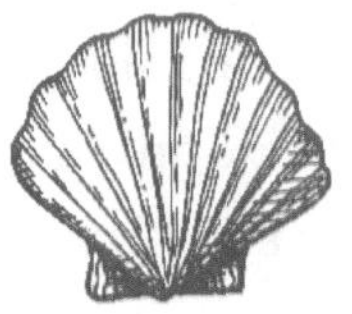

CHAPTER FOUR
ELLEN

Wednesday came and nervousness overwhelmed me on my first day of high school. My first time attending public school. I worried about being twelve and kids would laugh. When my mom stopped tutoring me at home, the private school evaluated me for placement in class and advanced me a year. My former classmates hadn't noticed or cared.

Mom helped pick out what to wear from the new clothes we bought in San Francisco. She said public school girls wore similar outfits; no uniforms like I used to have. Of course, they had a dress code: no shorts or pants, no crop tops. She chose a blue plaid A-line skirt with the hem below the knee, and a white short-sleeved blouse with ruffles down the front and on the sleeves.

After I turned twelve and my monthly period started, my body changed. Mom had bought me a trainer bra, but two weeks later, I had to get a larger one. That happened right after graduating from eighth grade, when summer began. What a relief I wasn't still in school.

The same thing happened to one of my friends when she had turned twelve. The girls accused her of padding her bra. One day, three girls had trapped her in the bathroom and tried to take off her blouse to see if they were right. She was mortified. I would have been too if that happened to me.

I tied a narrow blue silk scarf around my head like a band and checked in the floor-length mirror.

"You look nice, Ellen, very mature. No one will notice your age, I'm sure. You'll be fine," Mom said.

She had wanted to take me and pick me up each day. I convinced her to let me take the school bus. The school was too far for me to walk. Mom worried about me. I appreciated it, but I would soon be a teenager and this bit of freedom meant a lot to me.

She kissed my cheek and watched at the door as I walked up the long snaked-drive to the highway where the bus stopped. Choosing a seat at the back of the bus, I sat alone while kids found classmates they knew. Their loud voices filled the air. A few stared at me, probably because I was new.

When the bus let everyone out in front of the school entrance, I looked around, hoping to find Dana, the only person I knew. I didn't see her and headed into the building and found the classroom for my first period, freshman English. English was my favorite subject. I looked in and Dana was on the other side of the room, waving to me. She pointed to the desk in the row next to her. She wore a plain yellow skirt and blue and white striped shirt. I thought the two pieces were an odd combination. I noticed her scuffed brown and white saddle shoes, and she had metal barrettes in her hair.

Some girls still wore the classic black and white saddles, but some had loafers like my new ones, or Mary Janes. All wore anklets. Mine had white satin rosettes, which I liked. Satisfied my clothes and shoes fit in, I relaxed.

"Hi Dana," I took the desk she saved for me. "I asked my parents about the puppy."

"Yeah? What did they say?"

"The timing isn't right. We don't have a yard yet and until that is built, I'll have to wait." I made a sad face.

"That's too bad, Ellie. I'll let you know if there are any litters in the future, okay?"

I perked up at the thought there might be more puppies. "That would be terrific!"

We were sort of in the middle of the room. Dana introduced me to the girl behind her, Susan, with curly reddish-brown hair, brown eyes, and freckles. She seemed nice and her figure was mature. Nina sat in front of Dana. She had long black hair and dark eyes, wore braces, and her chest was flat as a pancake. I figured she was teased about that. Girls can be so mean. Nina didn't smile at all. Maybe because of the braces. I was lucky my teeth were straight enough not to need them.

The teacher, Mr. Stevens, stood up in front of the class. "Please take a seat. These will be yours for the entire year. Be quiet while I take roll call."

He started reading off names alphabetically, and each student said, "Here."

"Dana Anderson?"

"Here," Dana said.

More names were called.

"Nina Gallo?"

"Here," Nina said.

"Susan Murphy?"

"Here," Susan said.

Finally, he called my name, "Ellen Roth?"

I raised my hand. "Here."

When I turned to Dana, she gave me a strange look.

I whispered, "Something wrong?"

Dana shook her head. "Nothing." She turned her attention to Mr. Stevens.

I brushed it off.

While the teacher continued with roll call, I thought about how I would answer questions about my family. I'd been worried about it since we moved here. Back east everyone knew about our family, so they didn't ask me.

Mom and Dad said to stick to the story they had told me when they got married. That my parents had died and my dad took me in and when he married Mom, they adopted me. If anyone inquired about their deaths, they instructed me to say my mother died while giving birth to me, and my real father had been killed in an accident. I always went along with this story because I still didn't understand. Dad said that he was once married to her. It confused me and their answers didn't help. If I asked more questions, they said I'd understand when I was older. So that story was just temporary. Well, I'm older now, but they said to stick with the same story for the time being. Even though I wanted to understand and know more, something told me to just leave it alone.

Roll call ended. I couldn't take my eyes off Mr. Stevens. He looked like a movie star with his wavy yellow hair and vivid blue eyes and the cleft in his chin. When he walked down the aisles, he moved with a confident swagger. What a dreamboat.

"All right class, eyes front. The first part of our semester will start with a poetry assignment."

A few groans echoed in the room, all guys. I couldn't be happier. Poetry. That's my most favorite thing to do.

He continued. "Our first assignment will be due next Wednesday. The topic is," he wrote on the chalkboard, "What I Did for Summer Vacation, and it should rhyme." He handed a stack of papers to the first person in each row to pass back. "Here are some instructions and examples of how to write a rhyming poem."

What could I write about? All we did was move, and that didn't sound interesting. Maybe I could use a poem I'd already written. I'd have to go through all of my piles of papers to find one that would be suitable.

When class was over, I followed Dana out of the room.

"What's your next class, Ellie? I like your nickname better than plain Ellen."

"Yeah, I like it too. My next class is French, then biology. How about you?"

"I'm not taking French. I go to my Social Studies class."

"Okay. I'll see you in Biology class?"

"Sure." Dana gave me that strange look again, told me where my French I class was and went the other way.

Susan came up behind me. "I'm taking French. Can I sit next to you?"

I beamed at her. Another potential friend? Maybe school wouldn't be so bad.

At lunch in the cafeteria, I sat with Dana, Susan, and Nina, and a few other girls sat at the same table.

"Nina," I said, "are you related to the Gallo Wine family?"

"No, but I have a cousin on my mom's side who married a Gallo, and he works there in Modesto."

"Okay, I was just curious."

"But Lisa," Nina pointed to the girl with straight black hair and bangs, "she's a Higaki. They own the Flower Company, right Lisa?"

Lisa looked embarrassed. "Yes, my family moved our flower farm to a nearby town from Redwood City earlier this year. But our house is in this school's district."

"How do you know each other?" I said.

Susan piped in, "We live on the same street."

"That's close to the school?"

"Yeah. We walk to school." Susan smiled at Lisa.

Everyone was so nice. I was feeling more comfortable. Mom had given me money for lunch. The cafeteria food seemed strange to me. They served macaroni casserole with tuna, Jello, and a cookie. I wondered what my parents would think if they knew. Not the same as what my private school served.

Classes ended at 3 p.m. Susan and I sat together on the bus as it bounced along the road. I didn't notice her that morning, but I wasn't looking all that hard.

She did most of the talking, telling me all about her family, her sister who went to community college, and two brothers, all older and out of school. Going home, the bus went a reversed route. Her stop was before mine. I smiled and waved as she jaunted down the aisle and off the bus. Susan's street was east of the school in a neighborhood with lots of trees, and grassy lawns, and little children playing in the yards.

As soon as I walked in the front door, Mom rushed to me. "How was your first day?"

"It was good." I dropped my notebook on the entry table. "Dana takes most of the same classes and I met some of her friends. I told her the puppy would have to wait until our yard was done. She said she'd let me know if there were any future litters. Susan takes the bus too, so we sat together. She sure is a chatterbox."

Mom laughed. "How nice, sweetheart. That's nice to know there might be more puppies later." She followed me into the living room and we sat on the blue curved sofa facing the large windows overlooking the ocean. I had to admit, the view was amazing.

Mrs. C carried in a tray with tall glasses of iced lemonade. "I figured you'd be thirsty by now." She set the tray on the long glass-topped coffee table that had an enormous piece of driftwood as the base.

"Thank you, Mrs. C." I heard someone on TV call their housekeeper by the first letter of her last name. It sure made it easier to say, and it felt less formal and she didn't mind.

"I like English class the best. Our first assignment is to write a poem." I took a big gulp of the lemonade. The air inside the bus made me thirsty.

"You have many poems already written. Maybe one might fit."

"That's what I thought. May I go for my walk on the beach? I'll change clothes first, of course."

"Certainly. Make sure you return early enough to do your homework before dinner at seven."

I didn't bother asking about Daddy.

It had been two days since I turned in my poetry assignment and all I could think about was Mr. Stevens. I'd started wearing a little makeup. Only mascara and lipstick, like Susan and Nina. Dana didn't bother with makeup. She said, "Why should I wear it? I would still look like boring old me." She had low self-esteem.

Mr. Stevens began handing out our graded poems to each of us. When he came to my desk, he flashed me a huge smile while he handed me my poem. A big red A+ donned the top of the page. I giggled with glee, looking over at Dana. She smiled at me but hid her paper. At the end of class, when we filed out past the teacher, Mr. Stevens asked me to stay. Dana gave me an odd look. When everyone had left, I looked at Mr. Stevens expectantly.

"Ellen, I wanted to tell you how much I enjoyed your poem. You definitely have a flare for poetry. You don't need extra credit, but I hope you'll submit the five poems. Topics can be of your choice, but follow the guidelines I handed out. Would you like to do that? I'd really love to see more of your work."

"Oh, would I! Thank you, Mr. Stevens." I was on cloud nine as I floated out of the classroom. Dana was waiting for me. I told her all about it and asked her why she hid her paper from me.

"You don't want to see my grade." She frowned.

"Yes, I do, please?"

Dana retrieved it from her notebook. It had a big B+ at the top of the page.

"That's a good grade, Dana. Don't be ashamed. You can improve it. Are you going to do the extra credit?"

"I've always received As in school before. This is my first B. Maybe I'll do the extra credit."

"No, it's a B+ and high school is supposed to be more difficult."

"Not for you, apparently." Her shoulders drooped and forced a smile. "I'm happy for you Ellie, really, I am. Guess I'll have to work harder."

There was something in her voice. Maybe jealousy? I hoped not.

"I've been writing poetry for a long time, though. My mom writes poetry too, so I had learned some before this assignment." We kept moving to our next class.

"Oh, that's nice. Your mom helps you." She shuffled her feet.

"Doesn't yours?"

"My mom didn't do so well in school. I don't think she even finished high school. Please don't tell anyone I told you, though."

"Oh, I won't. It's none of anyone's business. My mom was my tutor when I was little, before she married my dad."

"Really?" Dana appeared suddenly interested. "I'm going to be late for my next class. I'll see you later, okay?"

"See ya."

I had a difficult time paying attention in my next two classes. My mind wandered, fantasizing about Mr. Stevens. He was much older than me, but his extra attention made me feel special. It had to mean something more than just my homework.

CHAPTER FIVE
DEE

The phone rang, and I rushed to answer it in the foyer. "Hugh?"

"Yes, Dee, it's me."

"You better not be calling to say you won't be here for Ellen's birthday."

"Of course not, darling. Jack left ahead of me to pick up Sylvi and they will be there soon. I just have a couple of things to finish up and I'll be off. Don't worry."

Something told me to worry. Ever since he opened the San Francisco office, he'd been breaking promises, being late, and his mind on other things.

"Well, okay."

"You don't sound like you believe me."

"Can you blame me? It's become chronic with you."

"What has?"

Seriously? I couldn't believe he was that unaware. "Being late and breaking promises." My voice broke, and I swallowed a sob.

An awkward moment of silence stung as I waited for his response.

"I'm sorry Dee. I'm doing the best I can to get this business off the ground. Please bear with me a little while longer. It's all going to work out."

"Yes, you keep saying that. Please hurry." When we hung up, I pulled a tissue from the box on the foyer table and looked in the mirror. "Damn, mascara always runs." I said under my breath, dabbing at the black streaks. "When will they invent one that's tear proof?"

"Did you say something?" Mrs. Chambers stood at the end of the hall. "Is Mr. Roth on his way?"

I turned and sniffled. "He said Jack and Sylvi will arrive first and he will be a little after." I forced a smile.

"Hmph." She adjusted her apron and returned to the kitchen.

I followed her. "Where's Ellen?"

"On the terrace. Don't worry, she didn't hear you on the phone with Mr. Roth."

"That's a relief. Need to watch my voice. I've been getting so upset lately. That's not like me. Is it?"

"Dearie, you have been under a lot of stress for the last couple of years. What with Mr. Roth flying back and forth and you left with organizing the sale of the mansion and the move. I understand, and I'm sure Mr. Roth does, too."

"I don't know about him, but I appreciate your support. What would I have done if you hadn't come here with us? By the way, when will you visit your son?"

"He's coming up here in a couple of weeks. I was going to ask for some time off."

"Of course, take whatever time you need. Shall I set the table?"

She waved me off with a smile, and I went to the dining room. Mrs. Chambers had already set it with clean linens and a floral centerpiece. I chuckled, thinking back to the first time I saw the dining room at Rothmorton Hall. That table sat nearly twenty people and only four of us used it every evening. This new house by the sea was a fraction of the size, but still spacious and modern. It had five bedrooms, one of which I kept ready for Sylvi and Jack when they visited. One is Hugh's den if he ever worked from home.

The remaining empty room would be a nursery, I hoped. When we were first married, it's all we talked about. Until two years in and nothing. When I finally got pregnant, I miscarried. We kept trying, and two years later I lost the baby early again. I was beyond inconsolable and went into a deep depression. That's when Hugh got the idea that we needed a fresh start. I agreed we needed a change, but it had never occurred to me where a fresh start would take us.

I felt more independent driving myself again, not having to wait for a driver.

The table looked nice, not too elegant, but classy with the new China and cut crystal I'd bought with brand-new linens to fit the table that sat eight. It had extensions for up to twelve if we ever had a dinner party. Though neither of us knew anyone in the town of Starlight Bay, yet.

"You look gorgeous, Dee," Sylvi said as she swooped in with her arms full of packages for Ellen.

I took the gifts and placed on a table in the corner. Jack followed behind, holding up a bottle. The gray hair at his temples had spread to a salt and pepper look the last few years, now that he was nearing fifty. I wondered if Hugh's hair would do the same in ten years.

"California's finest!" he said with a laugh.

Sylvi chuckled. "He's been trying out wines from all the California wineries he can find. There aren't that many. It's a sort of joke."

"Hugh won't touch it. He imports his favorites from Europe." Port was still my favorite after dinner drink.

"Hmmm, that roast smells divine. Did you make it or Mrs. Chambers?" Sylvi went to peek into the kitchen.

"We worked together on tonight's dinner. I'm so grateful for the last two years studying with our chef at Rothmorton Hall. Before then, I wasn't much of a cook." I laughed.

Jack went outside to smoke and chat with Ellen. I checked my wristwatch. Sylvi noticed.

"When will Hugh arrive?" She whispered.

I tensed. "He promised he would be here on time. Fingers crossed." I removed the apron and smoothed the full skirt of my new dress, a scooped-neck sleeveless little number in peacock blue.

Sylvi rolled her eyes. "We can only hope. I don't know how you handle it."

"Not very well tonight. I was pretty upset on the phone with him earlier. He is completely oblivious to his behavior. All he thinks about is that business. He was never like that before."

"Jack is that way too. This company is their baby—oops sorry, didn't mean. . ."

"It's okay. I think you're right. What with our lack of one, I guess the business is his replacement child." I hedged a tear and turned away.

"Aw, Dee, I can relate, which is why I kept this a secret. I don't want you to feel bad."

"What do you mean—Oh! Are you? I mean, really? After all these years?"

"Yes, I'm pregnant! I can hardly believe it myself. My doctors told me I was barren. I'm almost forty and scared because this is my first."

I rushed to her and threw my arms around her. "You are only thirty-six, silly woman. Did you know when you were last here? How far along are you?"

"Four months with a due date end of January. I suspected, but didn't want to jinx it. I got confirmation today."

Tears filled my eyes to the point I could barely see. "These are happy tears. I really am happy for you. You give me hope it might happen for me, too." Yes, I was happy for her. She deserved it. I deserved it too. My stomach tightened, pushing back years of disappointment.

"You said we'd wait." Jack's voice cracked through the room and his mouth turned downward.

"Sorry honey, it just came out." Sylvi grabbed him by his jacket sleeve and pulled him to her. He kissed her on the neck. All smiles again.

Mrs. Chambers came from the kitchen. "This dinner is ready to be served or it'll be ruined."

We all checked our watches and looked toward the front of the house. The phone rang.

I cringed while lifting the receiver, bracing for bad news. "Hello?"

"Dee, I'm leaving now. See you soon."

I slammed down the receiver without saying goodbye. How could he be so inconsiderate of his daughter's one important day? He had promised to come home on Friday in order to be here the entire weekend. And now it's Monday and still he couldn't be here on time.

"Mrs. Chambers, let's all sit down and start dinner. I'll call Ellen in. Hugh just left the city. It'll be another forty minutes unless he drives his usual breakneck speed."

It took every ounce of strength not to scream.

We had almost finished eating, keeping the conversation focused on Ellen and what she'd been doing and how school was going.

Just as I rose to get the birthday cake from the kitchen, Hugh breezed through the front door and down the hall. He held an elegantly wrapped gift. Mrs. Chambers took it and placed it with the others.

"Daddy!" Ellen jumped up from the table and dashed into her father's arms. "I'm so happy you finally came home. You missed dinner." She thrust out her lower lip.

"Sorry I'm late." He glanced at my angry face and flinched. "I wouldn't miss your birthday for anything, you know that." He kissed Ellen on her forehead and gave her a squeeze.

Mrs. Chambers threw Hugh a disapproving look, which he ignored.

"I'll have Mrs. Chambers make up a plate for you," I said, and went into the kitchen.

"I've already made one up, Mrs. Roth." She spoke low in a whisper. "See, he may be late, but he's here. Now wipe those tears and smile for Ellen and sit back down. I'll bring in the cake."

I nodded, brushing away my tears so no one could see, and sat down. Mrs. Chambers took the full plate of food and set it in front of Hugh. She cleared away the dirty dishes taking them to the kitchen.

Sylvi and Jack gave me an encouraging look.

"I see you brought a bottle, Jack." Hugh picked at the food on his plate.

"Sure did." Jack poured the Cabernet into Hugh's wine glass. "Dee? Sylvi?"

Sylvi shook her head. I nodded and lifted my glass for him to fill. I really needed something to calm me down.

Hugh pushed his plate of barely eaten food aside. "Are you all ready for cake?"

"I am!" Ellen said.

Mrs. Chambers came in with the double layer chocolate birthday cake ablaze with thirteen candles and set it in front of the birthday girl. Ellen's eyes sparkled in the flickering candlelight. I grabbed my camera from the sideboard.

We all sang the "Happy Birthday" song out of tune, of course.

"You're officially a teenager now. Make a wish, sweetie," Sylvi said.

"Take a big breath," Hugh said.

"I know how, silly," Ellen giggled, closed her eyes, moving her lips without sound making her wish. She opened her eyes and took a big breath and blew out all the candles.

I took several more snapshots, then cut the cake while Ellen passed the plates of cake around.

After the cake, we moved to the sofa in the living room for Ellen to open her gifts. Ellen reached for Hugh's gift first, tearing away the wrapping and bow.

"Oh my gosh, how creamy." She held up a Nikon 35mm camera. "I love it." She hugged Hugh and immediately got the film out.

"Now, now, Ellen," Hugh said. "You have other gifts. Then you can put the camera together."

Thrusting her lower lip out again, Ellen put the camera aside and picked up another package. "This is from Aunt Sylvi and Uncle Jack." She opened a jewelry box with a pair of amethyst earrings set in 14kt gold. "How beautiful. But they're pierced."

"I know," Sylvi said. "Your parents said you can get your ears pierced."

"Really? Gosh. Thank you."

The next gift was from me.

"Oh, Mom, I love this." She held up the solitaire amethyst necklace with two tiny diamonds, and a matching bracelet in 14kt gold. "It matches the earrings!"

"We coordinated," Sylvi said.

"The jewelry is for special occasions, not for school, okay?" I said.

"Sure, hope I'll have the occasion to wear them. And soon!" She giggled.

The rest of the gifts were clothing from Hugh and me and the last one from Mrs. Chambers. A scrapbook.

"What will I put in this?" Ellen asked Mrs. Chambers.

"Now dearie, you will have lots of special things to save in your scrapbook. You'll see."

"She's right, honey. I had one when I was in school," Sylvi said.

"What a thoughtful gift, Mrs. Chambers." I hadn't owned a scrapbook but knew its importance and glad she thought of the gift.

Ellen grew quiet, gazing out at the sunset. It was nearly 9 p.m.

"What's the matter, pumpkin?" Hugh asked.

"Oh, I don't know. I was just thinking about all the other parties we used to have at Rothmorton Hall. I'm glad you all are here, but I wished we could have had my party before we moved."

"There wasn't time, you know that." I looked at Hugh and saw the surprise, then guilt passed over his face.

Sylvi reached out and patted Ellen's hand. "You'll have plenty of friends by next year and we can do a big party."

"Well, sure we will." Hugh added. "We are all starting over and it will take time to adjust."

"I know. Well, I'm tired. I think I'll go to bed now." Ellen didn't smile.

She came around and gave us each a goodnight hug.

Hugh went to the formal bar in the room's corner. Behind the curved bar, he poured himself a scotch and me a port. I sat on one of the tall padded bar stools, crossed my legs, and leaned my arms on the padded edge. My reflection from the mirrored wall didn't hide a thing. At only twenty-nine, I looked tired with bags under my eyes. I slept horribly without Hugh next to me.

"Jack? Sylvi?" Hugh raised a glass.

"Club soda for me," Sylvi said. "I'll be abstaining for a while."

Jack smiled with pride and Hugh looked confused. "What am I missing here?"

Sylvi laughed. "I'm having a baby!"

"What? That's fantastic." Hugh shot me a glance, and I nodded.

"I'm so happy for them." I assured him with my smile.

"I plan on being a very careful and healthy Mom. No alcohol, though that may be unpopular these days. Some older obstetrics textbooks from the 1930s to 1951 mentioned something about it. It's considered old-fashioned. But at my age having my first baby, I'm not taking any chances."

"Probably a good idea. A toast to Jack and Sylvi." Hugh raised his glass and so did I.

It made me wonder if my drinking had something to do with my miscarriages.

After they left, Hugh and I sat outside for a while, like we did at the mansion. We gazed at the moonlight shimmering over the ocean and listened to the waves lapping on the sand.

"Are you really okay with Sylvi's news?" Hugh said softly.

"Of course, I feel a bit jealous. But the two of them have waited way longer than we have. I'm thrilled for her. It gives me hope for us."

"I'm glad to hear you say that. But, just to qualify . . . whether we have kids of our own, does not affect how much I love you, Dee."

"Saying that means a lot to me. I admit, sometimes I wonder if our lack of a child affects how you feel."

"Nonsense! Now don't think that way." He moved closer to me on the loveseat and put his arm around me.

My head on his shoulder, I cuddled close. "I know we've been fighting a lot, and it bothers me. I worry about what's happening to us."

"Nothing is happening to us, besides making major changes in our lifestyle and accommodations." He chuckled. "It's bound to cause stress and tension. But we will get through it with flying colors." He kissed the top of my head. "Oh, by the way, I bought a membership in the closest country club in Burlingame about twenty-five minutes east of here. Make sure you drop in there and look around."

"Okay. I've been wondering if there were any bridge clubs here."

"Probably, this club is for social events. They do have a driving range, no course. Jack signs me as a guest to teach me golf at his golf club.

We snuggled for a long time, and later in the master suite, we reconnected intimately. It had been too long.

CHAPTER SIX
DEE

After Ellen's birthday, I found myself bored, struggling to keep busy. Hugh had suggested getting involved with some charities in San Francisco. I avoided doing the drive, and getting involved in the country club made me cringe. What in the heck did housewives do in this beach town? I told Mrs. Chambers I was going for a walk into town.

Main Street connected with State Route 1 along the coast north of the drive down to our house. The walk to Main Street served as a replacement for the daily walks I made at Rothmorton Hall.

The sun shone brightly with a cool breeze off the ocean. I had opted for a cotton sundress and low-heeled sandals with a wide-brimmed hat to keep my face protected. My stark white skin stood out among the local beach goers with their summer tanned skin, but I didn't care. Sun-weathered skin was not a becoming look on me.

The town had its own style of quaintness drawing on the early twentieth century feel. Old-fashioned light posts along the sidewalks. The clapboard siding on buildings was painted in bright colors with striped awnings.

Most of the shops were open, and I took my time window shopping, thinking how different my tastes had changed since marrying Hugh. When I first met him, I didn't have a clue what was fashionable or cheap. Now, I shopped looking for designer labels instead of price tags.

The receptionist inside a beauty salon waved to me. Inside, I asked for a business card and assured them that I would soon set up an appointment. Hugh and I had a social event coming up.

On the window of the ice cream parlor, I noticed a flyer taped to the glass. It was an announcement regarding the local community meeting that evening. One of the agenda items was about the upcoming community theater production of *Carousel*. I went inside.

"Pardon me," I said to the young man behind the counter. "Where would I find the Town Hall?"

He was helpful, pointing to the building at the end of Main Street with the clock tower. He also directed me to a Visitor Information Center a few doors down and around the corner. I made a quick stop and gathered several brochures about attractions in San Mateo County. Hugh should have done this with me. There were a lot of things he should have done when we moved here. By lunchtime, I was hungry and returned to the house with plans to attend the evening town meeting.

The meeting was at 7 p.m., so Ellen and I had an early dinner, and I drove. I'd changed from the sun dress into something more sedate. A gray pencil skirt and cream elbow-length blouse, with matching gray pumps. I twisted my shoulder-length hair into a French roll.

There was plenty of parking. Several cars were parked in the lot, and a few couples walked toward the entrance. I quickly parked and followed. Self-conscious that I was going alone, I brushed aside my nervousness and pushed on. The meeting room was a large brightly lit space, with rows of chairs facing a raised dais. Several men and women, I assumed, were the town council, sat at a long table facing the assemblage. I took a seat in the back, thinking I was only an observer.

The meeting came to order, and business issues were discussed. The floor was opened to non-business topics. A man stood from the front row and went to a podium set to the side so he could address the council and those in attendance. He was quite good-looking, blond, and tanned.

"Uh, good evening, everyone. My name is Patrick Stevens the director of the fall production at the community theater. This year we will present the Rogers & Hammerstein musical *Carousel*. As most of you already know, the auditions were held last week and I've posted the cast selections. Tonight, I am seeking volunteers to help with the production such as set design/construction, lighting, makeup, hair, and costumes. We will also need musicians. I know the community has put on other musicals in the past and I'm hoping those who helped then will be available this year." He swallowed. "Are there any questions? Or anyone who would like to volunteer tonight for anything?"

An older man in a brown suit stood. "Do you have much experience directing musicals?"

"Why yes," Patrick said. "I have a dual degree in English and Theater Studies, with an emphasis on production and direction, though I have had many leads in high school and college productions. Since college, I directed a few plays and one musical at the San Bernardino Community Playhouse."

The man nodded his head. "Sounds great. You can count on my wife and me helping out. I do set construction, and she is an excellent set painter."

Patrick passed out a sheet of paper to someone in the front row. "Please fill out this signup sheet and pass it around? Anyone else?"

My hand shot up, and I stood, surprising myself. "I'd be interested in helping with costumes, though it would be the first time on a theatrical production. I designed and made my daughter's and other children's Halloween costumes for years. Also, I ran the sewing circle in Plymouth, Massachusetts.

Patrick raised an eyebrow. "Sounds good, Miss . . ."

"Oh, I'm Mrs. Dee Roth. We are new to Starlight Bay."

A woman sitting two rows in front of me turned around. "Mrs. Roth, with your leadership skills, if you would take the lead for costumes, I'd love to work with you. I'm Ethyl Graves and I'm sure I can find a couple others to help."

"Oh, well . . . Uh, I suppose I could do that." I swallowed hard, wondering what I was doing volunteering to head up the costumes.

More people stood to volunteer and the signup sheets were full. When the meeting adjourned, Patrick came up to me.

"Mrs. Roth." He stuck his hand out to shake mine, and I reciprocated. "Thank you for volunteering. Perhaps we could meet sometime soon to discuss the needs for the costumes? I'll have a schedule prepared which will be helpful."

Up close, he was even more handsome, like a movie star with the sunny yellow hair and chiseled features. Though Patrick was older, maybe fortyish.

"Of course, I need all the guidance you can offer."

We agreed to meet for lunch the next week on Tuesday.

I was eager to have something to do and plan for. When I arrived home, I was giddy.

"Well, aren't you in a spiffy mood?" Mrs. Chambers said. "I haven't seen you this chipper in months."

"You're right. I've been in a funk far too long. I just volunteered to help with costumes for the upcoming musical."

"That sounds right up your alley. Can I fix you a drink?"

"I'll get it. Thanks. Is Ellen still doing homework?"

"She was tired and went to bed early."

"I'll just take a peek and see if she is still awake." I opened the door a couple of inches. She was sound asleep. I'd wait until breakfast.

The following week, I met Patrick for lunch at a little café north of downtown. He was already there, sitting in a booth at the back. It was small, yet clean. Before I married Hugh, eating in diners and cafes was common for me. Life in Hugh's world spoiled me, and my expectations had hit a much higher bar. Dressing well meant more to me now, and my attire might have been a bit over the top. I would never go back to the old unsophisticated Dee.

Patrick waved me over as I entered, my full skirt barely making it through the narrowly set tables. Luckily, only a few people sat up front. He stood while I slid into the seat opposite him. I removed my gloves and the silk scarf from my hair.

"Thank you for meeting with me, Mrs. Roth. I apologize for the location, but it's quiet here, and the service is fast. I don't have a lot of time between classes."

"No need to apologize. That's right, you're my daughter's English teacher. I'd forgotten. Forgive me." I should have memorized all of Ellen's teachers' name and embarrassed myself.

"Ellen Roth? I should have known. You look too young to have a daughter in high school."

Not wanting to explain my not being Ellen's birth mother, I simply thanked him for the compliment. "I hope we'll have enough time to cover the key points for the costumes."

"Of course. I made a list here." As the waitress arrived with two glasses of water and menus, he took out a sheet of paper from a leather folio. He told her to come back in a few minutes for our order.

Patrick was a polite man and obviously well-organized. I found him quite attractive and friendly and he made me comfortable. After reviewing the short menu, the waitress returned, and I ordered a simple tuna sandwich and a side salad. Patrick ordered a burger and fries. From my own experience, a teacher's salary was meager in a small community.

"Here are some photos of the costumes I've done." I pulled the photo album from my tote bag and opened it on the table, flipping through the pages as I explained each costume and how I made them.

"These are marvelous!" Patrick looked pleased. "I especially like the fairy costume and this one," he pointed to the alien costume I made for a boy.

"That was a fun one," I chuckled. "I had never made anything for boys before. It was the son of one of my husband's clients. It was so well received, the following year I did costumes for several of the children at Ellen's school."

"You certainly show a wide range of skills. Are you familiar with the musical *Carousel?*"

"Yes, my husband and I saw it on Broadway three years ago for the revival. It was fabulous."

"How fortunate you saw it in New York. Is that where you're from?" He leaned in and looked at me with an intensity that almost made me blush. How silly.

"No, we lived outside of Boston. We only moved here last month and still getting acclimated to the local customs." I gave a light laugh. "I used to be a teacher in Illinois before I moved to Plymouth, where I met my husband."

"Really? What did you teach?"

"Elementary school, in the rural farming community."

"What a coincidence. I taught in rural Indiana before moving to California. What a culture shock it is. Don't you think?"

I nodded, surprised at our common backgrounds. I viewed him in a different light, especially when we started talking about poetry.

The food came, and we ate, and laughed and shared similar stories from our childhood living on farms and our dreams of something better. The time sped by and we hadn't even discussed the costumes. I agreed to meet with again after I had time to peruse his notes and we would get down to business then.

When we parted, I felt lighter somehow, elated even. It had been years since I talked with someone who understood where I came from and my interests. It was exhilarating. Since the town library was on the way home, I stopped in to see if they had material on the stage productions of *Carousel*. Some old magazines had a few photos, which I checked out along with some fashion books for clothing styles in 1873-1888. My excitement grew about the project and I couldn't wait to get home and sketch out some ideas for the costumes.

All my sketching supplies sat unpacked in the storage shed. Digging through them, I recalled how much satisfaction designing and sewing costumes had brought me over the years. Sketch pad, drawing board, and colored pencils in hand, I setup in Hugh's den, temporarily, until I could order furniture and equipment for my use in an empty room. Hugh rarely used his den. I was sure he wouldn't mind my taking his over, spreading out my research materials and photos on the floor and the drawing board on Hugh's desk.

"What in the world . . .?" Mrs. Chambers stood in the doorway with hands on her hips.

I brushed loose hairs from my face and looked up. "I told you I joined the community theater. They asked me to head up the Costume Department. Isn't that exciting?"

At first, she looked confused, then she smiled. "Yes, it is. I didn't realize you would be in charge, or what all that would entail. You look happy."

"I am happy and eager. Ellen will be home soon. Would you be a dear and tell her not to disturb me?"

Mrs. Chambers nodded and closed the door.

Once in my creative zone, I hated to be interrupted.

CHAPTER SEVEN
DEE

One of Hugh's clients, the Richelieus, invited us to a cocktail party at their home in Burlingame. Our first social event since moving here. I worried about leaving Ellen with Mrs. Chambers for the evening, but Ellen assured us she had plenty of homework to keep her busy, having started school that week. I also knew she would probably spend too much time watching TV, but it was the weekend, so I said nothing about it.

A sprawling Spanish-style home built in the 1920s had two stories, and a cabana by the Olympic-sized pool. We drove through the gated-entrance, where a valet greeted us and parked the car along the street outside the walled property.

"That reminds me, I called the contractor weeks ago to start the wall on our property. They should have started work by now. Have they called about it?" Hugh asked.

"No. I would have told you if they had. It seems to be a pretty safe community. I suppose there's no rush."

"Probably not, but I'll call on Monday."

As soon as we entered the home, servers dressed in white shirts with bow ties and black slacks offered hors d'oeuvres and champagne. I stifled a yawn, having hoped it would be different from the countless parties we attended in the Boston area. The home was the only thing a bit different. Definitely not something we would find on the East Coast. Dressed to impress, guests huddled in small groups of people they probably knew. I found it difficult being somewhere new and not knowing anyone. My hand looped around Hugh's arm for moral support.

He introduced me to the host and hostess, who were amiable. Mrs. Richelieu's eyes raked my dress up and down. Was she assessing my fashion sense?

My mind dulled, forgetting their names immediately, and I downed my second glass of champagne when a familiar voice came from the crowd behind me and I pivoted around.

"It's about time you arrived," Sylvi said. "You're wearing my favorite dress. You changed something about it though."

"Shh, not so loud. We had a little trouble finding the house." I said under my breath. "This is a dress from seven years ago. The rhinestone straps and belt are additions. Is it too much? The hostess did a one over on it."

The dress was the first designer dress Hugh bought me before we were married, a strapless long white velvet gown with gold lame trim.

"I'm the last person to advise you on couture. I'm a nurse, remember? You fit right in and do off the shoulder so well and with those long satin gloves. My shoulders are too bony."

"Is that why you cover them in black all the time?" I chuckled as my elbow dug into her side.

"Hey, that tickles. Black is never in poor taste."

"True. So, save me. I'm bored already and now Hugh has disappeared with the host."

"Jack is somewhere around. I know exactly what you mean."

"Do you know anyone here?"

Sylvi looked around and shrugged. "I don't think so. This is a relatively new client. And you know me, I am not a socialite. I do the bare minimum of social events."

I spoke low. "Hugh said he bought a membership at the Burlingame Country Club. Did Jack?"

"That one is near here. Closest to where you live. No, Jack bought into the California Golf Club in San Francisco. I think they did that on purpose to span their reach, you know."

"Ah, yes, you have the lingo." We both laughed. "The hostess is coming toward us. I've already forgotten her name."

"Doris Richelieu." Sylvi pasted a smile on her face.

The very tall fiftyish woman with dark hair and wisps of gray framing an overly made-up face, wore an allover silver sequined dress highlighting her well-defined figure. She breezed by somehow, remembering who each of us was, addressing us by our married names, and smiled. She didn't stop, however, heading toward the corner of the room where a few couples waved to her.

Sylvi and I exchanged glances. I was about to make a wise-crack when three women without their husbands introduced themselves. The women talked about their children, the lack of a proper beauty salon in the suburbs, and complained about driving to San Francisco to shop for clothes.

Much to my surprise, Doris later stopped by our group and invited me to join her bridge club. The ladies all lived spread out and not in one town, so they rotated from house to house each week, the hostess to provide lunch. I agreed and thought it would be nice to get to know them. I would fill in for a woman who was taking a break for surgery. It wouldn't be my turn to hold a meeting for several weeks.

When a couple of ladies who played tennis invited me for doubles at the country club, I tried to explain it had been years since I'd played. They didn't care, suggesting I might take a refresher lesson from the tennis pro.

I broke away from the hen gathering and wandered outside. It was cooler in the evenings and Doris's house was near the east bay. A brisk breeze swept over me, sending a shiver across my bare shoulders. Feeling hungry, I pulled my hand out of the glove slot and enjoyed a finger sandwich while sipping champagne. I was getting a rush from the alcohol and probably needed more food than that.

Hugh stood with an older man near the pool area. He saw me and motioned I should join him. He was smiling and animated. I quickly put my glove back on.

"Darling, I want you to meet someone special. He was one of my teachers in college."

I shook the man's hand and feigned interest. "Do you still teach?"

"Retired now, moved out here several years ago. It sure is a small world to have run into my favorite student."

I saw a brief return of the Hugh I'd fallen in love with. His gregarious nature shined while talking to his former teacher. He had been so serious the past year. We had lost the fun in our marriage. I'd recently read that the number of divorced couples increased by twenty-eight percent compared to a decade ago. Are we drifting apart and heading for that statistic? I took another sip of champagne.

The retired teacher moved on and Hugh turned to me, sliding his arm around my waist.

"Did I tell you how fabulous you look tonight?"

"How many drinks have you had?" I teased, leaning into him.

"I could ask you the same thing? Have you eaten anything since we arrived?"

"A little."

"Have you made any new friends among the ladies?"

"Acquaintances perhaps. Friends? Remains to be seen. A couple of invitations to a bridge club and playing tennis look promising though."

"That's good. Sorry I haven't been home much."

I just smiled and kissed his cheek. Jack and Sylvi found us and some dance music started by a jazz quartet on the patio.

Hugh took my glass from me and set it down, then guided me to the parquet dance floor laid out on the lawn. Soft lighting from the hanging lights made it almost romantic. I rested my head on his shoulder as we glided around the floor. Jack and Sylvi were dancing too. They looked so much in love. It was the baby she was carrying. Sylvi glowed with happiness.

Jack and Sylvi would meet us at our house to spend the night. We would all spend Sunday together.

On the drive home, Hugh was in quiet contemplation.

"I was noticing how similar the people here are to those we knew in Boston and Plymouth," I said.

"How so?" Hugh lit a cigarette and rolled the window down a bit.

"Well, you know, people with money."

"I need to be around people with money if I'm going to build this business."

"Right. I guess I expected people to more casual in California. But this party was just like the ones we went to back east. Except these people are self-made, not the 'old money' we knew before."

"You're right about the self-made thing. And I'm trying to be self-made here. Not relying on my family business."

"I admire you for that, and I want you to succeed. But . . ."

"But what?" He glanced at me with his brow knitted together.

"It's me, Hugh. I don't know how I fit in here. It took me a long time to feel comfortable as a society woman. I feel like I'm starting all over again."

He tossed the butt out the window and reached over to pull me across the bench seat. "Darling, you'll fit in just fine. Give it time. You've only been here barely two months."

"I know."

"What's happening with that musical you said you were working on?"

"Oh that! I've been working on designs for the costumes. Since the costume department has sewing machines and I don't, I'll be spending time there, some evenings and some days, when my helpers are available. I feel completely comfortable at the theater though. The people are more down to earth."

"I'm happy for you, darling. You should buy a sewing machine to use at home."

"I plan to."

"I'd love to see your designs. Show me tomorrow, okay?"

"Yes." I turned up the radio and snuggled close to Hugh. He was right. I needed to give everything more time.

Mrs. Chambers went all out preparing a Sunday brunch like the ones we used to have at Rothmorton Hall.

"What a spread," Hugh said. "Great job, Mrs. Chambers."

I think Mrs. Chambers blushed. That would be a first.

I talked low to Hugh. "She refused to let me help, said today was special. This is the first weekend we've all been together since we moved."

"That's right," said Jack. "We need to do this regularly."

"That's my plan, for sure," I said. "Where's Ellen?"

Mrs. Chambers entered the dining room carrying a tray of breakfast pastries and set on the sideboard. "I saw her going down to the beach about an hour ago. She promised to be back for brunch."

Sylvi went straight for the coffee urn to fill an extra-large coffee mug.

"Where did you find that?" I asked.

"I brought it. Since working at the hospital, I've taken to drinking lots more coffee."

"You enjoy being a hospital nurse again?" Hugh asked.

"I really do. It's not far from the Veteran's hospital. Isn't that the one you were in before you were discharged?" Sylvi asked Hugh and took a sip of her coffee.

Hugh's face went ashen. My face froze with a fake smile.

"Sorry. Shouldn't have brought that up." Sylvi grimaced.

Hugh acted like it was nothing as he shoveled scrambled eggs in a pile on his plate. "Uh, it's all right. When I first thought about moving to San Francisco two years ago, I wondered if it was suitable for us. I walked the streets for two weeks and even paid a visit to the VA Hospital. It was weird at first. But I wouldn't have followed through if I wasn't okay with it."

I relaxed knowing he was not bothered by it. The VA hospital is where he met his first wife, Nora, Ellen's mother. I never asked him why he chose San Francisco. I figured he had business reasons, and bringing up Nora was a topic better left alone.

Ellen appeared on the terrace and took off her shoes to shake out the sand and wipe her feet off with a beach towel before entering the house.

"There's Ellen," I said to cut through the sudden dearth of conversation. "Hurry and wash up and get a plate filled or you won't get any."

Everyone laughed at the expanse of food, like that would never happen.

"Is it okay I'm wearing shorts?" Ellen looked down at her short shorts.

"You look fine, sweetheart," Hugh said.

We all were seated, except for Mrs. Chambers, who was still organizing things on the sideboard.

"Fix a plate and have a seat, Mrs. Chambers. We won't eat unless you are sitting with us," Hugh said.

"Sit next to me, Mrs. C." Ellen patted the seat of the chair next to her.

"I'm coming, I'm coming," she said and sat down.

We never said grace, but Hugh surprised us all by saying a few words. "Thank you, God, for bringing us together today and may we all be happy and content."

Everyone mumbled an "Amen." Another first.

After brunch, Hugh and I discussed a schedule for him coming home regularly. We agreed on every weekend, Friday through Sunday nights, and Wednesday night. I agreed to spend only two nights a week at the theater for the costume work and days as needed to get the work done.

We went into the spare room where I had my costume project set up. A work table with my drawing board and supplies. Another table was cluttered with patterns, books, and fabrics.

"Here are my sketches for the ladies in the ensemble."

"Impressive. You've really outdone yourself for the show."

"That means a lot to me, honey." I attempted to straighten the mess.

"So, tell me. What it's like working with the new director." Hugh held up the sketches for the main characters.

"He really is marvelous. So talented and patient with me . . . uh, and everyone in the show. He even looks like a movie actor. You know that one, Paul Newman?"

"No, I don't think so." Hugh had a funny look on his face.

"From *The Long Hot Summer*? We saw it together."

"Oh, him." He nodded.

"I am really enjoying the whole process and being part of a musical."

"This Adonis, Patrick? Should I be concerned at all the time you spend with him?"

I knew he was teasing, but I sensed something more underneath. It reminded me of what had happened with our former chauffeur. Hugh's jealousy. He hadn't shown signs of it for years. Thinking I was mistaken, for it would ruin the wonderful time I was having. I needed to feel important.

Hugh left for work on Monday morning. As great as the weekend turned out to be, I thought of Hugh's words at brunch, *happy and content*. Would that ever be possible?

CHAPTER EIGHT
ELLEN

Monday came around again and school had been going pretty well. Nina had warmed up to me. She was what they called introverted, talked little, but she smiled more than the day I met her. She played the flute in the school band. I heard someone say band people were music nerds. The way they said it wasn't nice.

Dana was outgoing and made friends easily, which was a good thing because she would have me meet them, too.

My friendship with Susan grew closer than with the other two, but we all hung out together in our mutual classes and during lunchtime.

Lunch in the cafeteria was fun. An old diner on Main Street had closed and donated their jukebox to our school. We would listen to Elvis, Frankie Avalon, and Paul Anka.

"Did you hear *A Summer Place* will be playing at the local theater? We should all go," Susan suggested.

"Yeah. Let's go," Nina said. Her eyelashes fluttered. "Don't you just love that, Troy Donahue?"

"That film came out last year and my parents wouldn't let me see it. I doubt that's changed," I said.

"We don't get every movie in our tiny town. We have to drive up to a larger city," Susan said. "If your parents wouldn't let you see it, mine wouldn't either. But *Gidget* is coming in two weeks. Sandra Dee is in that one too. Maybe we should wait until then. I know my parents would let me see it. It's just for teenagers, I've heard."

"I saw *Gidget* when it came out last year. It was a blast! I had my hair cut to look like Sandra Dee's. I'd love to see it again, especially with all of you. And Sandra is the one who started using the word creamy all the time." I smiled, eager at the prospect of doing something with my new friends.

Susan added, "She did? That's swell. My folks would let me go as long as they approved of the film. They are so old-fashioned."

"Mine too," I said.

Nina sighed. "Yeah, my parents can be such a drag sometimes. Let's plan to see *Gidget*. How fun!"

Dana was quiet.

"What about you, Dana? Would you go?" I asked.

"I'll have to ask. Maybe. Depends on if I have to babysit or not." Dana tore her paper napkin into tiny pieces, not looking at us.

We agreed we'd plan for the movie in a couple of weeks. Dana said she'd have to let us know.

After lunch, I went to my next class and a folded piece of paper was on my desk chair. I picked it up and sat down, putting my books beneath my seat. When I read it, I almost fainted. My heart pounded, and I breathed quickly, and then coughed.

I grabbed my purse and books running out of the room into the hallway, and leaned against a wall while digging through my bag, searching for the inhaler. I squeezed the inhaler and breathed deeply, with my eyes closed and tried to calm down.

Only one sentence appeared scrawled on the piece of paper.

Ellen Roth is a Bastard Child!

It mortified me. Who wrote the note and why?

"Dee? Are you all right?" Mrs. Davis, my French teacher, looked at me with a worried expression.

I pointed to my inhaler, waiting for my breathing to normalize.

"Asthma? Would you like to go to the nurse's office?"

I nodded. Anywhere but back into that classroom. Who put that note on my chair? Mrs. Davis helped me to the school nurse and left.

Nurse Smith was a kind, older, plain-looking woman with brown hair streaked with gray and pulled into a bun. She guided me to a narrow bed in a private curtained area.

"I'll call your home for someone to come get you," she said.

I had crammed the note in my purse along with the inhaler, frightened someone might see it. It would take twenty minutes or so for the inhaler to take effect, and I hoped I wouldn't need to go to the emergency room if there was one nearby.

Mom must have flown. It seemed only minutes later she rushed through the door. Knowing exactly what to do to calm me, she sat next to me on the bed and held my hand, petted my hair, her voice low and soft.

"You'll be just fine, Ellen. Once you are breathing better, I'll take you home." She turned toward the nurse. "Would you check her pulse for me?"

Nurse Smith obliged. "It's almost normal. Ellen, do you know what triggered this episode?"

I couldn't tell them the truth. "I think it was someone's perfume, maybe?"

Mom looked at me funny. Usually smells weren't triggers, but she said nothing.

At home, on my bed, away from the school, I felt normal. "I'm fine, Mom, really."

She fluffed the pillows on my bed and brought me water, and put a lightweight cover over me. "We can never be too sure. It's my fault we don't have a doctor to call. There is a clinic here though, if you have symptoms again. I've called them and they gave me the name of an excellent local doctor for a checkup."

"That's good, Mom. You won't take me to the clinic today, will you?"

"I don't think so. You seem fine to me. I'll call Sylvi in a few minutes to ask her. I think she will be off duty now." Her brows knitted together. "Why did you tell the school nurse perfume caused the attack?"

Shoot. I hoped she would give me a pass and not ask about it again.

"Well, it might have. I'm not really sure what happened. Maybe it's anxiety over a test coming up."

"Hmm. Well, if anything is making you anxious or stressed, please tell me. Okay?" She smiled and smoothed my hair.

"I will. I'm really tired now."

"Then just rest. I'm going to call Sylvi."

Mom used the phone in her bedroom next to mine, leaving the door open. I got up carefully to listen from my doorway.

"Yes, the nurse asked her and she said someone's perfume . . . No, it's not a trigger. I asked her again at home and she then said she was anxious over a test . . . that doesn't sound like her either. Something upset her, but she's not telling . . . She seems fine, but tired . . . Uh-huh. I have a number for a doctor, just in case, and there is the local clinic. You don't need to come down. I'll let you know if you should. Thank you so much . . ." She hung up, and I went back to the bed, just before she came into my room.

"Sylvi says it sounds like you will be fine for now. But for you to let me know if anything upsets you like today."

"I will."

❧

The next day, Susan asked me why I wasn't in class. She was the only person I trusted completely at school to tell. During a break, we went outside under a tree near the bike racks. I showed her the crumpled note.

"Oh, my gosh! Who could have written this?"

"I don't know. Has anyone said anything to you about it?"

"No, not to me, anyway. I'm so sorry this happened. Why would someone do this to you?"

"The only people I know are the girls we eat with during lunch. Do you think any of them might be jealous, about, well, you know, maybe they know about my family's wealth?"

"Your family? I don't even know about it. I know you live in a pretty fancy house. But, lots of people do along the beach. Though I would have thought you'd go to a private school."

"I used to until we moved here. But my mom didn't want me boarding at the one they liked that's too far away."

"Yeah, that makes sense. I wondered about that."

"Because I don't use slang?"

"I guess."

"Maybe you can help me with that sometime?" I knew Susan would be a very special friend to me.

"Sure thing, Ellie. And if I hear anything about these revolting notes, you can count on me to tell you right away. We need to get to class. We'll be late." She gave me a quick hug, and we hurried to the next period.

❧

Each day, I watched to see if people were staring at me or whispering. Eventually, Susan told me she heard whisperings about it. Some girls didn't know what it meant at first.

"Sorry, Ellie. I said it was a lie and that someone was trying to hurt you. I told them not to believe it and tell others. They agreed it was mean to start a rumor about you and thought you were a real sweet girl."

"That's kind of you, Susan. I'm glad to hear at least a few people didn't believe the lie. I feel so humiliated and want to run and hide."

"Just hold your head up high. Like that song from *Carousel*. My sister Ann is in the chorus of the community theater production."

"She is? That's cool. My mom is designing the costumes." I'd used a few slang words when I spoke at school, hoping I was doing it right. I didn't want people to think I was conceited.

"Oh yeah. So, anyway, you know what's on that piece of paper isn't true, so don't give that person whoever wrote it the satisfaction. That's what my older sister told me."

"Oh gee, does she know about it too?" My face fell and my stomach rolled.

"No, she's a freshman in college. It's something she told me once, and I remembered. But I have some fun news to take your mind off it." Susan's face lit up.

"Like what?"

"Ann invited me to a beach party and said I could bring my friends. It's next Saturday, before the water turns too cold to swim."

"A beach party? Where?"

"North of where you live, but south of the point. It's where they surf. Lots of people go there from all over. It'll be fun and won't just be kids from here."

It sounded great, and it would definitely take my mind off the rumors. "I'll ask my parents. It's fine if your sister is older and driving, and there will be a group of us.

❧

In English class the next morning, Dana was quiet, her arms folded and barely spoke to me. I was afraid to mention the rumors. Maybe she had heard them and didn't want to be my friend anymore. I was convinced people, mostly girls, were whispering about me behind their hands.

Mr. Stevens smiled at me, but didn't ask me to stay after class. I wondered if he had heard the rumors. I shuddered at the thought. What if the teachers knew too? I kept my head down unless the teacher was talking, and didn't look around the entire period. Susan tapped me on the arm with her pencil and I turned toward her. She just smiled and mouthed, *don't worry*. I was lucky to have her as a friend.

When I got home from school, Mom was in the living room sitting on the sofa. From certain angles, looking out the windows, it looked like the house was floating on top of the water. I sat next to her and asked about going to the beach party.

"You say there will be a group of you going together. Who?"

"Well, Susan, a really, really, good friend, uh I think Dana, and Nina. These are the girls I eat lunch with every day. Susan's sister Ann, and her best friend Jane, go to college. Ann is eighteen and drives."

Mom put her finger to her forehead like she does when she is thinking something over.

"I'd like to meet Ann and Susan when they come to pick you up. If the others are with them, I want to meet them too."

"Oh, thank you, Mom!" I gave her a great big hug. "You're positively sensational."

She chuckled as she hugged me back. "I want you to have fun and make lots of friends. Just be careful and don't be persuaded to do anything you know isn't right."

"I will."

"You know, I've been worried about you lately. You seemed depressed and I could have sworn I heard you crying the other night. Were you?"

"Oh golly, no. Maybe it was my TV. I might have been a little down. My friend Dana has been acting oddly lately, but if she comes to the beach party, then it should all be good."

Lying to her was a terrible thing to do, and I hated it. The whole thing with the rumors tore at my insides. But I couldn't tell Mom or Dad, especially Aunt Sylvi. What would they think?

"Well, I hope so. Oh, and there's a letter for you on the foyer table."

I dashed to the foyer and picked up the envelope. Sure enough, a letter from my best friend, Kathy, in Plymouth. I tore down the hall to my room to open it. She'd sent a birthday card and a letter.

Dear Ellen,

I got your letters. Sorry you are so unhappy there. I miss you, too. It takes time to get used to a new place. Remember when my family moved to Plymouth. I was so unhappy until you came along. When you make new friends, it will get better. I promise. Freshman class is going well. Lots of homework. Bet you do too.

My parents said we might take a trip to California next summer and go to the amusement park, Disneyland. Have you been there? It's south of you. Maybe you and your parents can meet us down there. Wouldn't that be a blast?

Well, that's all for now. Keep in touch,
Kathy
P.S. Sorry I missed celebrating your birthday, hope it was special.

Getting Kathy's letter should have made me happy. It only made me miss her more and all my friends back east.

CHAPTER NINE
DEE

Ellen had returned to normal, and I waved goodbye as she walked up the drive to wait for the bus. The first meeting of the Costume Committee was this morning. Filled with excitement, I dressed in a blue floral print dress with a scooped neckline and slipped on a pair of espadrilles. Barrettes secured the sides of my shoulder-length hair, letting it fall naturally, and I stroked on a light red lipstick. A casual day working didn't call for anything more. I glanced at my watch, and rushed loading the car with my patterns, sketches, and sewing supplies, not wanting to be late the first day.

A white and green Chevy was the only car parked in the theater parking lot. My committee members, I assumed. Two heads bobbed up and down inside the car. When I got out of my car to open the trunk, the two ladies were on their way over, waving.

"Yoo-hoo, Mrs. Roth," Mrs. Graves called out. Short, curly brown, and gray curls framed her cheerful face, crowned with a cute white hat. She smoothed down her calico-print shirt-waisted dress over her full hips and scuttled over to me. "Do you need any help?"

"Good morning, Mrs. Graves. Yes, I could use a little help."

The two women reached my car and Mrs. Graves introduced her friend, Mrs. Birch.

"I'm very happy to be here. Ethyl told me all about you and I'm so eager to work with you." She appeared to be late thirties, with platinum blonde hair pulled into a severe-looking bun at the back of her head. Wire-framed glasses rested half-way down her nose, giving her the proverbial librarian look.

I eyed her brown and white polka-dot dress with big white buttons down the front. "Lovely dress. Did you make it?" I asked.

"Sure did." There was just a hint of pride showing through her expressionless face.

I handed my sewing kit to her and a bag of patterns. To Mrs. Graves, I held out some books and another bag of fabric samples I had found at the local fabric store.

She took them and her eyes grew large. "Oh my, you've been busy." She attempted to balance her large purse with the things I handed her.

"I have so much to discuss with you. My mind is brimming with ideas and I have sketches."

"Oh, you are an artist, too?" Mrs. Birch asked.

"Not exactly, but you'll get the ideas." We crossed the parking lot to the outside stage door, which I unlocked with the set of keys Patrick had given me, and down the stairs to the costume department.

Mrs. Graves switched on all the overhead lights and set her load down on an empty table. She went straight to the sewing machines to remove the covers. "These haven't been used since the last show. They need some oiling, I 'spect."

"Good idea." I placed my sketches and notebook on the same table and sorted through the various patterns and then spread out the fabric samples, gesturing to the ladies to sit. "Let me first thank you for volunteering and being here today. If you don't mind, could we address each other by our first names? Please call me Dee."

"I'm Ethyl, in case you didn't already know. We are less formal in private situations." She chuckled.

"Call me Betty," Mrs. Birch said with her mouth in a straight line. She was as somber as Ethyl was jovial.

"As far as our schedule. I will be down here in the evening on Tuesdays and Thursdays for measuring the cast members this week, and in the future, for fittings and such. During the day on Monday, Wednesday, and Friday, I'll be here 8-12 for the production work. It would be best if you could work the same hours until we have the majority of the work accomplished. What do you think?"

"Sounds good. Are you sure you haven't done this before? You seem to have everything well planned." Betty narrowed her eyes.

"Trust me, this is my first. Oh, and at some point, I may be joining a bridge club to fill in for someone temporarily once a week."

"We play bridge too," Ethyl said. "When your commitment is done with the other club, you could join ours."

"I'd love to join yours. I'll let you know."

Ethyl beamed at me.

"By the way, how do you know each other? Are you both from Starlight Bay?"

Ethyl chuckled. "I'm from here, born and raised. But Betty moved here . . ." She turned to Betty.

"Five years ago," Betty said. "My husband is much older than me and retired then. We used to live in the Los Angeles area. He'd always wanted to live up here."

"We heard you moved here in July," Ethyl said.

"My daughter and I moved once the house was completed and decorated. We came from Plymouth, Massachusetts. But, I'm originally from Illinois. Farm country." I was pleased by the affirmations from the two ladies when they heard farm country.

"We thought you all came from a wealthy background," Ethyl looked embarrassed. "I mean judging by the huge house on the beach."

"My husband comes from money in the Boston area, yes." I left it at that, not wanting to get too personal about my background, or Hugh's.

"Well, we're glad to have you." Ethyl nodded her head with approval and Betty did the same.

"So . . . about the dresses. I took the estimated number of hours to made one costume and multiplied it by the number of dresses we need for the main characters and the dancers and chorus. Then I divided it by three. If you know of anyone else, that could help, please let me know."

"My goodness, how many dancers and chorus will there be?" Betty scrunched her brow.

"Mr. Stevens said there are thirteen people in the ensemble. Men and women who perform as singers and dancers. For the women, we could use the same basic dress for all their scenes and change up the look with scarves and aprons."

"Terrific idea, Dee." Betty pushed her glasses up to look at the sketches. "These are marvelous drawings, and the fabrics you chose are colorful."

"I'm still working to convince my niece to volunteer. She's an excellent seamstress," Ethyl said.

"Please let me know about your niece. Now, have either of you seen the stage production or the film that came out in 1956?"

"I've seen both," Ethyl said. "The traveling Broadway production was in San Francisco and the film came here for a short while. It's a beautiful and sad story."

I nodded.

"I saw the film," Betty said.

"Good. If either of you have any suggestions regarding my designs and on fabric choices, please don't hesitate to speak up. I consider us a team. Okay?"

I think Betty might have cracked a tiny smile and Ethyl thanked me. These ladies were friendly and easygoing. Being from a farming community, I've always felt more comfortable with the working class and average housewives. No matter how much I worked at fitting into Hugh's world, I still doubted myself and my choices.

After the ladies left, I stayed behind to mull over more photos of period fashions writing notes in my book when I heard someone coming down the stairs.

"Did you forget something?" I called.

"It's me, Patrick." He reached the bottom of the stairs.

"Oh, I thought it was Ethyl. I wasn't expecting you today. We just finished our first session. They are lovely ladies. We should get along just fine."

"I'm pleased to hear it. You up for lunch?"

"I don't really have anything to show you, since I'm expected at home. Perhaps another day?"

"Sure, sure." His smile vanished.

"I'll be here tomorrow night to take measurements during rehearsal and I could show you my sketches."

"That's sounds fine. Enjoy the rest of your day."

I detected the tone of disappointment in his voice. We would be around each other a lot over the next several weeks. He'll be sick of me. With a laugh to myself, I collected my belongings and made my way back to the house.

CHAPTER TEN
ELLEN

Saturday hadn't come fast enough, as I did my best to ignore any weird stares and whispering at school. Fortunately, no one said anything to my face. Knowing classmates thought I was illegitimate was bad enough. Mom confirmed it was fine with Dad for me to attend the beach party. I was a little worried he might say no.

My excitement competed with my nervousness. I wore my two-piece swimsuit with a t-shirt and shorts over it, sunglasses, sandals, and a straw beach hat. In my beach bag, was my beach towel and a few personal items, including my inhaler. I hoped it wouldn't be needed. That would be embarrassing, with no place to hide. Oh, and I almost forgot my new camera!

A car pulled into the drive.

"They're here." I peeked out the glass window in the double door entrance. Susan and Nina, plus two other girls, were coming up the walkway. I opened the door. "Come on in. Mom wants to meet you."

"This is my sister Ann," Susan said. "And her friend, Jane." They strained their necks to see down the hall, and I chuckled to myself.

Ann was the oldest and the tallest, too. She wore her sun-lightened dark blonde hair in a ponytail. Jane, shorter than me, was almost eighteen. Her mousy brown hair looked cute in pigtails with red ribbons, and she wore a shift over her swimsuit. I knew it was a bikini, because the spaghetti straps tied around her neck showed.

"Come on back to the living room. She's waiting." Their expressions of amazement pleased me when they entered the spacious room.

"Oh, wow!" Ann gawked at the view from the windows.

"Uh, this is my mom, Mrs. Roth. Mom, this is my friend Susan Murphy and her sister Ann, who is driving, and her friend Jane Arden." I pointed at the last one trailing in behind. "And this is my friend Nina Gallo."

Mom stood and shook each of the girls' hands. They were all smiling ear to ear. She addressed Ann and Jane first. "I understand both of you are freshman at the community college."

They nodded.

"Have you declared a major yet?"

Ann spoke first. "I'm undeclared at present. But I'm leaning toward English and maybe go into teaching."

"That's quite commendable. Did you know I was once a teacher?"

Ann and the others looked surprised. It wasn't like I told everyone my tutor married my dad.

"You're the costume designer for the musical *Carousel*, right? I'm in the chorus," Ann said.

"Yes, I recall your name on the costume list. Isn't the show exciting?"

"I'm loving it."

Mom turned to Susan and Nina. "Both of you are freshman with Ellen. How is your first year going so far?"

They stammered awkward answers and Mom finally let us all go. When we were all in the car, I apologized.

"What for, Ellie?" Ann said. "Our parents did the same thing with me when I was your age. She's nice and a lovely woman. You'll have to tell us all about her being a teacher when we get to the beach. Let's go, okay? You all ready to have some fun?"

We all screamed with glee as Ann drove the car down the drive and to the highway.

Susan, Nina and I sat in the back seat while Jane sat up front.

"Where's Dana?" I asked.

"She said she had to babysit all day." Nina rolled her eyes.

"You don't believe her?" I said.

"I don't know. She's been acting odd all week. Haven't you noticed?"

Susan said nothing and looked out the window. "Hey see the boys out there surfing. That looks like a blast."

"Yeah, a blast," I said.

Ann drove up the highway north a few miles to Surfers' Beach. She parked in the dirt lot across the road from the beach area where dozens of teenagers tanned themselves on beach towels and played games on the sand. There was a volleyball net and several girls in bikinis and boys in swim trunks playing.

Ann opened the back end of her Chevy Impala. We gathered round to retrieve an ice chest filled with drinks and sandwiches, a large beach umbrella, and an extra-large beach blanket.

"I'm sorry, Ann, I didn't even think to bring any food." I was embarrassed.

"You're our guest, Ellie. Don't worry about it. Maybe next time you can bring something, okay?" Ann's sincere smile erased my concern.

"Thanks. Sure, hope there will be a next time. It's my first beach party."

"No way," said Susan. "I have a lot to learn about you, Ellie Roth."

I shrugged my shoulders. Maybe I would tell her all about my strangely sheltered life. But not today. I wanted to have some fun and excitement.

We carried everything across the road and down to where Ann and Jane's friends were waving for us to join them. As we passed through groups of partygoers, several transistor radios battled to be the loudest.

"Hey Ann, Jane," said a trim girl with pale blonde hair in a long ponytail and a tiny bikini. She looked almost naked. "We got here an hour ago, and this was the best spot we could get."

"This is a nifty spot. Thanks for getting here early." Ann introduced us to her friend, Gayle.

"Barb is already out with some guy trying to learn to surf. Can you dig it?" Gayle pointed out to the waves. Several guys and one girl were sitting on surfboards.

"Why are they sitting on the boards?" I asked.

"Waiting for the next wave to ride. Just watch," Susan said.

While the others put up the umbrella and laid the blanket on the sand next to Gayle's umbrella, I watched the surfers.

Not sure what to do, I pulled off my t-shirt and shorts, exposing my two-piece swimsuit, and sat under Ann's umbrella and retrieved the new camera from my bag. "Want your picture taken?"

All the girls screamed "Yes!" and started to pose together. I took several photos of the group, all with the ocean in the background.

Susan grabbed two Cokes from the ice chest and handed me one. "That's a real fancy camera you have."

"I got it for my birthday a few weeks ago. I'm still learning how to use it."

"When was your birthday?" Susan asked.

"August 29th. It was just the family. This is the first year I didn't have a big party."

"You have me and Nina, oh and Dana, of course. Now you know my sister and her friends. Pretty soon, you'll know everyone. It's a small town ... oh look." Susan pointed off the left of us.

"What are you pointing at?"

"Those boys are from the prep school way south of town. Aren't they dreamy?" Susan gawked.

She was right. Most of the boys were good-looking. They were all shirtless with short swim trunks.

Nina came over to sit with us. "What are you looking at?"

I leaned toward her. "Dreamy boys!" I laughed.

"Cool." She hid behind Susan, looking over her shoulder.

"Oh Nina, stop hiding. They'll never see you back there." Susan giggled.

"That's the idea." Nina grinned, though.

One boy just stared at us.

"That one boy is staring as much as we are," Susan said. "I think he's looking at you, Ellie."

"How can you tell he's not looking at you?" I elbowed her. He did kinda look like he was watching me, and it gave me a nervous flutter in my stomach.

The boy walked toward us, his shoulders broad and his back straight. He had dark hair and tanned skin, with adorable dimples in his cheeks. The way he carried himself full of confidence was like a prince. And then . . . oh my gosh, he stopped right in front of our umbrella.

"Are all of you from the girls' school?"

Susan giggled. "No, Starlight Bay High School."

He turned and looked right at me. "You wanna learn how to surf?"

"Surf? I don't know. It looks fun, but isn't it dangerous?"

He laughed. But it wasn't at me. "Heck, what's the point if it's safe?" He held out his hand. "Come on, you can watch for a while first, okay?"

It was the strangest thing. Like I was in a trance. My hand took his, and he pulled me up. I grabbed my bag and followed. Just like that. I looked over my shoulder at my friends. Their mouths were gaping open.

The boy went over to a long surfboard stuck into the sand. He dropped my hand and took hold of the board. The wind whipped up, and before my hat flew off my head, I caught the ribbons tying them under my chin.

"My name is Adam Greenberg. What's yours?" He brushed off the sand from the board.

"Ellie Roth?"

"Cute name for a cute girl."

Oh dear, the warmth of a full-on blush rose to my face. He called me cute.

"Thanks."

"Are you Jewish? Roth sounds like it might be."

"I'm not anything. We don't go to church." I wasn't about to tell a stranger about my parentage. Especially when I didn't know myself. "Are you Jewish?"

"Sort of. My dad is, but my mom is Protestant."

"I don't really care about things like that."

He stopped and looked at me up and down like he was assessing my value in dollars per pound. "You are really something. How old are you?"

"Thirteen."

"You look a lot older. I'm fifteen, will be sixteen soon. Then I can drive."

Gee, he thought I was older? My confidence returned, and I relaxed. "That would be great!"

"Let's go farther down to where my buddies are surfing. You can sit on the beach and watch."

"Cool." The rush of meeting and talking to a boy as handsome as Adam made me lightheaded. "Can I take pictures?"

"Sure thing."

For the next hour, I watched Adam and his friend catch a curl, so he told me. Susan and Nina sat with me and I took so many pictures, I ran out of film.

"What a gas, Ellie," Susan said. "You caught yourself a live one."

"What do you mean by that?" I scrunched up my nose.

"I heard it in a movie once. There are always more fish in the sea. They were talking about boys." She laughed and pushed me over.

"That's funny." I was gobsmacked over Adam. That's a word I heard in a movie I saw on TV. It just felt right. "Susan, your face is all red."

"Yeah, from the sun. It's my fair skin, reddish hair, and freckles. My mom insists I wear a hat all the time." She had the hat in her hand and slapped it on her head. "I just hate wearing anything on my head, makes my head hot."

"I know what you mean."

When Adam finished surfing, he wanted to show me how, but I was too chicken. He was so sweet and didn't even make fun of me. Instead, he invited two of his friends to join us. Chris had almost white hair with dark blue eyes and taller than Adam. I kinda stared at his muscular arms. He had just turned sixteen and drove his own car. Dan was Adam's age but shorter, with an average build, hazel eyes, and brown hair. Both went to the same prep school.

Dan took to Nina right away, and she liked him too, because she smiled with her braces showing. Dan didn't seem to mind. Maybe because he wore extra thick eyeglasses. When Nina took off her sundress, I noticed her chest wasn't as flat as in school. Susan whispered to me Nina's swimsuit had little pads that made her look fuller. That's why she was more relaxed around Dan.

Chris sat next to Susan, and they hit it off right away.

Adam and I spent the rest of the time talking about everything. My reaction to Adam confused me because of the feelings I had about Mr. Stevens. I had a lot to learn about myself: crushes, love, and life.

"I'm so sorry, Ellie, but I have to leave now," Adam said. "We've been here since early this morning. So, can I call you sometime?"

"I guess you can. I think we're the only Roth in Starlight Bay." I tried not to giggle, but I was so nervous. "Our house is on the beach south of Main Street."

"Groovy, Ellie Roth of Starlight Bay. I'll talk to you soon." As he walked away from me, he kept turning around to wave.

When I went back to the girls, they all crowded around me, asking tons of questions. "I'm starved, and then maybe I'll answer some of your questions."

I felt like I was floating on air. It was the best day of my life since moving to California.

Susan pulled me aside. "We should talk, in private before we leave."

"Gee, Susan, you sound serious. What's going on?"

Susan moved far out of the way to make sure no one could hear her.

"I found out who started that horrible rumor about you." Susan's eyes darted around us.

My stomach turned. "Who? How?"

"I was asking around and finally someone had heard directly from the source. I really hate to have to tell you this. You need to know that she is not your friend."

"Who is it, Susan?"

"Dana. But I don't know or understand why."

"Dana? I thought she was my friend?" My world started to spin around in circles in my head. I took hold of Susan's arm to steady me.

"Are you okay?"

"No, I need to sort this out. It doesn't make any sense." I turned and ran to the road and kept going toward home. My straw hat had blown back to flap behind me, the ribbons pulling at my throat. I didn't care. Why would Dana do this to me? What does she know?

Out of breath, I stopped for a minute, my beach bag hanging like a ton of bricks on my arm. I walked, tears streaming down my cheeks. A car horn blasted behind me. I turned around. The girls were in Ann's car as she drove around me and pulled to the side of the road. Susan jumped out of the car and ran toward me and wrapped me in her arms.

"Golly, Ellie, I'm so sorry. Come on, let's take you home."

I nodded and got into the car. Ann stared at me through her rearview mirror but said nothing. Jane turned around from the front seat. "You, okay?"

"Uh-huh." Worried that they knew why I ran off. I looked at Susan, who zipped her mouth closed with her fingers, so I knew she hadn't. Nina looked at me with pity. She knew.

When I entered the house, Mom, and Mrs. C came to the foyer.

"Did you have a fun?" Mom asked.

"Sure, I had a great time." I barely looked at them. "I'm exhausted. Can I tell you about it tomorrow?"

"Of course, honey. Are you hungry?"

"Not right now. Maybe later." They had to know something was wrong. Lying does not come easily to me.

Dana and her lies were on my mind. I had to speak with her. The sooner the better.

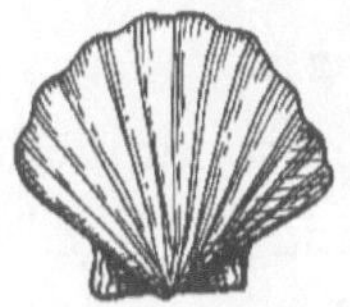

CHAPTER ELEVEN
ELLEN

At school on Monday, I pretended everything was normal in English and the other classes I had with Dana. Susan kept watching me. In French class, Susan made me promise to not tell Dana how I knew she had started the rumor.

In our last period of the day, Math class, I told Dana we needed to talk after school. It was important. She acted nervous and tried to get me to tell her what it was about. I just said it was private, and I didn't want to talk inside the school. She agreed to go with me to the track field. I didn't even care about missing the bus home.

As soon as class ended, Dana and I left for the bleachers. Neither of us spoke, which was strange. We usually talked non-stop. Step by step we climbed the bleachers, reaching the top row. The sun was behind us and its heat beat down on my back. Dana sat next to me, leaving three feet between us, like some kind of protective barrier. The only weapon with me was my voice and my anger.

"What do you want to talk about?" Dana crossed her arms, her mouth pinched in an emotionless straight line.

Dropping my books on the bench, I turned to her. "You started the rumor about me being a bastard, and I want an explanation. Why? I thought we were friends." My voice was steady.

"Friends?" she spat. "As soon as I heard your last name on the first day of school, I knew we could never be friends."

I flinched. "My last name?"

"I know who you are. Ever since I was six years old, I listened to my aunt and mother go on and on about the Roths and their little 'Princess Ellen.' You with your wealth and privilege."

"What could your mother and aunt know about me? I don't understand."

"I know exactly who your actual parents are. Hugh and Dee adopted you."

"Yes, I'm adopted. What's so terrible about that? My real parents are dead."

"It was terrible for me. Don't you understand? My aunt talked about the bastard child for years. I was sick of it. My father divorced my mom and abandoned me all because of what happened with my aunt and your parents. He got sick of it too?"

"I still don't understand, Dana. Who is your aunt?"

"Rebecca Slade." Dana got up and climbed down a few rows.

I followed her. "That name sounds familiar. But I don't know her. Stop and tell me what this is all about, please?"

Dana stopped. She breathed heavily and her hands had balled into fists. Then they relaxed, and she sat down again.

I sat on the bench behind her.

Dana turned to face me. "Aunt Becky was married to your real father, Hubert Slade."

My mouth dropped open. "My real father was your uncle? I remember something now. I read it in some old newspapers at the library back in Plymouth. There were rumors I didn't understand and did some research. Becky killed her husband, and they sentenced her to an asylum for the criminally insane. She'd been living in Plymouth and they captured her there. The articles in the papers didn't mention me or my mother, Nora." I had forgotten about it, because it was just too awful.

"Now do you understand?"

"No. I don't understand the connection, other than your uncle was my birth father. How my mother knew your uncle hadn't been explained to me, and it wasn't in the paper either. I'd assumed they were married, and that Becky killed him in a jealous rage over something. I didn't know why."

"Didn't they tell you the whole story?"

It was plain that Dana didn't believe me. "No. They told me when I was older, I would understand."

"You're older now, so I guess I'll be the one to tell you." Dana put her hands on her hips and smirked. "Your real father, Hubert, was married to my Aunt Becky. But Hubert got your real mother, Nora Roth, pregnant. Nora was crazy, just like Aunt Becky. They were in the same institution."

"That's a lie. I would have been told." Would they though? My parents hadn't told me much about her. Was Nora really crazy? I felt sick to my stomach. Dana's words swirled around my head. I thought I might vomit.

"Just ask them. Anyway, Aunt Becky knew that a rich man adopted Nora's baby, which is you, and you lived like a princess. All the while, my mom struggled to support us after my dad left. I've had nothing, and you had everything. All I'd heard from Mom and my aunt were terrible things about Uncle Hubert and what he did to women. They hated him and blamed him and Hugh Roth for all of Aunt Becky's problems."

"What? Why did they blame Hugh? My dad." I wanted to defend my dad, but Dana kept talking.

"My Aunt Becky blamed Hugh because he put his wife Nora in the same hospital. If she hadn't been there, none of that would have happened. She said Uncle Hubert and your mother had an affair. You know how babies are made, don't you?"

My face went hot and my stomach turned somersaults. "Y-y-yes, I think so." I held my stomach. "How does that make me a bastard?"

"Because they weren't married to each other, that's how." She laughed with wild eyes at me, a wicked blood-curdling laugh.

I shuddered. "Stop it, Dana. I don't want to hear anymore. None of it matters, because what you did to me was a terrible thing and I don't deserve it. Maybe *you* are just as crazy as your aunt. I hate you. I'll hate you forever."

I screamed at her, grabbed my books and hurried down the bleachers as fast as I could.

Dana yelled to me. "At least now you know the truth!" She cackled like a witch. I could hear her all the way to the school parking lot.

Maybe I knew the truth, maybe I didn't. Becky was insane. How could anyone believe anything coming from her? I needed my mom, Dee. She was my true mother. The only one I'd ever known. Whatever it was, I had to know the truth.

It felt like déjà vu, walking alone on the side of the road, far from home, just like last Saturday on the beach. What Dana told me seared through my mind. I must have walked a mile when I saw Mom's car coming toward me. She stopped and waved me over. I got in the car, not knowing what I would say.

"Honey, what happened? When you didn't come home on the bus, I came looking for you." She put the car in gear and, after a car passed us, made a U-turn.

"I'm sorry. Something came up."

"Something came up?" She shot a sideways glance at me. "Whatever it was, you look white as a sheet. We'll talk when we get home."

My eyes stared straight ahead, avoiding Mom's questioning eyes. My head hurt from everything Dana told me. Mom turned off the highway at our drive and to the house. Neither of us spoke while walking to the front door. Mrs. C was gone to visit her son, so we would be alone.

Mom went in ahead of me and I dropped my books on the foyer table.

"Let's sit in the living room. Want anything to drink?"

"Sure, a Coke?" I went to one of the two strange modern chairs next to the window overlooking the ocean. They had only three legs and no armrests. Dad loved them, but they weren't comfortable. I stared at the ocean while fluffy clouds filled the sky and little patches of brilliant blue peeked through.

Mom handed me the green glass bottle of Coke. Her face lined with concern. "Okay, so tell me what's going on with you." She sat in the matching chair opposite me.

I took a deep breath and told her everything Dana said about her mom, Aunt Becky, Uncle Hubert, and the horrible rumor she had spread through the Freshman class. I continued to stare out the window, afraid to look at her. When I finished talking, I looked down at my hands in my lap.

"Ellen." Her voice was just a whisper. She reached over and took my hands in hers, forcing me to raise my eyes. Her eyes glistened with unshed tears and she looked as if she'd seen a ghost.

"This is a bizarre twist of fate that we moved to the same town as Becky Slade's sister."

"It is. But I'm still confused. Some of it didn't make sense. Did Dad's first wife really have an affair with Dana's uncle?"

"She has some of the story wrong. I'm so sorry you had to hear any of it from someone who wanted to hurt you. It wasn't fair to you at all. Your father and I should have told you sooner the disturbing and sad story about your real mother, and the man who fathered you."

"You're my real mother," I choked.

"Thank you, honey. I meant your birth mother. However, Dana doesn't have the whole story and some of what she'd heard from her mother and aunt isn't entirely true. The story needs to come from your father, the man who has loved and cared for you. Do you think you can wait until he comes home?"

All I could do was nod my head. "Oh, Mommy!" I burst into tears and fell into her arms as she rocked me back and forth, petting my hair.

She told me to ignore Dana and the rumors the next day at school. She promised everything would be worked out. We had a peaceful dinner, then snuggled on the cozy sofa and watched a movie. Although I dreaded facing Dana, I trusted in Mom's word that everything would be fine.

CHAPTER TWELVE

DEE

The anger I felt toward Dana consumed me. How dare she spread rumors about my darling girl and tell her the horrid story of Becky, Hubert, and Nora.

After Ellen left for school, I called the operator to get the number for Connie Anderson, Dana's mother. No one answered. I kept calling until someone did.

"Is this Connie Anderson, Dana's mother?" I struggled to keep my voice calm, not wanting to alert her.

"Yes, it is. Who's calling?"

"I'm the mother of one of Dana's classmates, and I would like to meet with you to discuss the vicious rumors she spread at school about my daughter."

"What? Are you sure it was my Dana?"

"Positive."

"Who's your daughter?"

"Ellen Roth." I gave her a moment to let that sink in.

"Who are you?"

"I'm Mrs. Hugh Roth. Shall I come to your home? Or would you like to hash this out in public?" The strength of conviction coursed through me.

"Dee Roth? You live in Starlight Bay?"

"Didn't you know?"

"This is unbelievable. I moved Dana here a year ago to get away from all that craziness."

"Well, your daughter has continued the tirade on Ellen. It needs to stop."

Silence.

"Are you there?"

"Yes, I think it would be best if you come here. Let me give you my address. How about 1 p.m.?" Before hanging up I jotted down her address.

Ellen had told me Dana didn't take the bus. She lived walking distance from the school. The address took me to an apartment building. Connie said their apartment was on the first level in the back of the parking lot.

The woman who opened the door looked nothing like how I remembered Becky Slade. Connie had straight brown hair in a short bob with bangs and wore what looked like a uniform.

She let me into a tiny, but neat, living room.

"You look just like the photos in the society column," Connie said.

"What paper?"

"The Boston Globe."

"I thought Becky was in New York," I said.

"She is. One of the attendants at my sister's asylum would give her copies. She showed me whenever she found something about your family."

I was sitting on the edge of the sofa, as if I was readying for a dash out the door. "I'm sorry, but that sounds creepy to me."

"Becky's mind has been . . ." She made a strained expression and looked at the ceiling, "frozen in time. All she thinks or talks about is what happened all those years ago with her husband and yours and Ellen."

"I'm sorry to hear that. Rehabilitation would be difficult then?

She laughed. "She's so far gone, there's no help for her. They keep her sedated most of the time. I just couldn't take it anymore and stopped visiting. After my divorce, I brought Dana out here."

"I see. What a bizarre coincidence we all moved to the same town. We moved here the end of July once the house was built."

"Oh, you built a house here?"

"On the beach."

"Lucky you." She swallowed hard and looked me in the eye. "Please believe me. Dana never mentioned your daughter to me."

"I believe you. If she wanted revenge on Ellen, she wouldn't have told you anything."

"Revenge? Is that what you think? I know she's been depressed and lonely. I work at a local motel and as a waitress, to support us. Dana's father still lives in New York but doesn't help with support. He was sick of the whole scandal with Becky, and I probably made it worse talking about her all the time, too."

I opened my purse and pulled out the wrinkled note and handed it to Connie. "This is one of the notes left on Ellen's desk one day."

Connie read it and gasped. "Holy Mary," she muttered under her breath. "There were others too?"

"We think so, and by word of mouth." I took the note from Connie and put it back in my purse. Hugh would want to see it. "It was a girl who told a friend of Ellen's that the rumor came from Dana. When Ellen confronted Dana, she admitted it and then told the story as she knew it to Ellen. Dana said she had been sick of hearing all about Uncle Hubert's little princess Ellen, and how protected she was from the scandal. She's jealous and wanted Ellen to hurt as much as she has all these years."

Connie pressed her hands to her cheeks and shook her head. "Really? She said that? I had no idea Dana was so affected by the scandal surrounding Becky. I thought she was acting out because she was unhappy about us moving here and that her dad bailed on us. She was only seven at the time of the arrest and trial. But before all of that happened, my sister lived with us for a short while after she left the sanitorium, before going home to Hubert. She disappeared before the police found him dead. I didn't know where she went. Perhaps Dana overheard Becky talking about it. This truly shocks me. But doesn't Ellen know the story?"

"Only part of it, as you only know part of it, too. We've been waiting, perhaps too long, to tell Ellen everything about her parentage. Before yesterday, Ellen only knew her birth mother had died during childbirth, and her birth father was killed by his wife. Ellen knows Hugh had once been married to her mother. We hadn't told her they were still married when she was born."

"Ellen must be devastated by what Dana told her. I am so sorry." Connie's eyes began to tear.

I almost felt sorry for Connie and all she had gone through. But Ellen was my daughter and her feelings came first.

"To say the least, yes, she was a mess. She didn't know about Becky and Hubert. And, she never knew about all the things Becky had done. We protected her from it."

Connie got up and went to a bookshelf, retrieving a folder. She gave it to me.

"What's this?" I asked.

"The transcript from Becky's trial. I'm guessing you and Hugh didn't want to know anything about it, and I don't blame you."

"You're right. We didn't. In fact, Hugh refused to press charges for everything Becky did to us and to Hugh's property before she was arrested. He didn't want it in the papers. He figured they would punish Becky enough for the murder of Hubert."

Connie didn't blink an eye. "I know about that. But it didn't matter, because it's all in the transcript, anyway."

I snapped my head up from the unopened folder. "How?"

"Becky confessed to everything she knew about Nora, Hugh, and Ellen, and all the terrible things she did in Plymouth."

My hand went to my chest, my heart was pounding. "Is Dana aware of the folder's contents?"

Connie sighed and slumped into her chair. "I don't think so. I've kept it under lock and key all these years. You can have those. I don't want them anymore. For me, it's all in the past. I want to concentrate on the future."

"I'll give these to my husband. He'll want to know what's on record." I paused to take a deep breath. "Now, what will be done about Dana?"

"When she gets home from school, I'll have a long talk with her. Then take her to your house so that she can apologize to your family." She leaned forward, her eyes begging forgiveness.

"That is an excellent suggestion. We will need to set a date and time so my husband can be at the house. He works in San Francisco for long hours sometimes."

"Of course. I-I don't know what else to say, that I haven't already. I look forward to when we all meet." She looked older than when I first arrived. If I had met her elsewhere, I would have thought her a nice, hardworking mother. She had the misfortune of having a nutty sister and then a daughter who sought revenge.

I stood with the folder under my arm. "Let's tentatively set the meeting for tomorrow at 5 pm. I'll call you to confirm. Oh, and where are your dogs? Dana hoped we would buy a puppy, but we don't have the space yet."

"The dogs? I sold them all. Someone made me an offer I couldn't refuse, since we really needed the money."

"I see. Dana must have been upset by that. From what Ellen told me Dana really loved them."

"I told her the dogs were just to make extra money and to not get attached. But you know how kids are." She shrugged her shoulders showing no regret.

I felt a bit sorry for Dana. Connie didn't come across as a compassionate parent. When I left the apartment and got into my car, I sat there, shaking. My emotions were all over the place. I hated having the folder in my possession, though I was curious about what Becky had said in court. My next action would be to call Hugh.

CHAPTER THIRTEEN
HUGH

Hugh checked the rearview mirror as he backed out of the parking space and exited the garage in the basement of his office building. He'd promised to leave early enough to make it home by 5 p.m. Dee said it was important he be there. Something to do with a classmate of Ellen's and her mother.

Dee explained he would be upset about it and she didn't want him driving while angry. She knew how he could get. He tried to stay calm, since he didn't know what it was about.

The drive was easy and the weather clear as he pulled his Roadster into the drive. Only Dee's car was parked on the pavement.

"Dee?" Hugh called the moment he walked through the front door.

Dee wore a dress in Hugh's favorite color, aqua blue. Her skirts swished as she walked quickly into the foyer. "Record time, honey. Thank you." She kissed his cheek and placed in his hand a lowball of his favorite Scotch.

"Will they be here soon?"

"Not exactly. I asked you to be here at five, so I could fill you in beforehand. You will not be happy about what's transpired. Have a seat."

"Now I'm really worried." He furrowed his brow and squinted at her.

Dee talked while Hugh listened, his expression growing more and more incredulous. When she stopped, he took a few moments before responding.

Hugh cleared his throat and downed the rest of his drink. "So let me get this straight. Becky Slade's sister, Connie, moved to Starlight Bay a year ago and her daughter goes to school with Ellen. And she, uh Dana, spread a rumor about Ellen. What rumor?"

Dee retrieved the note from her purse and handed it to Hugh. His eyes popped while reading.

"Damn it!" He went to the bar and slammed the note on the counter, then refilled his empty glass. "Why didn't you tell me about this last night?"

Dee looked surprised. "I was handling the situation with her, and that was more important. Let's not get sidetracked before they arrive. There's plenty more." Dee sat on a bar stool and recounted Dana's conversation with Ellen.

Hugh ran his hands through his hair. "How despicable. Where's Ellen?"

"I sent her down to the gaming room to wait until I call her back in. She knows that Dana and her mother are coming here."

"Why are they coming?"

"Connie wants Dana to apologize for what she did to Ellen."

"Good. And—?"

"I thought we should be in agreement regarding the story."

"The story?"

"That's what I wanted to discuss with you. Dana needs to tell people at school she spread a lie and she was sorry. We won't make a formal complaint to the school, which would save her from being suspended, or worse."

"Okay. How do we know Dana won't tell more of the story?"

"Because Connie moved them here to start over on a clean slate. Sound familiar?"

Hugh leaned on the bar and swirled the ice in his glass. "She wants the whole Becky thing kept in the past, too."

"Not only that, but we have information about Becky that Connie doesn't want known here."

"Right, all the crimes Becky committed."

"Exactly. We all need to agree to the same story and protect each other."

Hugh gazed at his beautiful and extremely smart wife. "I am so lucky to have you in my corner. That's a solid solution to this mess. Do you think they will agree?"

"I do. But there's something else." She crossed the room to get the folder about the trial and handed it to Hugh.

Hugh's brows shot up. "What's this?"

"You won't have time to read all of it before they arrive. But Connie gave it to us."

Hugh opened it and scanned the first couple of pages. "Good God."

"I know. Surprising, isn't it?"

"So, Connie knows."

Dee nodded, then checked her wristwatch. "They'll be here any time." She opened the door to the downstairs and called Ellen to come up.

When Ellen entered the living room, Hugh embraced her, kissed her forehead.

"Sweetheart, I'm so sorry all this happened and that your mother and I didn't tell you these things sooner. It must have been a terrible shock."

Ellen sat on the sofa. "It's okay now, but when Dana told me those things and accused my birth mother of being crazy, I thought I'd go nuts, too."

Hugh spoke in a gentle voice, telling her about Nora, how they had met, and then married. He explained Nora had been a prisoner of war and it had changed her and how she ended up at the same sanitorium as Dana's aunt.

"How sad and terrible she went through all that. So, my mother wasn't really crazy?" She slumped against him with relief.

"No honey, she was there to get better emotionally. You know what that means?"

"Yes, but how did she know Becky's husband?"

Hugh swallowed hard and cleared his throat. "Hubert was not a good person. He was known to take advantage of women. Your mother was not strong enough to defend herself and he . . . well, he took advantage of her."

"You mean she didn't want him, but he made her anyway, against her will?"

"Yes. You are a very smart young lady."

"Since they weren't married to each other, then it's really true then."

"What's true?"

"That I'm illegitimate, like the note said, a bastard."

Dee took one of Ellen's hands and Hugh took the other.

Hugh continued, "One could say that, but legally, I was still married to your mother when she gave birth to you. So, technically, you are my daughter."

"Oh, so why did I call you Uncle Hugh?"

"My father had suppressed Nora's death and spread a lie that our marriage had been annulled and she had left Rothmorton Hall. He sent you away. After my father died, it took me two years to find you. I made a terrible mistake by perpetuating the lie, claiming you were an orphaned relative. It was just easier than the whole sordid tale."

"Wow. That's some story. It sounds like something from a movie or a novel." She looked down at her hands.

"It's a lot to take in, honey." Hugh worried she would be upset with him. "I don't expect you to fully grasp why I did what I did. I thought I was protecting everyone. But I know it was not the right thing to do."

She looked up. "No, Dad. I think you did what you needed to do at the time. I couldn't have understood all that when I was little. I see why you kept the secret." She glanced over at her mother.

Dee wiped a tear from the corner of her eye. "We love you more than anything, dearest."

The doorbell rang, and everyone jumped. Dee went to greet them at the door.

"Ellen," Hugh whispered, "Everything I just told you about your mother is still a secret from people. It's just too big a story to explain."

"I understand. It's not something anyone needs to know."

"If you need further explanation, ask me or your mom."

Ellen smiled and hugged him again.

Dana appeared at the entrance of the living room, her eyes on the floor with her arms crossed. Her mother followed behind. Dee made the introductions.

Connie shook Hugh's hand. "I really am pleased to meet you, Mr. Roth. Thank you for allowing us to come to your home." She turned to her daughter. "Dana has something important to say to you all."

Ellen and Dee took seats on the sofa. Hugh sat on a bar stool. Connie stepped back.

Dana lifted her head and glanced around the room. She coughed in her hand and wiped it on her dress. "I-I first want to apologize to Ellie . . ." She faced Ellen directly. "I did a terrible thing to you and you were right when you said you didn't deserve it. I blamed you for my unhappiness and know that was wrong. When we first met, I was really excited about it and thought we would be great friends. Hearing your name in class made me angry. I couldn't see how we could be friends given what I knew about you. My mom didn't know I had overheard her and my aunt talking many times over the years. We should have talked about things. Instead, I held it all in and that was wrong.

"Ellie, can you ever forgive me? If you can't, I understand, and I'll try to stay out of your way at school." She turned to Hugh. "Mr. Roth, I apologize to you and Mrs. Roth too, because Ellie is your daughter, and you have every right to be angry with me . . ." Dana looked at her mom, who smiled and nodded. "Oh, and one more thing. I'll tell people at school I spread the rumor and that it was a lie. That's all I have to say." Dana stepped back and lowered her eyes once more to the floor.

Ellen stood. "Dana, I accept your apology and I forgive you. Let's just see how things go, okay?"

"That's very mature of you, Ellen," Connie said. "Thank you."

Dee took the floor and shared her ideas for moving forward from that day. A unanimous agreement was reached to maintain strict confidentiality regarding their family secrets, vowing to never disclose any information about each other to outsiders.

Everyone has secrets.

Hugh offered Connie a drink and Ellen took Dana outside to the beach until it was time to leave.

That night, in their bedroom, Hugh and Dee struggled to release their anger from the incident.

"I'm exhausted from the last two days." Dee said, while changing into her nightgown. "All I want to do right now is sleep." She sat on her side of the king-sized bed and wound her alarm clock.

"I really wish you had told me right after you found out about it." Hugh spoke the words slowly and calmly so not to make Dee defensive.

Dee looked up sharply. "Really? You want to rehash all this after it's been resolved amicably?"

"Well . . . this was a serious situation, and I was just a phone call away and only a forty-minute drive."

"Oh, now it's *only* a forty-minute drive? One you refuse to make every day, while I handle life here on my own. You don't appreciate what I do while you are gone." She sniffed away a sob.

"That came out wrong. I appreciate all you do and especially handling the Connie meeting alone. I just should have been here." Hugh stood in his boxers and tee shirt while he hung his suit on the mahogany valet stand.

"You certainly said a mouthful. It's too bad we had to waste a Wednesday to deal with such an unfortunate mess." Dee stopped and stared at him.

Hugh sighed. "You know what? I'm emotionally spent over this, too. It's sad we can't enjoy what little time we have left before I return to the city in the morning."

"I hate to agree with you on that, but I do. You had to start this before going to bed." Dee stormed past Hugh into the bathroom without a glance.

Hugh slipped into silk pajamas, then crawled under the covers on his side of the bed.

When Dee got into bed, without a word, she turned out her light on the nightstand and plumped up her pillows, hitting them hard and loud.

Hugh noticed, but said nothing as he turned his light out.

They both rolled over with their backs to each other.

Hugh promised himself they would work through this. They always had before.

CHAPTER FOURTEEN
DEE

It's not over, till it's over.

The next day, I received a call from the school.

"Mrs. Roth? This is Mrs. Steel, the principal at Ellen's school. It's been brought to my attention, a derogatory rumor about Ellen has been spreading through the school instigated by Dana Anderson. We've spoken to Mrs. Anderson on the phone and she said both your families were aware of it and that you had come to a resolution between you?"

"Uh, yes, we did."

"That's fine, but the issue needs to be addressed by the school. We need you and Mr. Roth to come in to my office today at 3 p.m. after classes end. Mrs. Anderson will be here as well."

"I can be there. But I doubt my husband can get away from his office in San Francisco."

"If he doesn't mind, you can come in by yourself. We've informed your daughter this morning to be here, too."

"Is that necessary? I think she's been through enough humiliation."

"It's important she is there for confirmation. Only if we need her. She can wait outside my office while the rest of us talk."

"That should be fine. I will be there for sure."

We had hoped involving the school wouldn't be necessary. I supposed it was a good thing the school cared. I dialed Hugh's number at work.

"Hugh Roth speaking."

"Hi, it's me. There's been a glitch to our plan to eradicate the rumor about Ellen."

It sounded as if Hugh slammed his fist on the desk. "Now what?"

I cringed. "The principal at the school wants us there today to discuss the rumor. They know it was Dana. Connie will be there too. If you can't make it, I can go alone."

"Do you want me to drive down? What time is the appointment?"

"3 p.m."

"Damn, I have an important meeting at two o'clock and I don't think I could make it. I'm sorry."

"No, no, that's fine. I can handle it. If Connie can do it by herself, then certainly I can."

"I have faith in you, Dee. Call me as soon as you can after the meeting."

I dressed for the occasion in a lightweight gray skirted suit and gray low-heeled pumps. Nervous flutters roused in my stomach. I had thought the confrontation about the rumor was over and I did not relish rehashing any details.

It was unfortunate we hadn't been given more warning, so I could have talked to Ellen beforehand.

By the time I arrived at the administration building, the campus was busy with students leaving by car and bus. I wondered if any of the students knew about the meeting.

Ellen sat outside Mrs. Steele's office and I went to her, but the door was open. Connie and Dana were already there. Darn, I wasn't even late. I smiled at Ellen as Mrs. Steele came out to greet me.

"Please come in, Mrs. Roth."

Dana looked worried, but Connie was calm. Neither spoke. I took the empty chair next to Connie.

Mrs. Steele shut the door and took her seat behind her desk. She clasped her hands in front and pursed her lips.

"Although you handled this situation between yourselves satisfactorily, you should have contacted me. This school and the district do not tolerate vindictive behavior.

She looked directly at Dana. "What you did was shameful. What is your response to this?"

Dana was clenching her hands so tightly they turned red. "I am very sorry for what I did. I've apologized to Ellen and her parents, and I've been telling classmates that the rumor was a lie I started."

"As you should be, and I'm pleased to hear of your apology and that you are trying to clear up the rumor. Why did you do it?"

Dana shot a glance at her mother, who nodded her head and touched Dana's hand. "I guess I was jealous of her. Uh — she comes from a rich family and uh — well, we just barely get by." She hung her head low.

I breathed a sigh of relief. Dana's answer didn't open the door for Mrs. Steele to prod further, judging by her expression.

"And, Mrs. Roth, you are satisfied by Dana's apology?"

"Yes. She promised to tell classmates the rumor was a lie, and that she was sorry for starting it. I'm glad to hear she's already doing so. That's probably the best that can be done. May I ask how you found out about it?"

Mrs. Steele jotted some notes in her notebook, then retrieved two small pieces of paper, similar to the crumpled note Ellen gave me.

"Mr. Powers, the biology teacher, noticed students passing notes around in one of his classes, giggling and laughing. He intercepted the notes and recognized the handwriting to be Dana's. When he questioned some students, one of them said she saw Dana write the note."

Connie spoke low to her daughter, but loud enough for me to hear. "How many of those notes did you pass out?"

Dana hung her head. "Five."

I was surprised there had been so many and by the look on Mrs. Steele's face, she concurred.

"Usually, we can't stop rumors because we can't confirm absolutely who started them. In this case, we have concrete evidence. I'm afraid we will need to punish Dana."

"Will you suspend her?" Connie's face had gone pale through this whole ordeal and I felt her pain the same as I felt Ellen's.

"Suspension would be too harsh. Detention would be a suitable punishment. She is to report to detention hall, one hour at the end of each school day for two weeks, starting tomorrow."

Dana inhaled sharply and turned to her mother. "Oh no! Mom, I'm so sorry."

"Is this necessary?" I asked.

"It is," Mrs. Steele sighed. "Failing to punish would give students the impression that they can freely engage in improper or mean actions facing no consequences."

"Two weeks is a long time, but I agree with you on punishment." Connie dabbed a tear from her cheek.

"I'm glad to hear you say that. Most parents try to manipulate the situation." She handed a green sheet of paper to Dana. "This needs to be signed off by the teacher each day and returned to me at the end of the two weeks. I hope you've learned your lesson."

Dana mumbled a yes and another sorry and took the sheet.

When we all departed, I said nothing to Connie. I weakly smiled at Dana as they walked away from us. I mean, what was there to say that hadn't already been said.

As soon as we got into the car, Ellen let out a big sigh. "Glad all that is over, hopefully."

"When your classmates learn of Dana's detention, that should quell the whispers and pointing."

Hugh returned home early that night, explaining he would work from home on Friday. That made me so happy. I threw my arms around him and dragged him into the bedroom and filled him in on the meetings and Dana's detention.

"What a relief that mess is resolved. But what about the other two notes that were passed around?" He looked worried as he removed his tie and shirt.

"Hopefully, they were tossed. The principal believes that by putting Dana in detention, the situation will calm down or the rumors will shift their focus to Dana." I followed his lead and went to my dresser to select a nightgown.

"That would serve her right." He removed his shoes and inserted cedar wood shoe trees.

"On another more positive note. The cast usually holds a big party after the closing performance and they are having trouble finding a large enough facility."

"We could hold it here. Is that what you are hinting at?" He grinned.

"Would you be okay with it? It won't be your usual society crowd, but these people are so genuine and they would be extremely grateful."

"Anything for you, darling." He gave me a peck on the cheek.

"I'll tell Patrick when I see him. And I'll work with Mrs. Chambers on the details. Instead of taking advantage of her, wouldn't it be a better idea to find a nearby catering company?"

"Absolutely. I'm sure a caterer in San Francisco will come down here. I'll have my secretary look one up for you."

"You are the best husband." I gave him a big kiss on his soft lips. Things were looking up. "I'm going to take a shower."

"Would you like company?" Hugh winked, removing his trousers.

"Excellent suggestion."

CHAPTER FIFTEEN
ELLEN

On Friday morning in English class, Dana kept her eyes forward and didn't even say hello. I ignored her, too. We kept our distance, but difficult since we sat next to each other.

Susan and Nina noticed and sent me questioning looks. Susan pointed to Dana's back and mouthed, *what's going on?* I shrugged. I knew Dana would be in detention after school, and I needed to act like I knew nothing about it. Everyone would know soon enough.

Paying attention in class had become difficult for me, what with my confusing feelings for Mr. Stevens and daydreaming about Adam. I wondered if I would ever see him again.

We were supposed to be reading Shakespeare's *Macbeth*, though I had already read it at my private school last year. It was my least favorite play because of the dark themes. I much preferred *A Midsummer Night's Dream*, a delightful and funny romance. My parents took me to see the stage play when I was ten.

"Ellen, you're next," Mr. Stevens said.

My head jerked up. I hadn't been paying attention during the out loud reading. "I'm sorry, I lost my place."

A few sniggers ran through the room, but Mr. Stevens slammed his ruler on his desk. The sniggers stopped, and he told me where to pick up. I stood and read the next page. That had never happened to me before. I was sure my embarrassment was apparent. When I touched my face, it felt red hot.

When class was over, Dana rushed out of the room. Nina went on to her class and Susan and I walked together as usual to French class.

She whispered in my ear. "Okay, now give. You refused to tell me anything all week about what I told you at the Beach Party."

I pulled Susan into an alcove so no one could hear. "It's a long story. But I will tell you that Dana starts detention today for spreading the rumor."

Susan's eyes grew enormous. "Really? Oh, I want to know." She shimmied her shoulders. "Please."

I shook my head. "We'll be late for class. After what happened in English, I'd rather not be humiliated again today."

Susan said no more and followed me to an uneventful French class. In Biology and History class, Dana behaved the same and so did I.

Lunch break finally came, and I joined Susan and Nina at our favorite table. Two other girls from Biology class sat with us. Dana sat in the corner, alone.

"I just feel weird," Nina said. "Anyone know what's going on with Dana?"

Susan opened her mouth, and I shot her a dagger stare.

One girl whispered. "Someone said Dana is telling people she had started the rumor, and it was a lie. Can you believe it?"

"Really?" Susan took a bite of her peanut butter and jelly sandwich she brought from home.

"That explains why she's been acting weird ever since the rumor started," Nina said under her breath and looked at me. "Did you know?"

I averted my eyes. "I'm just glad the truth is out, and that Dana is clearing it up," I said. "Could we please not talk about it anymore?" I shoved a big spoonful of the green Jello in my mouth.

Everyone nodded in agreement and ate their lunch. Conversation moved to the current movie at the theater. The two girls from Biology got up and left. They had a class clear across the campus.

"*Gidget* is showing at the movie theater now," Nina said. "We should all go next Wednesday."

"We could walk there from the school. Maybe someone's mom could pick us up and take each of us home?" Susan suggested.

"I'll ask my mom. She doesn't go to the theater on Wednesday nights," I offered.

"Cool. Let us know on Monday," Nina said. "I need to get to class. Ugh!" She made a face, and we all laughed.

At home, Mom was in the kitchen with Mrs. C preparing dinner.

Mrs. C smiled at me just before placing a pan covered in foil into the overhead oven.

Mom kissed my cheek. "Hi, honey. Your father worked from home today and will stay for the weekend. In celebration of that and the resolution of you know what incident, we are making his favorites. Would you wear something nice tonight?"

"Sure, Mom. Can I ask you a favor?"

"Of course." Mom was busy cutting vegetables on the big island in the middle of the kitchen. She wore her prettiest ruffled pink apron over a floral print shirtwaist day dress.

"Susan, Nina, and I want to see the movie *Gidget* next week, and we need someone to pick us up after and take us home."

"You saw it last year, right?" She stopped and put her hand on her hip. "How are you getting there?"

"Yeah, I'd like to see it again with my new friends. We'll walk together. It's not that far from the school."

"I'm not sure. Your father comes home for dinner on Wednesdays. I want to be home and I don't want you to miss it either."

"There will be time."

"I'll need to discuss this with your father first. And don't pout."

I tucked my lower lip back in and started to leave the kitchen.

Mom returned to her cutting, but had a curious look on her face. "Did you talk to Dana today?"

I stopped and turned toward her. "No, we didn't talk in class and she avoided everyone at lunch. Except I heard she told some kids she was the one who started the rumor and lied."

"Good. I'm glad she is following through on her promise to clear things up. I do feel bad for her. But she brought it on herself." Mom turned to me and opened her arms wide.

I stepped into her hug. She smelled of carrots and celery mixed with her favorite perfume, Miss Dior. My nose twitched from the strange mixture. I kissed her cheek and pulled away, grabbing a carrot to munch on.

"I like your hair like that, in the French twist," I said. "You should wear it like that all the time. It hides the gray hair," I giggled.

"What gray hair? I'm not yet thirty!" She laughed. "Your father is counting his grays, so far, only at the temples. But don't tease him about it."

"You two make me laugh," Mrs. C chimed in. "Now Ellen, you get along so we can do our work."

"I'm going to change and go for a walk on the beach for a little while. Okay?"

They both just nodded their heads as I headed to my room.

I pulled on a pair of white shorts and a pullover top, and grabbed my beach bag and inhaler on my way out of my room. In no time, I was on our stretch of beach with my bare feet skimming the top of the shallow waves.

A figure walked toward me, waving. It was Adam. My heart pounded.

"Well, hello!" I glanced up at the terrace and couldn't see anyone watching. But I was afraid someone would see us. "What are you doing here?"

"Hoping to find you," he grinned ear to ear. "And here you are."

"Let's walk back this way out of eyesight of my house." I kept going, and Adam turned around and walked by my side.

"Is that your house up there? I wasn't sure. I came down here on Wednesday hoping to find you. You told me you walk on the beach every day after school."

"You did? Wednesday was a crazy day." My insides were fluttering like crazy that he had been trying to find me. I was sure glad he didn't come when Dana was with me. That would have been awkward.

"I know you said to call, but I wanted to see you in person." He shoved his hands in his shorts' pockets.

"I can't stay down here for long. They expect me to change for dinner. My dad will be here for the weekend."

"What do you mean? Isn't he here all the time?" He gave me a baffled look.

"He works a lot and sometimes spends the nights in San Francisco. Not as much as he used to, so I want to spend as much time as I can when he's here."

"Sure, I understand. My dad travels occasionally. Hey look, I was wondering if you want to go to a movie with me. Maybe this week, if you can?"

"Oh . . . I already have plans to see *Gidget* in our town theater on Wednesday. You remember my friends Susan and Nina from the beach party?"

"I remember. They're cool. Hey, that film is about surfing. I'd see it and bring my two buddies. We could all see the film as a group. It would be fun."

It took me a split second to make up my mind. "That would be creamy."

I fluttered my eyelashes, and the thought of a date with Adam made my skin shiver. Well, I shouldn't call it a date, since I wasn't allowed to date yet. It would be a group date. I hoped Mom would let me go and pick us up. I crossed my fingers and wished it would all happen.

"We'll have a blast." He stopped. "Well, I gotta go, too. My older brother is waiting for me up on the road."

"I didn't know you even had a brother. How old is he?"

"Twenty-one, a senior at UCLA and doesn't have class on Fridays, so he comes home to have his laundry done." Adam laughed.

"His laundry? And to drive up here so you can accidentally run into me?" I laughed at that.

"Yeah. Something like that." Adam winked and my stomach fluttered again.

"My friend Chris will drive on Wednesday. Boy, I can't wait until I can drive myself and I won't have to be chauffeured everywhere."

"Yeah, me too. So, I guess I'll see you Wednesday after school."

Adam jaunted off along the sand, taking long strides up the slope, turning to wave to me.

Gosh, he was so cute. I could barely stand it.

At dinner, Mom brought up the movie and Dad looked confused.

"What's the issue, darling? Any reason she can't go with her girlfriends and you pick them up?" Dad cut into his chicken cordon bleu and took a bite. "This is perfectly delicious."

"I'm so glad you like it. My first time making it and I wanted it to be perfect." She patted Dad's arm, looking relieved.

Why was she worried about the dinner? Dad loves everything she does.

Mom took a sip of her wine. "Well, Wednesday is the night you come home during the week."

"I think it's all right for her to go and you pick them up. It doesn't matter when we have dinner. Maybe I'll take the two of you out when you get home. Give Mrs. Chambers the night off." He glanced at Mrs. C, who was trying hard not to pay attention to their conversation.

"I'd love to have Wednesday night off, Mr. Hugh. Thank you," Mrs. C said.

"That settles it."

Dad looked pleased with himself at solving what I considered a non-issue. Why was Mom so resistant to my request? Was something going on between them I didn't know about?

On Saturday, Mom was busy working on a costume in her sewing room. She had just bought a new sewing machine. Aunt Sylvi showed up saying she would pierce my ears so I could wear the amethyst earrings she gave me for my birthday. She set it up in the breakfast nook.

"What's all this Aunt Sylvi?"

"I'm a nurse, so this operation needs to be sterile."

My eyes bugged out, and I took a step back. "Operation?!"

Aunt Sylvi laughed. "I'm kidding on the operation part. But it's best to use sterile tools to avoid infection. See here?" She pointed to the bottle of rubbing alcohol, a large embroidery needle, a clothespin, and cotton balls.

"What's the clothespin for?"

"To numb your earlobe. We could use ice if you'd prefer?"

Mrs. C was in the kitchen and had gone straight to the freezer, bringing in an ice tray. "Here you go. That's how most folks do it, if the clothespin doesn't work. Right, Sylvi?"

"That's right. Thanks for the ice. Which do you want, Ellen?"

"How would I know? This is my first time. Let's try the clothespin first." As soon as she clipped it to my ear, I flinched. "Ouch, that hurts too much."

"Okay." She removed the clothespin and wrapped a napkin around an ice cube, then held it behind my ear. "How's that?"

"Much better."

It didn't take her long to pierce both ears. It still pinched a bit, but I didn't cry or anything.

"There. All done." Aunt Sylvi held up a hand mirror to show me.

"Oh, I have earrings too?"

"These are simple gold wires to wear until the piercing heals. You will need to clean your ears every day and move the wires periodically to avoid sticking. Okay?"

"Gee, Aunt Sylvi, they look cool. Thank you." We hugged each other, and she kissed my cheek. "I love you Aunt Sylvi."

"Love you too, sweetheart."

Mrs. C was no longer in the kitchen. She'd finished cleaning and went to her suite at the back of the house.

"Do you have some time just to talk?"

"Sure." Aunt Sylvi put all her tools away and sat opposite me at the breakfast table. "Did you want to talk about something in particular?"

"Yes. What with all the craziness that happened with Dana, I've been thinking a lot about my birth mother, your sister, Nora."

"I guess you would be."

"Dad never talks about her. Maybe it hurts too much. And from what I've heard, they didn't really know each other for long, before she went into the mental hospital. You knew her all your life, and I just figured you'd know more."

"That is a very mature assessment of the situation and you are probably right. Your father knew Nora from a husband's perspective. I knew Nora as family and a sister."

"What was she like? Do you have a picture of her? Dad said he never had one taken of them."

"I have one photo I've carried around with me for years. Come with me."

I followed her down the hall to the first bedroom on the left. Mine was just beyond hers. I'd only been in her room twice. Mom had it decorated specially for her. Soft hues of green and gold dotted the bedspread and, through the open bathroom door, the towels, and rugs.

"This is a serene room," I said.

"A good word to describe it. That's how I feel when I'm in here." Aunt Sylvi went to her jewelry box on the mirrored dresser and removed a gold locket on a long chain. She opened it and placed it in my hands. "She was just eighteen when that photo was taken. I was fourteen at the time."

"It's so tiny." I gazed at the face of a pretty young woman. "She was blonde too, like me?"

"Just like you, or you like her, curly too." She sniffled. "Sorry, I always get emotional when I look at that picture."

"I wish I could have a copy."

"I don't know why I never thought of it before. Nora used to have a picture of both of us. Hugh might have kept some of her things. I assumed it was all thrown away, but maybe not. Dee would know since she handled all the non-saleable items from the mansion."

"Yes, she might know. Hey, maybe I could take a picture with my camera?" I ran from her room to mine and brought back my camera. We tried several ways to get a clear shot.

"When the roll is done, let me know when the film is developed. I'd like to see how they turned out." Sylvi took the locket and placed it in her jewelry box and closed it. Her hand rested on the lid for a moment.

"Please tell me more about her." I sat on the tufted chair in front of her dressing table.

Sylvi chuckled, as she sat on the foot of the bed. "She was so independent and what you'd call flamboyant."

"Flamboyant?"

"Everything she did, she did with gusto, flashy, and tons of energy. She liked to wear bright intense colors, too. In high school, she was a cheerleader and one of the loudest, as I recall. And she was athletic, played tennis, and on the girls' swim team. She even played softball for a while. She loved adventure and right after the bombing of Pearl Harbor, Nora signed up to be a Navy nurse."

"Wow, she did all that and became a nurse, too?" I wondered if Dad knew all of this.

She nodded her head. "I idolized her and aspired to be like her. But we weren't interested in the same sports. I became a nurse and followed her into the Navy, too. Our personalities clashed sometimes. Nora was the one to hold grudges. She was still upset with me about something when I joined the service. Can't even remember what it was. Something I did, or said that she didn't like. She could be judgmental of me. But I loved her anyway."

"We both lost someone special. It would be wonderful to have a little sister or brother. If I do, I won't let anything get in our way."

"I bet you wouldn't, either."

"What about your parents, my grandparents?" I'd always wondered if there were more family.

"Oh, gosh. It's kinda sad, actually. You sure you want to hear about them?"

"Yes, of course."

"Nora and I were little. She was around six and I was barely two. Our father died in a work accident. Our mother was forced to support us all by herself, and she was not fully equipped to do so. Her parents had disowned her when she ran away to marry our father. She was already pregnant with Nora." The corners of her mouth turned downward.

"You didn't know your father at all, either?"

"Sounds like a habit in our families of missing a parent or two. But Mom managed until Nora was in college. She got sick and died. I was there till the end and the experience influenced me all the more to be a nurse, not just Nora."

"That is very sad. Do my parents know all of this?"

"I don't think I ever talked about Nora and my parents. They never asked, like you, little dear. I haven't really thought about all of that for quite some time. Not since I found out Nora had died."

Tears welled in Aunt Sylvi's eyes again, and I moved to sit next to her. "Sorry, I'm making you sad by asking about them."

She put an arm around me. "We both have losses to deal with. Tears are a part of the territory. Thank you for making me remember a lot of things I'd pushed down inside me."

We sat there for some time, letting the silence embrace us in our sadness. My loss of a mother who was her sister, and her loss of her whole family. I realized how lucky I was to have Aunt Sylvi in my life.

CHAPTER SIXTEEN

When Monday came around, I told Susan and Nina everything had been arranged. "However, I didn't tell my mom about the three boys that are meeting us at the theater." The looks on their faces were priceless.

"What boys?" Susan asked.

"Yeah, how'd you get three boys to go to the movies with us?" Nina said.

I told them about meeting Adam on the beach and that he invited himself and would bring his two friends. The girls squealed so loud I thought my ears would burst. Everyone in the cafeteria stared at us.

"Calm down. I should have waited until after school to tell you. But I just couldn't. Isn't it positively dreamy?" I knew I overused dreamy and creamy, and needed to learn more slang words.

"Golly," Nina said. "Is he bringing those two friends of his we met at the beach party?"

I nodded. Again, the two girls squealed with glee. I laughed, and we talked about a mile a minute, trying to decide what we would wear to school that day.

"Let's keep this to ourselves. Don't tell a soul," I said low. "Or there will be rumors said about us."

Eyes wide, they nodded and zipped their lips with their fingers.

On Wednesday, while walking to the movie theater, I told Susan and Nina some of what happened the week before, about Dana.

"So, I met Dana on the bleachers and came right out and asked her," I said.

"And she admitted it to you?" Susan said.

"She did. Because she's jealous of me. She hated me for coming from a rich family." Of course, I would never repeat to anyone the real reasons.

"Really?" Nina said. "How strange."

"I told Mom, and she talked to Dana's mom. And then they came to my house and told my dad." I tried to be nonchalant about it.

"What did they do?" Susan said.

"Was your dad angry?" Nina said.

"My dad was so cool. Dana made a formal apology to me and to my parents. And then Dana and I went down to our beach. But she didn't say a word to me. We just sat there until we were called in. I guess they were talking about it and all." I hoped that was enough information that they wouldn't ask more questions.

"After they left, my parents thought the incident over until they got a call from Principal Steels's office. We had to go in and meet with her, along with Dana and her mom."

"Jeepers, that's crazy, Ellie," Nina said. She was the only person I knew who said jeepers.

"Apparently, a teacher intercepted two notes being passed around, and he identified Dana's handwriting. That should be a lesson to anyone," I said, looking around to make sure no one was within earshot of our conversation. Only little kids on bicycles. We had taken an alternate route out of the way of the high schoolers walking home.

"How long does she have to do detention?" Nina asked.

"Two weeks. My mom said she deserved to be punished and I shouldn't feel bad for her. But I do, anyway."

"You mean you aren't angry at Dana for what she did?" Susan said.

"I was at first. Then she apologized and now she's being punished. What's the point of me holding onto any anger? Makes no sense. I wonder if maybe she and I could still be friends?"

"Ellie, you need to forget about being friends with Dana. She's ruined all her friendships, us included. It's something she needs to deal with. Not your responsibility," Susan said.

"Gee, Susan, you sound like my mom. I think you are right, though. Thanks." I pulled up my shoulder bag. Glad that we all put our books in lockers before leaving school. Though how we were going to finish homework was beyond me. I would ask Mom to take us back to the school for our books.

Susan waved her hand in front of my face. "You daydreaming again?" She laughed.

"Sorry. Oh my, look ahead. They got there before us." I pointed to the three boys standing near the box office.

We were nervous, and it showed. Susan couldn't look at them and Nina was giggling.

"Hey there, Ellie," Adam said. "Gee, you look pretty in that color. Uh - you all look nice today."

What a nice boy he was to include my friends.

"You remember my friends from the beach party?" Adam said.

"I remember you Susan," Chris said.

Susan blushed. "Hi."

"I remember Nina for sure." Dan adjusted his thick glasses.

Nina giggled again, saying nothing.

"We got the tickets already," Adam held them up. "Come on, we'll get some popcorn and Cokes, okay?"

Adam looked so smart and handsome in his school uniform. I had completely forgotten about the uniform I used to wear to school in Massachusetts. I barely noticed his friends. My eyes were all on Adam.

With our drinks and popcorn in hand, we entered the darkened theater. The boys acted like they had planned things out. They made sure it was boy, girl, boy, girl with an empty seat between each twosome. Adam took the aisle seat next to me. Susan and Nina were clearly very happy with who they were sitting with.

Right before the film started, Adam whisper in my ear. "Did you just get your ears pierced?"

Gosh, he noticed and my friends hadn't. "Last weekend. They're still healing. These are temporary wires."

"You look pretty." He smiled so sweetly. If I'd been standing, my knees would have buckled. I also noticed that Adam didn't use a lot of slang. He spoke politely and mature, I thought. Maybe that's why we clicked the way we did.

When the film got to the part where Sandra Dee was all alone with that older man, the Big Kahuna, I looked at Adam as if we were in the movie. I wondered what that would be like. Though I wasn't planning on anything like that happening between us, yet. And Sandra Dee chickened out in the movie, anyway. I would do the same thing, probably. Run out of there. But Adam took my hand and held it for the longest and I was in heaven.

While the credits were running, Adam leaned in to whisper again. "Would you go with me to my school's Fall Dance on Saturday, November 6th?"

I gasped. "Golly, sure I'd go. My parents would need to give permission, and I'm sure my dad would want to meet you. They don't know about our meeting on the beach last weekend," I said.

"Sure. It's just a school dance. They only have one in the fall and one in the spring, so it's kinda special. I'll go to your house and ask properly. Whatever it takes so you can go with me." He squeezed my hand one last time and let go. My hand tingled in a good way.

"Call me and then we can set a day when my dad's home," I said.

When the lights were up, we all walked out together and I stopped short. Mom was parked in front of the theater waiting. She'd already seen us and waved.

"Adam, that's my mom's car out there on the curb. Act like we just ran into each other." I turned to Susan and Nina. "Walk next to me, now. My mom can see us."

We girls quickly said goodbye to the boys, then walked out together and got in the car.

"Good evening, Mrs. Roth," Susan said.

"Thank you for picking us up," Nina said.

I slipped into the front seat. "Hi, Mom. That was a great movie."

"Yes." The girls in the back seat said in unison.

Mom said hello as she pulled away from the sidewalk. "Who do I take home first?"

"Would you mind taking us back to the school so we can get our books from our lockers? Then take Susan home first." Maybe Mom didn't see us with the boys . . . maybe.

When we arrived home, Dad's car was there and so was Mrs. C. She had the dining table all set for the four of us.

"I guess we aren't going out?" I asked.

"Change of plans. We'll go another time, maybe this weekend. Go wash up and we'll eat soon." Mom dropped the car keys in a bowl on the foyer table.

"Did you have fun, sweetheart?" Dad stood in the hallway between the living room and the entry.

"Yes, we all enjoyed the movie. I'm off to wash up." Boy, things sure changed fast around here. I put my books on my desk and freshened up in my bathroom.

Dinner was relatively quiet, with a few comments from Mrs. C and Dad. Mom didn't say a word.

"Delicious dinner." I took the last bite.

"You are most welcome, dearie," Mrs. C said.

"So, Ellen, who were those three boys walking out of the theater with you and your friends?" Mom had raised her brows.

I swallowed and took a gulp of water. "Oh, them? Uh, funny coincidence. Adam and his school buddies, Chris, and Dan, who we met at the beach party, saw the same movie." Did I sound normal or guilty?

"A coincidence? I thought perhaps you had planned to meet them there, and you just forgot to mention them." Mom was being strangely accusatory.

Dad looked clueless, his face a blank page. "They were at the movie? How surprising. Bet that was fun." He smiled.

My eyes darted back and forth between the two. Mom doubted me and Dad seemed to be pleased. I shot a look at Mrs. C. She wasn't paying any mind, as she was already clearing the table.

"Well, Adam is a really nice guy, super intelligent, and goes to the Prep Academy. And . . . uh, well, he asked me to go to his school's Fall Dance in November. I know it's weeks away, but he wanted to be sure I was available . . ." My voice just died off as I looked at my parents. Mom's mouth had dropped open and Dad, well, his eyes were about to pop out of his head.

"Ellen, you already know what I think," Mom said.

"Yes, I know, that I'm too young to date but . . ." I faltered.

"Now, darling, let's not be so hasty," Dad said to Mom. "Going on a date alone with a boy is hardly the same thing as going to a formal dance at the Prep Academy. I went to a few of those in my day. As I recall, they were a lot of fun and there were several adult chaperones."

Dear Dad saved the day.

"Oh Daddy, thank you, but don't worry, Adam wants to come to the house to meet you and Mom and ask your permission. You know, the proper way."

"Well, he sounds like a fine young man." He took Mom's hand in his. "See, darling, we will meet the boy. When does he want to come?"

I was beyond excited, yet didn't want to show them. "He said he would call and find out when is best for you."

"Perfect." Dad turned to Mom. "You have said nothing."

"Sounds marvelous. I was just being cautious. My only concern is for Ellen's welfare," Mom said. But she didn't look pleased. Her mouth was a straight line, and she had that crease between her brows.

We had dessert, and I excused myself to do some homework.

I danced in circles down the hall to my room and closed the door. I squealed into a pillow and wanted to call Susan, but I'd have to wait until the next day.

CHAPTER SEVENTEEN
Dee

I checked to make sure Ellen's lights were out and joined Hugh in our suite to get ready for bed. Ellen's explanation for the boys' presence at the theater didn't sit right with me. I couldn't put my finger on it.

Hugh was out on the terrace, smoking his last cigarette of the day.

"Hugh," I called to him.

He poked his head in. "What darling?"

"I don't believe those boys showed up at the movie coincidentally."

Hugh tossed his cigarette across the rail and went in, closing the sliding glass door. He wore only his pajama bottoms.

"What are you talking about? That's what Ellen said. Why would she lie about a thing like that?"

I laughed. "Aren't you cold from standing outside without a shirt?"

He shrugged.

"Ellen is only thirteen and . . . it's those teenager hormones."

"Hormones? You mean the boys?" Hugh laughed loudly and with gusto.

"Make a joke. I'm serious. She's a very pretty girl, and this Adam met her only two weeks ago and he suddenly shows up at the theater? I just want to make sure they take things slow."

"If he likes her, and does that, it just shows that he's the kind of man, er, boy who goes after what he wants. That's not a bad thing." Hugh paused. "But I agree. If we can help it. It was a while ago, but I do remember being a teenager."

"At least we agree on that point." I sat on the side of the king-size bed and rolled down my stockings. Hugh watched me.

"I love how you do that." He winked. "Back to our topic. We just got through the Dana incident and now we have Adam to contend with. I don't know if I'm ready to deal with teenagers." He pulled on his pajama top and sat on his side of the bed.

"It's a part of parenting, honey. We need to figure this out to avoid alienating Ellen. The more we try to keep them apart . . . The more they will want to be together. We don't want our own *A Summer Place*." I shuddered at the thought.

Hugh looked confused. "What do you mean by that?"

"In that film, Sandra Dee gets pregnant, and she runs away with Troy Donohue to get married."

"What? I haven't seen the movie. Who did you see it with?"

"Remember, I'm the one with time on my hands. I saw it alone last year. Where were you?" I narrowed my eyes at him. "One of the reason's I wouldn't let Ellen see the film then. It was showing here a couple of weeks ago. I was relieved when she said the girls wanted to see *Gidget*."

"Well, I'm making up for all the time I've ignored you." He slid under the covers and scooted over to my side. "Hurry and come to bed."

"Back to Ellen."

"You're right. We certainly don't want the worst to happen to Ellen."

"We need to talk calmly to Ellen, so that she understands the importance of taking things slow and not rushing."

"How did you get so smart at being a mom?"

"Oh Hugh, I'm not. But I remember what it was like being a teenager in a restrictive environment." I rose and went to the door of the bathroom.

Hugh took a moment. "I remember too. That's how I ended up joining the Navy!"

"Exactly! I won't be long. Keep my side of the bed warm for me, won't you?"

Late Friday afternoon, Adam called, and I answered.

"Mrs. Roth? This is Adam Greenberg, Ellen's friend."

I was pleased he said he was a friend. "Yes, Adam. We've been expecting your call. Mr. Roth will be home this weekend. Would you be available to stop by on Saturday, say 2 p.m.?"

"Yes, ma'am. I look forward to meeting you and Mr. Roth."

"Do you have our address?"

"Yes, I do."

"See you then."

Well, I had to admit it. He impressed me with his handling of the call. We'll see how he handles Hugh's interrogation. I chuckled.

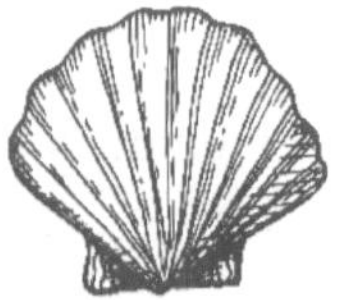

CHAPTER EIGHTEEN
HUGH

Hugh sat on the terrace reading the newspaper, dressed in a yellow golf shirt, casual slacks, and his comfy deck shoes. It had been a while since he had a leisurely weekend, and he almost regretted the upcoming meeting with Adam.

While lighting a cigarette, he recalled a similar situation from his prep school days. There was a cute girl in his class he wanted to take to the movies and he had to meet with her parents first, too. Hugh was not a confident boy and the girl's father came on strong, intimidating him. His father and that man were alike, forbearing and gruff. But he stood firm and got the date with the girl.

Hugh chuckled at the thought and wondered if he should take the same position with Adam, or take pity on him. Another chuckle.

Dee and Ellen had gone for a walk on the beach to give Hugh and Adam time alone to for their talk.

Mrs. Chambers opened the terrace door. "Adam Greenberg is here to see you."

"Good, I'll come inside."

Hugh finished his cigarette and stepped inside.

Adam stood in the middle of the room with his hands shoved in the pockets of his beige slacks. Hugh gave the boy a once over, then let out a satisfied grunt at the boy's clean, short-sleeved collared shirt, and his straight, dark hair neatly combed to the side.

"Adam?" Hugh said.

"Mr. Roth, a pleasure to meet you." He stuck out a hand, and they shook vigorously.

Adam's palm was damp and Hugh assumed nervousness. Good, he thought. Hugh motioned to the two armless chairs by the window, offering one to Adam. Hugh remained standing, thinking it would put him at an advantage as he asked questions.

"I understand you've already met Ellen on more than one occasion." He attempted to lead Adam to admit to a not so coincidental meeting at the movies or another meeting between them.

"Uh, yes, Sir. I-I met her at the beach party a couple of weeks ago and again the other day at the movies. That was a happy coincidence." He gave a nervous smile.

"Hm, uh yes, a coincidence." Hugh paced. "Where do you and your family live? In Starlight Bay?"

Adam shifted in his seat and pulled at his collar. A bead of sweat rolled down his temple. "We live south of here, a few miles. My father is a doctor, and he has patients all over the county."

"A doctor? What is his specialty?" Hugh crossed his arms and tried to look down his nose, like his own father would have done, but he didn't feel comfortable. He needed to loosen up.

"He's a cardiac surgeon, Sir."

"What hospital?"

"He's in private practice and is affiliated with several hospitals along the bay."

Ellen had made an excellent choice in this young man, he thought. "So, tell me about this dance you want to take my daughter. You don't drive yet, I gather?"

"Uh, no, I don't, I'm fifteen. It's the Fall Dance my school holds every year. Sophomores, juniors, and seniors can attend with a date, I mean, a guest. My parents will be chaperoning along with another couple. So, they will bring me to pick up Ellen and after the dance, we will bring her home."

Hugh blew a sigh of relief. "That's really great to hear, Adam. My wife and I were a bit concerned, since Ellen is only thirteen, and we think she is too young for dating. This situation sounds well planned out, and I look forward to meeting your parents."

Adam relaxed and beamed a bright smile. "So, you're giving permission?"

"Of course. I appreciate you coming here to meet me." Hugh saw Dee and Ellen coming up the steps from the beach. "And just in the nick of time. My wife and Ellen are returning from their beach walk." Hugh waved them in, happy to have gotten through the interview with Adam.

Before entering, they changed their shoes at the door. Both of them wore sundresses in bright colors and the walk in the sun gave their complexions a cheery glow.

"Hi Adam." Ellen was nervous too. She swished her skirt back and forth like she used to when she was little.

Hugh winked at Ellen and his wife.

"Mrs. Roth, nice to meet you." Adam shook her hand.

Dee offered something cold to drink.

"I wish I could, but my older brother drove me here, a senior in college. He's waiting for me outside in his car." Adam shot a glance toward the hall.

"My dear boy, he could have waited inside," Hugh said. "I wondered how you got here."

"Oh no, Mr. Roth, he didn't want to impose."

"Daddy, what did you tell Adam?" Ellen asked.

"I told him you can go to the dance. It's not for weeks now. What will the two of you do until then?" Hugh knew those two kids would not want to wait until November.

Ellen and Adam gave sidelong glances at each other and shrugged.

"Well," Dee interjected. "Adam, feel free to visit Ellen any day of the week until the dance. She looked at Hugh for his approval.

"I agree," Hugh said.

Adam nodded.

"Thanks, Dad." Ellen ran over to kiss Hugh on his cheek. He gave her a hug. "I'll walk Adam out to his brother's car. Okay?"

Hugh and Dee smiled and nodded as the young couple made their way down the hall to the front door. Dee plopped down on the sofa and Hugh joined her.

"How was it?" she said.

"Great. He's a mature and polite young man, and his parents will be their chauffeur and chaperones at the dance. It couldn't have been better planned. And your suggestion to invite Adam here was pure genius." He leaned over and kissed her firmly on the mouth. "Adam's father is a surgeon, so I'm doubly pleased."

"Now we can relax for the rest of the weekend."

"Yeah, until the next scary parenting dilemma." Hugh laughed and held Dee close.

"I sure hope the next one doesn't come too soon. There's too much going on right now with the musical. I have a tower of dresses to hand finish this next week and fittings for a dozen girls." She exhaled.

"It must feel great to be needed doing something you love, darling." Hugh kissed her forehead. "I'm proud of you and can hardly wait for the opening night."

Dee's head popped up. "Oh, that reminds me. I need to get with Mrs. Chambers on the details of the cast party!"

CHAPTER NINETEEN
ELLEN

Adam and I spent a glorious time together this past week. He came over twice after school, Chris drove. I invited Susan to join us. We hung out on the beach, swimming if the water wasn't too cold, played ping-pong or cards in the gaming room, and just had fun together. If Mom was busy with her costumes, Mrs. C watched us, though she tried to pretend she wasn't. I knew it and that was okay with me. When it became too difficult for Adam to find a ride, we resorted to phone calls, which I found satisfying. We got to know each other better. Although I was attracted to him, knowing they watched us kept things cooled down. He hadn't even kissed me yet. Golly, I wasn't sure I was ready even though I liked him a lot.

Two weeks until Mom's opening night and I had shown no interest in what she was doing. Mom had been begging me to go with her to rehearsals, but I had an excuse for one thing or the other, or because of Adam.

At school, Susan reminded me that her older sister, Ann, was singing in the chorus. She and her mother were going, and they invited me to join them. I thought it would be neat to surprise Mom, so I didn't tell her.

Mom had left the house at seven. Susan would come for me at 7:30 p.m. The sound of their car horn let me know they had arrived.

"Who's that blaring their car horn?" Mrs. C asked.

"I forgot to tell you I'm going to the rehearsal with my friend Susan. Her mother is driving."

"That's nice, dearie. Does your mother know you are going to be there?"

"Naw, I'll surprise her."

"I'm sure she will be happy to see you there."

Mrs. C followed me out the front door. Susan's mom got out of the car and hollered to Mrs. C. "Don't worry, I'll have her home early."

Mrs. C nodded and went back inside the house.

Susan had opened the front passenger door and moved to the middle of the bench seat. I got in and shut the door.

"Who is that lady?" Mrs. Murphy asked.

"That's Mrs. C our housekeeper."

"Of course, you have a housekeeper," Mrs. Murphy muttered, rolling her eyes.

I detected a slight sarcastic tone but ignored her. I had learned not everyone can afford a housekeeper anymore. Someone told me it used to be fairly common in the olden days like the 1940s, but after the War things changed.

The theater was near the school, as it shared the auditorium for events such as graduation, and band and orchestra concerts.

We had to be quiet inside while they rehearsed a dance number. The dancers wore full petticoats as practice before rehearsing in the finished costumes. A small orchestra in the pit consisted of adults and student musicians. I had gone to several stage performances with Mom and Dad in Boston. Those were enormous theaters with large professional orchestras. Not knowing what to expect from Starlight Bay Community Theater, they sounded pretty good.

We took three seats in the back row. It was dark, but I finally spotted Mom sitting with Mr. Stevens down front. Mom had told me my teacher was the director. I knew Mom was in charge of costumes, but it never occurred to me the two of them would know each other all that well. I mean, it surprised me to see them sitting together. Mr. Stevens was talking close to her ear. The look on his face . . .

My stomach turned somersaults, and I felt sick. I couldn't see Mom's face. I felt uncomfortable when Mr. Stevens lay his hand on her shoulder and she didn't push it away. What was going on with them? I shuddered at the worst possible thoughts, horrid thoughts. Is that why Mr. Stevens didn't have time for me after class anymore? Is he interested in my mom?

I had never felt that kind of rejection before. It was excruciating.

The dance scene was over and the house lights brightened. Mr. Stevens and Mom stood. When she turned around and saw me, she waved excitedly for us to join her.

"Hey, there's your mom, Ellie. Let's go down there," Susan said.

"Oh, I'd love to meet your mom, Ellen," Mrs. Murphy said.

I had no choice, since the two were on their way down the aisle toward my mom. Mr. Stevens wasn't paying attention. He had gone up onto the stage to speak with the dancers.

Mom gave me a big hug. "Why didn't you say something at dinner you were coming tonight?"

"Uh . . . Surprise!" I managed a laugh and introduced Susan's mom.

"I'm so honored to meet you, Mrs. Roth. I've heard wonderful things about the costumes you are making for the production."

Mom gave an embarrassed smile. "Thank you. It's been great fun. You'll love the show. It's nice to see you again, Susan, and meet your mother."

"We can't wait to see the entire show. Can we Susan?" Mrs. Murphy said.

"Oh no, it's all very exciting, Mrs. Roth. When does the chorus sing? My sister Ann is in the ensemble," Susan gushed.

"I remember she told me on the day of the beach party. She will be in the next scene after the dancers are done." Mom gave me an odd look.

My body felt stiff and my stomach was still upset. I didn't know what to say. I glanced up at the stage just as Mr. Stevens turned around and saw me. He waved and smiled. How could he pretend so easily? Maybe he is an actor, too.

"Would you all like to go backstage to see some costumes that are completed?" Mom offered.

"Would I?" Susan said.

"We'd love to," Mrs. Murphy said. "Is Ann backstage?"

"Either in the wings or in the green room."

"Green room?" Susan and her mother said in unison.

"That's where the cast waits until they are called on stage," Mom said.

We followed my mom through a side door and down some stairs.

"Is this where you and your sewing ladies work?" I asked.

"Yes, dear. Sorry for the mess. We have quite a lot of dresses to make." She moved some fabric and long, full-skirted dresses aside.

"We don't mind. They are beautiful." Mrs. Murphy's and Susan's eyes bugged out.

Mom really was a talented seamstress. I tried to focus on the conversation while my mind was spinning over what I thought I'd seen between Mr. Stevens and Mom.

"I wish I could sew like this," Mrs. Murphy said.

Susan picked up one of the dresses and held it in front of her. "Wow, this would be so cool to wear. I should have auditioned for the show. But I can't sing or dance." She laughed.

"Susan, that's not true. You have a lovely voice," her mom said.

"You're supposed to say that," Susan said.

"Maybe next year you can audition for the next musical," Mom said in her sweet, supportive voice.

How could I think such a terrible thing about my mom? I loved her. She's a special person. Maybe it was Mr. Stevens and not her. Not sure what to think, but wishing I could have run out of there.

"They are about to start the next scene if you want to go back out into the auditorium to watch." Mom stood at the stairs.

Susan and Mrs. Murphy agreed, and I followed them. But Mom stopped me.

"Is everything all right with you? You seem upset about something."

She was intuitive. It wasn't easy hiding my emotions from her. "I think something I ate disagreed with me. My tummy is a little upset."

"When you get home, take some Pepto-Bismal. There is a bottle in my medicine cabinet in our bathroom."

"Okay. Thanks. I'm really excited about your costumes. You are doing a swell job!"

I finally calmed down to enjoy watching more of the rehearsal. Susan nudged her mom and pointed when they saw Ann on stage in the ensemble. She was pretty good.

When it was time to leave, Susan and her mom went to the ladies' room while I waited outside at the entrance under the canopy. Coming out of the backstage door, I saw Mr. Stevens and Mom. They were huddled together talking, but for a moment, it looked like Mr. Stevens leaned in and kissed her. I backed up and turned away, horrified. How could he? How could she?

I dashed to Mrs. Murphy's car and got in; glad she hadn't locked the doors. As soon as they dropped me off at home, I barely said goodnight and ran to the front door. I let myself in with my key. Mrs. C was in the kitchen. Not wanting to see her right away, I snuck in quietly, tiptoeing through the hall to sit on the terrace. The image of Mom and Mr. Stevens together fixated in my mind. It was awful. I sat on the loveseat and burst into tears.

The sound of the sliding glass door startled me and I tried to hide my tears.

"There you are," Mrs. C said. "You were quiet coming in. How was the rehearsal?"

I wiped my eyes. "Fine."

"Dearie, whatever is the matter?" She sat next to me and took my hand in hers.

"I can't tell you. It's just too terrible."

"You know you can tell me anything. Is it a secret? Is it Adam, or a boy at school? I saw your notebook today, with initials written all over the cover."

Oh, my goodness. She saw that? I shuddered with humiliation. "I'll tell, if you promise not to tell anyone." I trusted Mrs. C. Aunt Sylvi was very understanding, but she was too close to Mom and Dad. I just knew she would tell.

"Of course, dearie, I can keep a secret." She stroked my hair like when I was a little girl. It comforted me and my sobbing stopped.

I took the hanky she offered and blew my nose. "Those aren't a boy's initials." I feared looking at her. Dare I tell?

"Not a boy? I don't understand."

"P.S. stands for my English teacher, Mr. Stevens. I wrote those initials when school first started, before I met Adam." I hiccupped.

"Oh, I see. A schoolgirl crush on your teacher is a common thing. There's no need to be embarrassed about that." She took out a second hanky and dabbed my wet cheeks.

"Really? Did you have a crush in school?"

"Oh yes, there was a handsome teacher that all the girls fawned over. He had dark wavy hair, much like your father's. He wore a mustache, as so many did in those days. But it was short-lived."

"What happened? Did he reject you?"

She laughed. "Oh no! It would have been inappropriate for a teacher and a student to even talk about such things as a crush. I got over him as soon as the first boy asked me to go for ice cream."

"Really? I've been so conflicted about my feelings ever since the beach party."

"What happened there, dearie?"

"You know, Adam. He came here to meet Daddy?"

"Yes, I remember him."

"Isn't he simply dreamy? He goes to the prep school south of here and I'm really excited to go to his school's dance. He's so nice. But before I met Adam, I thought I was in love with Mr. Stevens, and now I think about this boy all the time."

"That is perfectly natural, too. Adam is your age and you have more in common. He seems very nice."

"It's all this other stuff that's been going on."

"I see. All that nastiness with Dana is over, isn't it?"

"Uh-yeah, that . . . and . . ."

"Something else has you cryin'? Did something happen at the rehearsal?"

"Yes." I wanted to tell Mrs. C that I thought Mom was having an affair. But it would be so damaging, especially if I was wrong. But it sure looked like he kissed her from where I was standing. I had to tell someone.

Mrs. C put her hand on mine. She knew just how to comfort me. She was like a grandmother to me.

"Uh . . . The way I saw him acting with Mom upset me."

"In what way?" She looked perplexed.

"Well . . . I saw them in the parking lot and it looked like he kissed Mom." I just blurted it out so fast I couldn't stop myself.

Mrs. C's eyes nearly popped out of her head. "That couldn't possibly be. You must have misunderstood."

"That's not all. They were sitting up front in the auditorium when I first walked in. With his hand on her shoulder, he looked at Mom like Daddy does sometimes. Like he loved her. I know I didn't get that wrong."

Mrs. C leaned back and crossed her arms like she does when she was thinking about a recipe for dinner. "How did your mom react to him? Could you see her expression?"

"Not in the theater, but she didn't push his hand off or anything, that she didn't like it. But in the parking lot, he had his back to me and I could see Mom's face. After what I thought was a kiss, she laughed. That's strange. Isn't it?"

Mrs. C sighed with a look of relief. "I think you've misinterpreted what you saw. A woman would never laugh if a man kissed her. She might smile if she liked it, or slap his face, if she didn't."

"Really? Oh, just like in the movies? I've seen that happen." I'd begun to feel much better and my stomach stopped hurting. Maybe I'd misunderstood. I hugged Mrs. C. "Thank you for listening and helping me understand. I was angry and thought the most horrible things about Mom. And . . .I think I understand now about my crush on Mr. Stevens and why he stopped spending so much time with me after class. I thought it was because he was in love with Mom. Now I can see that he probably realized I had a crush, and he didn't want to encourage me."

Mrs. C stood up and gazed down at me. "You've made a mature observation of his actions. I'm proud of you." The corners of her eyes crinkled as she smiled.

"I love you Mrs. C."

Feeling grown up, I hugged her and went to bed. I hoped that Mrs. C was right, and I'd nothing to worry about. Something tugged at me. I no longer believed Mom had any romantic feelings about Mr. Stevens, but I wasn't completely convinced about him.

CHAPTER TWENTY
HUGH

Thursday was the opening night of *Carousel.* Hugh drove down from the city with Jack and Sylvi who planned to stay over until Saturday morning. On the way, they stopped to pick up Ellen at the house. Dee had been at the theater most of the day.

Pressed for time Hugh went up to the front door alone.

"Daddy!" Ellen ran out when she saw him.

"Don't you look all grown up? New dress?"

"Yes, you like it?" She twirled the full skirt around as the porch light shone on her shiny pink silk dress with tiny pink satin bows clipped to her curly bob. "I know these don't match exactly, but I wanted to wear the jewelry I got for my birthday." She touched the amethyst earrings and necklace.

"I think they look perfect. Can I get a big hug?"

"Careful, Daddy, as long as you don't mess up my hair."

"Now you sound just like your mother."

They both laughed as they got in the car. Sylvi had moved to the back seat to sit with Ellen.

"What are you two laughing about?" Sylvi asked.

"Just an inside joke," Hugh said.

"I went to the theater on Monday to watch the rehearsal and saw Mom's costumes," Ellen said.

"You did? How fun," Sylvi said.

"It's very professional. I'm sure you will be impressed with the performance. Though not as fancy as the shows in Boston."

Hugh was bursting with pride at how mature his daughter sounded. His excitement rose at seeing the culmination of his wife's work.

Ellen handed out the tickets Dee had given her as they strolled into the entrance to the theater. Their seats were down front and center. Hugh looked around for Dee, but she must have been backstage. He had a seat for her, but Dee had already warned him she might have to stay backstage in case of any costume mishaps.

Right before the curtain went up, Dee crept in from the side door and took her seat next to Hugh. With a happy expression, he took her hand and held it during the entire first act.

Hugh felt Dee cringe when a dancer struggle with a shoulder strap that came undone. She whispered to Hugh she would have to go backstage to fix it.

During intermission, after Dee left, he and Jack went outside for a smoke. They both agreed the show was impressive for a small-town community theater. The director apparently knew what he was doing.

Back in their seats for the next act, Hugh hoped Dee would return, but she didn't. Must have been other issues she needed to handle. Disappointed, he turned his attention to the enjoyable performance.

After the last curtain call, they all went backstage to congratulate Dee. The crowd pushed them in until Ellen broke away to visit friends in the cast. Hugh searched for Dee until he noticed her standing next to a tall, handsome, blond-haired man. From Ellen's and Dee's descriptions, he figured the man to be the director, Patrick Stevens.

Dee had her back to Hugh, and the man was leaning into her, his hand on her back, just a little too low. An uncomfortable heat spread through Hugh. He'd felt that whenever his former chauffeur, Ben, would talk to Dee. He has been terribly jealous back then. Those feelings returned while watching this man with his wife.

"There's Dee, let's go congratulate her. Dee!" Sylvi shouted over the clamoring voices. "Oh, she just saw me." Sylvi pushed ahead, and Jack followed.

Hugh hung back, keeping his eyes on the director, wondering what designs he had on his wife?

"Oh, Hugh!" Dee called to him and waved.

He pulled himself together and smiled, maneuvering her away from Stevens. Hugh kissed her and put his arm possessively around her waist.

"Let me introduce you to the director," she turned, "Patrick Stevens."

Hugh kept his left arm around Dee and shook Patrick's hand. "I've heard a lot about you and the show, Mr. Stevens. It was marvelous."

"Please call me Patrick."

Hugh nodded, turning back to Dee. "And you, darling, did an outstanding job on the costumes. I'm so proud of you." He kissed her again."

Dee gave him an odd look.

Hugh wasn't usually so demonstrative in public, especially in a crowd. His need to show Patrick that Dee belonged to him overcame his usual sense of propriety.

The conversation remained light and mostly about the show. Patrick remained neutral but continued to hang around Dee, much to Hugh's discomfort.

Ellen broke through their little group and threw her arms about her mother, forcing Hugh to take a step back. "Oh, Mom, it was sensational and your costumes looked fabulous onstage!"

"Thank you, dear." Dee didn't stop smiling the whole time. Her face, flushed from the excitement, made her glow. Hugh thought she looked more beautiful than ever.

Several people had crowded around Patrick to congratulate him, much to Hugh's relief.

"Shouldn't we get home, darling?" Hugh said to Dee. "Mrs. Chambers has a light supper and dessert waiting for all of us."

"That's right. She mentioned it to me this morning. I'm famished. Haven't had a bite in hours."

❧

At home, Mrs. Chambers welcomed everyone with hot cocoa, tea, and plenty of food. Ellen grew drowsy, her head nodding and just like the old days at the mansion, Sylvi and Jack took her to bed and tucked her in. Hugh had his arm around Dee as they lingered at the dining table.

"Mr. and Mrs. Roth," Mrs. Chambers said. "My son confirmed he will drive up tomorrow to take me to the Friday night performance. I'm so eager to see it. He also volunteered to help on Saturday for the cast party. Whatever you need."

"I'm so glad he's taking you," Dee said.

"We can use an extra pair of hands. Thanks," Hugh said.

Mrs. Chambers cleaned up the last of the dishes and bid a goodnight.

Dee yawned.

"You must be exhausted, darling," Hugh said.

"I am, but I've barely been home all week, what with all the work at the theater. Care to join me on the terrace? I need the sound of the ocean."

Hugh followed her outside, and they stood at the railing, letting the ocean breeze flow over them. "I've been missing this."

"We both have." She leaned into him, raising her head, their eyes locked.

Hugh bent down and kissed her in a deeply passionate embrace.

Dee moaned.

For a while, they cuddled, listening to the waves roll in on the beach. The moon peaked out from the clouds and its light shimmered on the water.

Hugh woke knowing Saturday would be another important day for Dee. The opening of the show was a big success for her. Despite what he thought was going on between her and Patrick, he needed to stay focused on the cast party. This would be the first event they hosted since moving here. It would be an important event for Hugh too. Even though most of the guests were just the average people in town. He was aware of the elitist tone, but as a businessman, he understood the importance of appearances, regardless of personal beliefs. A successful party could affect all avenues of his business, including his plans to get into the cruise travel insurance business.

Dee was running about the house checking that everything was spotless and in order. Mrs. Chambers followed. "Mrs. Roth, the show was simply marvelous. My son and I enjoyed it immensely."

"I'm so glad the two of you liked it." Dee nearly ran into Hugh in the hallway.

Hugh stepped aside to let her pass and chuckled while Mrs. Chambers continued chattering about all the details of the show she liked or thought could have been done differently.

He waved to Mrs. Chambers' son to direct him on a few tasks and looked around for Dee.

"When do the caterers arrive? It's almost noon," Hugh called down the hall.

"They arrive at six." She appeared in the open front doorway. "No need to shout, honey. We have hours to prepare, relax. This isn't our first party, you know." She chuckled.

Hugh sighed and met her halfway. "Sorry, I thought you were in our suite. I'm feeling a little stressed."

Dee shut the door and kissed him on the cheek. "I went through the back way to check the front yard. It looks nice. Oh, I just remembered. Pull our alcohol from the bar. They provide a full inventory to make sure there's enough." She stroked his arm. "You remember. Things are the same on the West Coast."

"I remember. Just being silly." He lifted her fingers to his lips.

"Besides, I should be the one nervous. All these people know me and I want to make a good impression, too."

"How many people are expected? Are they bringing guests or is it just the cast and crew?"

"I invited everyone, plus one guest. I don't know for sure, but I told the caterer over one hundred. The children in the play may not attend, as it depends on their parents and the late hour. If they do come, probably won't be for long."

"Okay, just checking, I had figured up to 120. We'll be fine." He squeezed her hand and kissed her cheek. "I'll go downstairs to check on the gaming room, make sure everything is set up in case anyone wants to play. The caterers bring additional tables and chairs, right?"

"Yes, they were ordered."

"Good. The Tiki torches are set up downstairs. We'll have the servers light them, ok?"

Dee rolled her eyes at Hugh.

"Unbelievable how cold it turned suddenly. Glad I purchased several portable heaters for outside. Hope that will be enough out there."

Hugh turned to leave when he remembered the band. "Oh, and the band . . ."

"They come at ten to set up and start for the early guests after curtain calls. I wanted to be there, but Patrick said Monday would be fine to check the costumes."

"Good." Off he went downstairs, using the indoor staircase. He made a mental note to remember to keep the door open so guests knew they didn't have to use the outdoor steps. That reminded him to double check the lights on the steps worked.

Hours later, guests were arriving in a steady stream. The caterers were busy and doing a great job. Hugh had changed into his dress suit. Dee reminded him not to wear the usual tuxedo. He followed what the men wore to the opening. After all, he was the host. The caterers provided a coat check system and Hugh worried no one would go outside, even with the heaters.

"Honey, stop worrying, everything will be just fine," Dee said.

Dee was stunning no matter what she wore, and she dazzled in a modest pale green cocktail dress that shimmered with a lacy neckline. The two stood together in the foyer welcoming guests. Hugh tried to remember who was a character in the musical, but Dee thoughtfully introduced them as both character and their actual names. She knew everyone, and Hugh should have assumed she would.

He gazed at this incredible woman, his wife, and realized he needed to remember just how remarkable she was. All the time spent away over the past two years had put unnecessary tension in their marriage.

And then Patrick Stevens arrived without a guest, which Hugh half expected.

Patrick wore the same suit he had on opening night, and there was no denying he was handsome. What did Ellen call him? Movie star handsome. Hugh was friendly toward him, keeping his growing distrust in check. As the arrivals trickled off and it appeared most were there, Dee and Hugh separated to mingle.

The band played current and old tunes. Couples were already dancing on the terrace. Some with their coats on.

Hugh dashed downstairs and found about a dozen of the younger crowd dancing on the patio and some playing ping-pong. That made him happy as a clam.

When Hugh returned to the terrace by way of the outdoor steps, he couldn't find Dee. Then he noticed her dancing. With whom else? Patrick. His arm wrapped around her waist and gazing at her like a lovesick puppy. Hugh's insides tightened and his hands rolled into fists. He looked around, and no one was watching them. Forcing himself to relax, he grabbed his first glass of champagne from a server passing by. He needed to calm down. Making a scene would be the worst.

Plastering a smile on his face, Hugh made his way through the dancing couples and tapped on Patrick's shoulder. Patrick turned sharply, frowning at first. When Patrick saw who it was, he surrendered like a gentleman, and Hugh took his place.

Hugh's smile turned genuine and looked into her green eyes. "You look happy, darling." He whispered in her ear and hugged her close. "Are you cold?"

"I'm happy and warmer now that you are close to me, though it's not as chilly as you thought. The heaters work, if you stand close enough."

He steered them to the nearest unit.

"The party is a great success. Everyone says so and look at them . . . they are all smiling. Isn't it wonderful?" Dee smiled.

"If I'm correct, this is the first party we've done together since we were married that you were truly happy about."

She pressed her cheek against his. "Maybe that's because these people are my friends. They'll be yours too, if you want."

"Of course, I do. I'm sorry I never noticed you weren't happy at all those social functions. You fit into the life so easily, I assumed you liked it. But seeing how happy and satisfied you've been ever since joining the theater . . .well, I'm delighted."

Dee pulled back. "I wasn't unhappy. But fitting into your social world wasn't easy for me. I had to work at it pretty hard."

"From here on in, I won't pressure you into any social or business events you aren't comfortable doing." He twirled her around and pressed her against him.

"Oh, I love when you twirl me." She laughed.

Hugh puffed with pride. He was the luckiest man in the world. That was until Hugh spied Patrick standing in the shadows of the terrace watching them dancing. He did not look happy. In fact, he looked positively murderous. Or was Hugh imagining it because of how the light fell on Patrick's irritatingly handsome face?

When the band ended for a few moments and started again, they were playing *Blue Moon*, one of Dee's favorites. But Ellen dashed out to the terrace.

"Daddy, will you dance with me?" Her face glowed with her youth and beauty in the same pink satin dress she wore for the opening. She had insisted on wearing it again, and Dee agreed.

"Absolutely, sweetheart. Darling," Hugh said to Dee, "will you excuse me while I dance with this stunning creature?"

Dee stepped away, kissed Ellen on the cheek, and went into the house.

"Ellen, you look beautiful. Sorry I've been so busy today."

"I understood. I love this party. My first one like this in ages. The people are so friendly. Susan's mom is here and my friend Ann, who was in the ensemble. Remember?"

"Yes, you told me at the opening. She did an admirable job. Do you think you will audition for any future productions?"

"I'm not talented that way, Daddy."

"How do you know? You have a beautiful voice and you can learn to move and dance on the stage." Hugh twirled her around. "See, you can do that."

She scrunched up her cute nose. "Maybe. Depends on what the next show will be. Mr. Stevens hasn't said anything about it."

Just hearing that man's name made Hugh tense. "That's right, he would probably be the director again."

"Why wouldn't he, Daddy?"

Hugh evaded answering. He was working out how to get that man out of their lives.

After the last guest departed, the caterers were occupied with cleaning, washing glasses and dishes, and packing up. Mrs. Chambers navigated the shutting down of the party and settling up with the bill using the blank check Hugh gave her.

Ellen had gone to bed ages ago. She wasn't used to staying up past ten, but she lasted till midnight, not wanting to miss anything.

Hugh and Dee were tired and gravitated outside and sat on the cushioned loveseat. He pushed a heater closer. She had grabbed a fur stole from the closet. Hugh was warm enough with his suit.

"It's supposed to get down to forty-nine degrees," Dee said. "Can you believe it?"

"At least there won't be any snow." He cuddled up close to her, trying to keep quiet.

The urge to warn her about Patrick pulled on Hugh and he couldn't hold it in any longer.

"That Mr. Stevens . . .er, Patrick . . ."

"What about him?"

He tried to choose his next words carefully. "He seems quite taken with you."

Dee pulled back and narrowed her eyes at him. "If you mean, he respects my talents and encourages me, yes, perhaps."

"I'm sure he respects your talents, as you have many and they are great. What I mean is . . . the way he looks at you, so intently."

"Hugh, don't do this."

"What? Protect you? You are my wife. I should protect you from someone that may want . . . "

"This sounds just like your crazy notions about Ben. You were wrong about him then and you're wrong about Patrick. He's a nice man and we get along fine. We're friends."

"Is that what he thinks?" Hugh treaded on dangerous waters. Alienating Dee was not what he wanted.

Dee moved away from him. "You better not be implying there is something going on between Patrick and me."

"No, not between you." He paused, weighing his next words. "I think it's pretty obvious, at least to me, uh, from his side, there is definitely something. I just don't want you to encourage him."

As soon as the words left his lips, he knew he'd pushed too far.

"Encourage him? I don't like where this is going. You are ruining a perfect evening for me with your jealousy over . . . over nothing!" She pushed away and threw her hands in the air. Then, in a huff, she stormed into the house.

Now he'd done it. There was something off about Patrick. Hugh was going to prove it.

Regretting their argument, he tried to smooth it over before they went to sleep. Dee wouldn't talk to him after she spent an extra-long time in her boudoir. That private place Hugh had built especially for her inside her closet, just like Ellen's, only twice the size.

She slipped under the covers and turned off her light.

"Dee, I'm sorry, please, let's not do this again. I hate it when you turn your back on me." He touched her shoulder. She didn't flinch or pull away. His hand glided down her silk sleeve. Her hand took his and wrapped it around her waist, but remained with her back to him. He took the invitation to spoon her, and that's how they fell asleep.

It was better than nothing.

All day Sunday, Dee was polite, but definitely reserved. Hugh said little and they put all their attention on Ellen until Hugh left early Monday morning for the office.

He hoped his next night home on Wednesday would go better.

CHAPTER TWENTY-ONE
DEE

Still feeling the burn from Hugh's comments after the cast party, I was unusually cool with him on Sunday. Now that Monday is here, my guilt over the argument overcame me. I hated being angry with him. I loved Hugh with all my heart. There is no room for anyone but Ellen. He should know that. The very idea Patrick had feelings for me was just ludicrous. I've made it perfectly clear I was happily married. Hadn't I?

With Ellen off to school, I drove to the theater to meet Ethyl and Betty to inspect the costumes. Before storing them for later use, we would make any necessary repairs and take them to the dry cleaners. I wore a long-sleeved cotton shirt with the sleeves rolled up over a casual pair of capris and canvas shoes.

"Here we are, Dee," Ethyl said, carrying a basket full of baked pastries. "You're dressed casual today. I love it. And, what a fabulous cast party you and Mr. Roth gave all of us. It will be food for conversation for months to come, if not years."

I'd never seen Ethyl wear anything but a dress, mostly calico prints. Perhaps she didn't feel comfortable in pants, some women didn't.

"I agree, Ethyl," Betty said, following behind with a large thermos of coffee as usual. She went to the kitchenette, where cups and such were stored. "Woo-wee, someone did not wash out their cups!"

"Bet it was a man," Ethyl chuckled.

"You ladies keep me in stitches. I could use another cup of coffee." I reached for a clean mug and unscrewed the thermos cap. "Thanks for bringing this. I'm still sluggish from the past week. What a whirlwind it was."

For the next few hours, we went over every costume, set aside the ones for repairs and the rest in bags for the cleaners.

"Okay, now let's divide up the repairs and we can do them from home. They are mostly hand sewing jobs, right?" I said.

"Great idea." Betty sorted through those she felt comfortable doing. "I'll take these."

Ethyl did the same. "And these I'll take."

"Didn't leave much for me." I waved my finger at them as if they were little girls.

"You've done so much and deserve lots of time off," Betty replied.

Ethyl agreed, and I said a gracious thank you.

Betty got serious and looked behind her as if she were checking to make sure we were all alone.

"Do you think Mr. Stevens will want to do the next production?" She said low.

"Maybe. I don't really know. He hasn't said." I kept my face steady and my voice calm, not wanting them to know how I really felt. Which was what? I didn't know anymore. Hugh's suspicions made me question everything about Patrick. Hugh's perceptions were usually correct, despite his error regarding Ben, that one time.

"Well," Betty took a deep breath. "While I don't usually gossip, this information could be important later."

"Okay, Betty, spit it out," Ethyl said.

"My grandniece goes to the college in San Bernardino. You know, the one Mr. Stevens came from. She told me about some incident that happened with him that year. Apparently, it was all hushed up, and then Mr. Stevens left suddenly without saying farewell to his classes. When I told my grandniece who was directing our production, she was surprised to learn he was teaching at a high school."

"What was the incident?" I leaned forward.

"I don't know all the details, but it involved at least one female student. The girl reported that he had pursued her relentlessly despite her not being interested. It was against school policy and cause for dismissal. You know, students and teachers." Betty crossed her arms and leaned back in her chair. "He may have done a superb job as our director, but do we want him teaching our teen-aged girls?"

My mouth dropped open and Ethyl's face went ashen.

"We sure don't!" Ethyl said.

All I could do was nod my head. I was speechless.

On Tuesday, I told Mrs. Chambers I would go to the grocery store. She happily allowed me the privilege. When I returned home, my arms were full of bags and the phone was ringing as I reached the front door. I fumbled for the keys, but the phone kept ringing. Where in the world was Mrs. Chambers? Finding the keys, I hurried in, placed the grocery bags on the foyer table and picked up the receiver.

"Hello?" I panted, out of breath.

"Dee?"

It was Patrick.

I took some deep breaths. "Oh, hello, Patrick. I just walked in the door. I had expected to see you at the theater yesterday. Betty, Ethyl, and I were there all morning."

"Yes, I thought you might be. That's why I waited to call you today."

How strange. Why did he wait to call me? "Did you need something? I have costumes I planned to repair today."

"Dee, you are a wonder and so committed. Would you meet me for lunch in about thirty minutes? At the Coast Club Cafe? I have some things to discuss with you."

He sounded different.

"I suppose so. Not for very long." This was perfect timing to get everything cleared up, so I could tell Hugh he was wrong about Patrick.

"Great," he said. "See you soon."

I quickly emptied the bags of groceries onto the kitchen counter when Mrs. Chambers came in from outside.

"There you are. The phone was ringing off the hook."

"I'm sorry, Mrs. Roth, I was watering the plants on the terrace and didn't hear the phone. I think maybe my hearing must be going."

"I certainly hope not. You need to get your hearing checked soon. The call was Mr. Stevens. I'm meeting him to wrap up some things post-show. You know." My voice shook with apprehension at the meeting with Patrick. I never had before. Why today?

"Of course. I'll take care of these groceries. Will you be out long?"

"Not planning on it. I've lots to do here." I adjusted my hat, grabbed my gloves, and headed back out to my car.

The cafe was south of our house a few miles. I'd only seen it while passing. Again, not the nicest place around, but it was popular. On a Tuesday, there were only a few people there. Patrick was on his lunch break, so I knew we wouldn't be there for long. Though I recall him saying he had an open period after the lunch hour. He said he used that time for grading tests and meeting with students. Oh gosh, meeting with student girls? Like my daughter. I pressed on the gas pedal, feeling a sense of urgency. Patrick's white Fairlane was there. The school is farther away from the cafe than my house. He must have called from here.

He had a table in the back, like the other times I had met him for lunch. Only two other times. It wasn't regular. Usually, I would see him at the theater.

He stood and waved. I forced a smile.

When I got to the table, Patrick came around and held the chair for me, like any gentleman would.

I sat and removed my gloves. The waiter brought two glasses of water and menus. Food was the last thing on my mind. I laid the menu down.

"What did you need to discuss with me? I have everything under control closing out the costumes and once—"

"Dee, this isn't about the costumes. I know you will handle all that perfectly, as you have with everything you do. Because you . . . are perfect."

He leaned forward, his right hand moved across the table toward mine. "Don't you know?"

I pulled my hand back into my lap. "Whatever do you mean?"

"I have feelings for you. No, to be honest, I'm in love with you. I know you feel the same for me." He looked intently at me.

He's in love? Hugh was right.

"I'm sorry you feel that way, really. But you are mistaken. I've never given you cause to believe I feel anything more for you than respect and my friendship." At that moment, whatever respect and friendship I had toward him had vanished. The situation had become quite uncomfortable.

"I don't believe you, Dee." His voice changed, edgy and weird sounding. "I've seen it in your eyes, felt it in your touch. You've never rejected my touch . . . until just now."

"Your touch? A handshake? A dance? You've misread my innocent and common actions. I am a happily married woman." No longer feeling embarrassed for him, all I wanted to do was get away from him. I'd made a terrible mistake meeting him.

"What about those times you complained about your husband being away so much? How happy you were to be useful again."

"I don't recall ever complaining to you about my marriage. And yes, I was happy to be involved in the show and use my talents. Again, you've misinterpreted innocent comments, which now I see I shouldn't have said."

Patrick's eyes turned dark and his shoulders rigid. "I know I've made you happy." His voice was urgent and raspy.

I lowered my voice. "You've never been married, or you would understand that couples make compromises because they love each other, as Hugh and I do, deeply. It's a forever kind of love." I stood just as the waiter started toward us. "I'm leaving now." I waved away the waiter.

"Dee, don't go, please." He stood and reached across the table.

I shrank from him. "I'm sorry, really, I am. But please, don't make a scene. And never call me again. My obligation to you is over. I will complete my responsibilities to the theater." With that, I turned and hurried out of the cafe.

On the way home, my hands shook on the steering wheel. How could I have been so blind, so trusting? Hugh was right.

CHAPTER TWENTY-TWO
DEE

Sylvi and Jack arrived late the night before. We had a nightcap together and then retired. All week I had put off talking to Hugh about what happened with Patrick and the gossip from Betty. I wasn't ready for his *I told you so*.

We were all going to the Fall Harvest Banquet and Dance at the club. Hugh had invited Jack and Sylvi as our guests. Since it was so close to Halloween, costumes were optional. I was all costumed-out and passed. Same with Hugh, but Sylvi and Jack decided to rent some professional costumes in San Francisco.

Hugh had left a note on his pillow that he and Jack had gone to the putting range for a couple of hours. I dragged myself out of bed to get some breakfast, hoping Sylvi would be up.

In the breakfast nook, Sylvi was there, still in her robe. So was I.

"You look like death," Sylvi said. "That show sure wore you out."

"Gee, thanks a lot. I can't believe it was a week ago and I'm still exhausted. The problem is, Hugh and I had a falling out right after the cast party."

"Arguments happen. Too bad it happened right after your evening of success with the show. Are you all right?"

Sylvi was the best. She always knew the right thing to say. I looked for Mrs. Chambers, not wanting her to overhear, but she must have gone to water the plants.

I kept my voice low. "He was just being Hugh, you know, jealous. Not for the first time. He had some ridiculous idea that Patrick Stevens had designs on me. I thought it ludicrous."

Sylvi said nothing. Her face said it all.

"You agree with him?"

"I certainly do now," Mrs. Chambers said behind me.

"What?" I turned sharply to find her standing in the middle of the kitchen with her hands on her hips. "How did you get in here so fast?"

"Just never you mind. Where is Ellen?" Mrs. Chambers asked, looking around.

"I saw her going down for a walk on the beach earlier," Sylvi said.

"Good. Because I promised I wouldn't say anything about what she told me. Now that I know Mr. Hugh thought much the same thing as she did a couple of weeks ago, I can't keep my mouth shut."

"Oh my god, what did Ellen see?" Things just turned from Hugh's imagination, which turned out to be true, to something else, the eyes of our daughter.

Mrs. Chambers took a seat at the breakfast table with us and spoke low. "Just in case Ellen shows up unexpectedly, we need to keep this between us, and Mr. Hugh, I suppose. She thought she saw Mr. Stevens kiss you, Mrs. Roth."

I laughed out loud. "That's ridiculous . . . she did? Oh dear, when?"

"It was the night she went to watch the rehearsal. You and the director were outside the stage door in the parking lot."

I thought back to what it could have been that Ellen saw to think he had kissed me. "Oh that. It was nothing. He said I had chalk on my face. I use it to mark fabric. He leaned toward me to brush it off. I recall that I laughed about it." It was one thing for Patrick to misread me and another thing people could see in his actions. My heart ached for Ellen to have thought there was something between Patrick and me.

"That's what she saw. She could only see that back of him leaning in to you. I explained it away that a woman wouldn't laugh if a man kissed her."

"That's true," Sylvi piped in. "Ellen must have sensed something prior to that for her to assume it was a kiss."

"She did earlier that night," Mrs. Chambers said. "She said he looked at you, Mrs. Roth, just like your Mr. Hugh looks at you, like he was in love."

I was floored. How could I not have noticed? It wasn't just Hugh. "What did you tell her?"

"That she misunderstood what she saw. You and Mr. Roth are very much in love, and there was nothing between Mr. Stevens and you."

"You're right, there isn't. Did she believe you?"

"She believes it," Mrs. Chambers said.

"Thank you, for putting Ellen's concerns to rest." I said.

"What are you going to do, Dee?" Sylvi asked, taking a piece of toast and spreading butter on it. "Sorry, I'm starved."

"Actually, I already did something and planned to talk about it to Hugh, eventually. I realize, I need to tell him right away. I've been procrastinating because I thought it was only Hugh imagining it. But, if three people are thinking the same thing, there might be others and you know how rumors start. They are hard to stop. And Hugh and I had our fill of rumors for one year."

Sylvi looked confused.

"That's a story for another day."

"Okay. I'll remind you." Sylvi scooped three eggs and four sausages onto her plate.

I stared at her.

"Hey, I'm eating for two, remember?"

Saying nothing, I smiled at her, a tug of my own demon jealousy about her pregnancy.

"Well, I have a hair appointment today, so I need to get hopping." I finished my coffee and hurried to change into a day dress and left for the salon.

Three days I'd been stewing over the scene with Patrick, not knowing how to tell Hugh. I was still processing Patrick's unbelievable confession he was in love with me and how he refused to believe I didn't feel the same. In truth, it gave me the creeps. I thought of the story about the college girl in San Bernardino.

I would tell Hugh tonight.

❧

The dance was our first event together at the club and it was a big to-do. Hugh looked so dashing in his tux.

Jack came as a giant white rabbit. "I'm Harvey, you know from the play with James Stewart?"

"And the movie," I said. "I love it. You're hysterical, Jack." My sides ached from laughing so hard. "You know that Harvey doesn't actually appear in the play or the movie?"

"I know that." Jack rolled his eyes. "I'm Elwood P. Dowd's imagination."

Hugh looked at Jack like he was nuts.

Sylvi wore her narrow fitting black satin dress that fell to the floor and a headband with big black cat ears. She had painted whiskers on her face and wore black fur gloves from the costume place that had white plastic claws fitted into the tips of the fingers. Very realistic, I thought.

Sylvi wiggled her whiskers. "This is the last time I'll be able to wear this dress, probably forever. It's too tight about my middle. Does it look bad? Soon, I'll have to wear maternity clothes, ugh! They are not flattering, at all."

"You still look good and you're making be laugh. Love the whiskers."

"Yours is new." Sylvi turned me around. "Love it."

"From my last shopping spree in Boston, not knowing whether I would ever get a chance to wear it here."

A designer dress in satin with layers of tulle in my favorite color, blue, that reached my mid-calves. The neckline swept across my chest just a tad off my shoulders. Rhinestone studded heels and an evening bag to match. On my ears, I wore the blue sapphires and a necklace of sapphires and diamonds Hugh had given me for our fifth anniversary.

There was no time to talk to Hugh alone before the dance, but I did tell him I had something important to say later. He looked worried.

I kissed him. "Don't worry, it's good news." Probably not good, but I didn't want to spoil the whole evening.

We all relaxed and had fun. The other couples at our table, which included Doris and her husband, chatted with lively enthusiasm. Doris reminded me about the bridge club.

"Sorry, Doris. I've been busy with the theater production in our town. I was in charge of costumes for the entire cast," I told her.

Doris gave an impressed gasp. "You didn't? How marvelous! I've never been to a community theater. Was it any good?"

"Maybe not by big city standards, but everyone enjoyed it." I didn't appreciate the woman's obvious snobbery, but I had grown accustomed to similar comments over the years. "I can attend the next bridge meeting if you still need me."

"Fabulous, my dear. I'll give you a call next week with the details." Doris turned to the woman next to her. Her way of telling me I'd been dismissed.

Shrugging my shoulders, I gave my attention to Hugh.

The men were talking politics, what with the presidential election around the corner. Hugh and I were privately non-partisan, though he planned to vote for John F. Kennedy.

Doris's husband raised his eyebrow at Hugh. "Well, if you support him, I hope he's the right man for the job. We don't fuss over parties at this club, otherwise, we wouldn't have as many members. We try to keep things civil," he said in his gruff voice and let out a boisterous laugh. A burly man with kind eyes.

I motioned to Sylvi to join me in the powder room. There were several women in the spacious lounge area, all in white, with a circular upholstered bench in the center. Most of them were adjusting their hair and makeup in the mirror that extended the full width of the wall. I went into the adjoining room and took a stall at the far end. I heard a couple of ladies leaving stalls while chatting.

"Did you hear about a new member's wife? She was having lunch with a man that was not her husband?" the older sounding woman said.

"What new member?" said the other woman in a high, squeaky voice.

"The Ross's, no, Roth, I think. It was at some out of the way place near Starlight Bay."

"Who told you this?"

"One of the ladies at my table said she recognized her tonight."

"How can she be sure it wasn't innocent?"

"I don't know. But why would she mention it if she didn't think it was questionable?"

"Some women just like to gossip and spread rumors. I would be careful if I were you."

"You are the only one I told," the older woman said in a huff. The sound of their clicking heels on the stone floor quickly dissipated.

I couldn't move. Who saw me with Patrick and then recognized me tonight? I finished my business and found Sylvi in the lounge. By then, we were alone.

"Dee, you look like you've seen a ghost." Sylvi came toward me, concerned.

"Not a ghost, but I'm shocked, as if I'd seen one. I'll tell you later. Do I need a retouch?"

"Just lipstick. I don't know if I can wait until later."

"You'll just have to." I went to the mirror and pulled out my lipstick. My hand trembled so badly I smeared the deep red color.

"Here, let me." Sylvi wiped off the excess with a tissue and reapplied the color. "There, perfect. Wow, you are really shaken up. Do you need a drink?"

"As soon as we return to our table. Stop staring at me like that."

"Like what? Just curious."

"Okay . . . I'll tell you."

I checked behind us, making sure no one had come into the powder room, and whispered what the two ladies had said.

"That's terrible." Sylvi's faced was aghast.

"Let's go. The men must be thinking we fell in by now." I gave a small chuckle.

"Funny."

As we exited, we walked past two women, one older, the other younger, and her squeaky voice confirmed it. The look on their faces told me they were the ones I had overheard. Served them right to be caught spreading vicious rumors with me in earshot, or at least they were worried about it. I smiled politely. "Good evening," I said, and continued on.

I nudged Sylvi with my elbow and shot a look at the two ladies. Sylvi caught on and squeezed my hand. When we reached the table, she whispered to me. "Oh, if I could just say something to those two biddies to shut them up."

Mouthing a 'thank you' to her, I placed my evening bag on the table.

Hugh stood. "A dance?"

I nodded, and he guided me onto the large dance floor. The ballroom at the club easily seated three-hundred for dinner plus a dance floor.

"I love dancing with you, Hugh."

"You looked upset when you came back to the table."

"Did I?"

"You can't keep secrets from me, Dee."

"You will have to wait until later." I forced a smile.

He twirled me around and then back into his arms. "No. You will tell me now. Let's go outside."

Reluctantly, I let him take my hand, and we went out on the lighted patio. It was cool, but not cold and no wind. Hugh, always the gentleman, took off his jacket and put it around my bare shoulders. We took a bench out of the way from the people dancing outside to the music coming through speakers.

"You look gorgeous tonight."

I smiled.

"Now, tell me what's upset you."

"I heard something distressing in the powder room. But first, I owe you a huge apology."

"About last weekend? I owe you one, too."

"Let me be first."

He stopped and knitted his brows together. "Okay."

"You were right about Patrick."

"I know. But what changed your mind?"

"Because of what he told me when I met with him on Tuesday. But it's worse than I thought. I know now, it isn't just you that noticed Patrick's behavior. Both Sylvi and Ellen thought the same thing."

"Ellen? What gave her the impression? Isn't she too young to notice these things?"

"She is a young woman, and she has feelings. She told Mrs. Chambers she saw Patrick look at me the same way you do, like he's in love with me."

"No kidding? Sorry she noticed. And Sylvi too?"

"Yes, on opening night. That's not all. I overheard a couple of ladies in the powder room talking about me."

"Do we know them?"

"I don't, and they don't know me personally, but apparently one of them was told something by a woman here who knows who I am. She saw me having lunch with Patrick. Probably on Tuesday."

I felt Hugh tense next to me.

"I told you each time I met with Patrick. There wasn't anything to hide. The woman, whoever she is, thought it was inappropriate. And you know how rumors start. So, yes, I'm worried."

"We need to stop this, somehow. I don't want your reputation tarnished over some fly-by-night, or anyone. Tell me what happened on Tuesday," his voice rose.

I looked around us, but no one was paying us any mind. "I agreed to meet him at a café south on the highway."

"What did he have to say?"

"He said he was in love with me."

Hugh scowled.

"And that he was sure I felt the same way. I assured him he was mistaken. He's in denial. He refused to believe me."

"I want to punch him and ruin his pretty face." Hugh's hands balled into fists.

"Now calm down. I told him never to call me again, and I left before the waiter came for our order. I was shaking like a leaf."

Hugh pulled me to his side on the bench. "Darling, I see how this has upset you. I'm so terribly sorry and my anger doesn't help either."

"You have every right to be angry, but now these two women might spread lies of what the meeting with Patrick was really about. When I think back on it, someone could have misconstrued it as a lover's quarrel." My face fell into despair.

Hugh hugged me. "Hopefully, Patrick got the message and those ladies will keep what they heard to themselves."

"I doubt it, unfortunately. Oh, and I almost forgot. Betty Birch told me on Monday some disturbing information about why Patrick left San Bernardino College. A female student reported him for inappropriate behavior."

"Damn, I knew there was something off about him." Hugh's face grew stormy.

"Well, thanks for not saying I told you so." I kissed him lightly and stood. "Let's go back in. I'm cold."

Most of the people had gone back inside. It had turned suddenly chilly. We mustered through the rest of the evening, putting our worries aside to enjoy the event. I worried about the gossip and what Patrick might do next.

CHAPTER TWENTY-THREE
HUGH

Hugh gazed at his sleeping wife, thinking of their lovemaking when they came home from the dance. Despite all she had told him about Patrick and gossip in the powder room, they put it behind them to rekindle their passion. A much-needed recommitment of their love and marriage.

He rolled over and tried to sleep. Two hours of tossing and turning, Hugh couldn't sleep, too full of anger. Not at his beloved Dee, but at that blasted Patrick. Usually, he would have been elated at being right. However, Patrick's declaration of love unsettled Dee and him too. He couldn't blame Patrick for his feelings. Dee was a beautiful and talented woman. People can't control who they love. Patrick needed to accept Dee didn't feel the same and control himself, and stay away from her.

There must be some way to get him out of their lives. Determined to find some dirt on Patrick, he decided to have the incident in San Bernardino looked into. Quietly, he slid from under the covers and went to his home office and sat at his desk, swiveling back and forth. He stopped, grabbed the Yellow Pages, and turned to the section on private investigators.

On the following Tuesday, Jack had scheduled an early morning tee time at the California Golf Club in south San Francisco. He and Hugh were to meet with the president of Bauer Cargo, Thomas Bauer.

Golf was never Hugh's game. When he wanted to quit playing, Jack stepped in and convinced him to learn enough to play with potential clients. That was how things were done, he said. Jack was a great player and teacher, but Hugh still hoped his handicap wouldn't be held against him. At Rothmorton Insurance, there were other people to do marketing and business development. Hugh had to buck it up for his own company until it was large enough to hire the experts.

Jack knew what Thomas looked like from the photo in Bauer Cargo's annual report. They checked in and waited on the first tee until Jack spotted Bauer coming their way. A large barrel-chested man with a full beard, wearing a red cardigan, over a white-collared shirt, and slacks, similar to what Jack and Hugh wore. Jack's a Palmer fan, so he wore Arnie's favorite, a pink shirt under a green cardigan. Hugh preferred navy blue over white. San Francisco courses were open year-round, but Hugh hated playing in the rain and the clouds were growing dark overhead.

"Mr. Bauer," Jack stuck out his hand. "Jack Clayton, we spoke on the phone. This is Hugh Roth, President of Roth Enterprises."

"Call me Tom, while I beat your ass on the course," he chuckled, grabbing hold of Hugh's hand and giving it a forceful shake. "My V.P. has been biting at the bit to get a policy from Rothmorton."

Hugh and Jack glanced at each other and smiled.

The three of them were next to tee off. Hugh retrieved a ball and tossed it in the air. The ball landed closest to Tom.

"Tom, I guess you go first," Hugh said.

"Thanks, Son." Tom pulled the appropriate club from his bag the caddy carried.

Hugh hadn't been called son in years. Tom was probably twenty years older, and despite being nearly forty, it made him feel young. Jack went next, and then Hugh. Hugh's first drive wasn't as far as the other two, but still on the fairway.

They walked down to their balls and Hugh talked about his company's relationship with Rothmorton. Tom listened intently. Jack added a brief overview of Roth Enterprises' financial position should they take on Tom's ships.

Everything seemed to be going well until the sky broke open and caught them in some rain for several minutes. Opening their umbrellas, they proceeded to the next hole. The business talk lulled. After they played the first nine holes, Tom suggested returning to the clubhouse for coffee and breakfast and continue the discussion.

The hostess seated them at a table along the window overlooking the course. Hugh's stomach was rumbling, since he hadn't eaten before arriving at the course. He was nervous before such important meetings. As usual, Jack was cool as a cucumber. They talked about other personal interests, and Hugh mentioned his hunt for a sailboat to replace the yacht sold in Plymouth.

"Well, well, well, I think I can help you with that." Tom pulled out his wallet and flipped through a few business cards, then handed one to Hugh. "I just met with this fella, a broker, at the San Francisco Marina. Been looking for a new toy myself. He'll fix you up. Be sure to tell him I sent you. Never know, if you buy one from him, he might give me a discount on my next one." He chuckled and scratched beneath his graying beard.

"Much appreciated, Tom. I'll definitely contact him," Hugh said.

Jack winked at me. "Tom," Jack interjected. "We'd like to put together a formal proposal for you."

"Sure, sure. Do that and I'd like both of you to fly up to our offices in Seattle and get the full tour of our cargo ships in person. When can you have the proposal ready for the presentation?" Tom looked at each of us and waited.

Jack glanced at Hugh, raising his eyebrows as a signal for him to answer.

"We've been working on something for you. I suppose it could be ready by next Monday. Of course, it would need a final review by Rothmorton's underwriters. How would that work for you?"

Hugh had just started work on the project. It would take long hours that week to finish it. Hugh was eager to lock in this deal before the end of the year. But he knew Dee would be unhappy with him gone a whole week plus a weekend so soon after promising to the new schedule. He hoped she'd understand.

"Splendid, Hugh. I'd toast on it, but it's too early in the day, even for me."

They all agreed and laughed.

The rest of the morning was social chitchat, and then Jack and Hugh returned to the office to get busy on the biggest deal they'd had yet.

Hugh called Dee right away.

"Really, Hugh? Why couldn't you make it a week later to give you more time to prepare? After everything with the Dana and Patrick situations, I thought you understood the importance of being here at home."

Hugh could hear Dee's nails tapping on the table near the phone. "I do understand, darling. But this deal is of utmost importance to the success of our company. I know we need time together and with Ellen. After this presentation is done, I'll come home for a full week. What do you say?" He wished he was standing in front of her so he could influence her with his pleading face. It usually worked.

"Well, all right. What else can I do? You've promised your client. Good luck, honey," Dee hung up.

Tired of all the tension, he focused on the contract. Hugh and Jack worked steadily through the week on the presentation and scheduled Hugh's flight to Seattle for that Saturday night.

Hugh settled into his seat on the flight to Seattle. Leaning back, his mind immediately went to Dee. She and Ellen meant everything to him. He hated all the problems that had fallen on his family since moving to California and began to doubt his decision. The errors in judgment he'd made years ago kept coming back to haunt him. The whole mess with his late wife, Nora, her death, and how his father had kept it a secret. How Ellen came into being and all the secrets that had piled up over that. When he finally came clean with Dee and Ellen, he thought their lives would finally be smooth sailing. Then this Patrick character had to mess things up.

Hugh knew he risked more fighting with Dee by working so hard on the new contract. He convinced himself that when the project came through, he'd spend more time at home.

The stewardess stopped by, asking if he wanted another drink. He shook his head, finished his glass, and handed it to her. As his eyes drew closed, much needed sleep overcame him.

Hugh woke to the pilot's voice over the speaker announcing they were about to land in Seattle. As the plane lowered toward the runway, a screeching noise from beneath the plane jarred everyone. A stewardess came out of the cockpit and signaled the other stewardesses to get to their seats. The pilot's voice told everyone to assume crash positions.

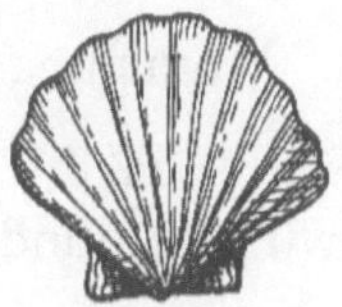

CHAPTER TWENTY-FOUR
ELLEN

Never in my life had I been so nervous about a party. In this case a prep school dance with a dreamboat. Adam made me tingly all over whenever we were together. I'd not danced with him before, but Dad gave me some practice dancing at the cast party and a couple times when he was home.

Mom took me into the city to shop for a special dress and I stood staring at it hanging on the closet door. Not a prom dress, which I hoped to attend in my junior year, but for this special dance. Mom and Dad assured me it was just right. Lavender ruffled tiers of organza in a tea length with a sash and bow at the waist. The neckline swooped across my shoulders in a single layer of organza. I had wrist length white lace gloves, too. Mom and Aunt Sylvi helped me get ready. The amethyst jewelry looked perfect with the dress.

"Wish Daddy was here tonight."

"He would have been if the meeting in Seattle wasn't crucial for his business. Let me get the camera out so I can take pictures when Adam comes."

I was sure Mom was upset with Dad for choosing business over me. He was there for me during the Dana crisis, and he met Adam, giving permission for me to attend the dance. That was plenty for me.

"You are such a lovely young lady. You make me proud," Aunt Sylvi said.

Sylvi went ahead and Mom and I strolled down the hallway, arm in arm, to the living room. She went to the closet to get the camera and something else that surprised me.

"This is to keep you warm." Mom put a white velvet cape with a white fox collar around my shoulders. It hung just to my waist.

"It's perfectly divine." I twirled around and around till I was almost dizzy.

"What a beautiful cape, Dee. You look marvelous in it, honey." Aunt Silvy kissed my cheek.

The doorbell rang and Mrs. C let in Adam and his parents. Adam introduced them to us and we sat for a few minutes while Mr. and Mrs. Greenberg told Mom and Aunt Sylvi about the dance and where it would be held.

It was hard to pay attention. My eyes were on Adam in his sharp-looking black suit and his hair perfectly combed and shiny. He gazed at me, letting his dimples show, but I could tell he was trying to hide his nervousness.

Mr. Greenberg stood. "It was a pleasure to meet you, Mrs. Roth and Mrs. Clayton. I hope we meet Mr. Roth another time. We really should be going."

"The dance ends at ten and we will bring Ellen home to you as soon as we can," Mrs. Greenberg said.

Mom stopped us and had Adam and me stand together in front of the family painting. "I'll have copies made for you," she said to the Greenbergs.

She kissed me on the cheek, and Adam took my hand as we left the house. The Greenbergs also drove a Lincoln Continental. Adam whispered it wasn't brand new like my mom's, as if it mattered to me. I didn't care if they drove a Chevrolet. He and I sat in the back seat and he held my hand between us. I thought it nice his parents didn't stare at us.

No one talked during the drive, except for a few whispers from Adam.

"You look gorgeous, Ellie," he said. "All the guys will be green with envy that I'm bringing a girl like you." He squeezed my hand and I'm sure I blushed bright red, and was glad it was dark outside and in the car.

As soon as we were all in the ballroom, Adam's parents encouraged us to mingle or dance while they stood off to the side with the other chaperones. The elegant room with crystal chandeliers reminded me of the music room at Rothmorton Hall. An orchestra sat on a stage at one end of the room. Around the dance floor were round tables covered in white linens and small lamps in the centers.

Adam guided me to a table where his friends, Chris and Dan, were sitting with two pretty girls. They looked older than me.

"Hey, Ellie, great to see you again," Chris said and turned to the girl with long wavy blonde hair. "This is Mary." She smiled but said nothing.

She probably wondered who I was and why Adam had brought someone so young to this dance.

"Hi, Ellie," Dan said. "This is Sandy."

"Welcome Ellie, I understand you go to Starlight Bay High School," she said, as she fluffed her teased short dark bob.

"I do. The private school is too far from where we live now. I don't mind. The people are nice." At least the few girls I made friends with were nice. Not sure why I felt the need to explain why I went to a public school. Maybe I wanted them to know I was more like them than they assumed.

"Yeah, Ellie's family moved here from the Boston area this summer," Adam added.

Did he think that would make them accept me? Maybe. I really only wanted to dance.

"Boston? Interesting." Mary raised an eyebrow. I guessed it impressed her for some reason.

The orchestra was playing one of those new twist songs, and everyone was doing it.

"You know how to twist?" Adam asked.

"Sure do." I grinned.

He grabbed my hand and I followed him out onto the dance floor where dozens of kids were doing the twist. Adam could do it perfectly. I followed what everybody else did. It was so much fun. When the song ended, a man stood at the microphone and sang "It's Now or Never" the Elvis tune. Adam stood a foot from me and put his hand at my waist and I put my hand on his shoulder and we held each other's hand. He led with a simple step, which I had no trouble following, just like with my dad. One couple danced really close to each other. The boy had his arms wrapped around the girl. But it was short-lived when Mr. Greenberg pushed his way through the dancers and pulled them apart.

Adam stifled a chuckle. "That's why I'm holding you so far away," he said. "There are very strict rules about how close we can be to each other."

"Oh. This is my first school dance," I said.

"I guessed it would be. You dance great. Did you take classes?"

"Back in Plymouth, we did last year, but I couldn't go to the dance because I was sick."

"Your asthma?" He said it with so much compassion.

"Yes."

The next song was fast again. "Do they mix up the songs fast and slow all night long?"

"Maybe, I don't know. I guess we'll find out."

Chris and Dan and their dates appeared on either side of us. The boys sent him goofy looks, which Adam shrugged off.

When the next song was slow again, he leaned into my ear. "They like to give me a hard time because this is the first dance I've been with a girl."

"Oh, Adam, that makes me feel really special." I was giddy inside.

During a short break, he took me back to the table and went with his friends to get some punch and cookies for us. Mary and Sandy were talking to each other. I looked around the room like they weren't there.

"Ellie, what does you father do?" Sandy said.

I turned to her. "He used to be the Chairman of the Board of a large insurance company in Boston and then started a new company in San Francisco. What does your father do?"

Sandy brushed her hands along her satin dress. "He's an attorney. A partner at a big firm in Monterrey. Have you been there?"

"Not yet. Do you board at the girls' school then? That's a long way to commute." I wondered what the school was like and if I was missing anything by attending public school.

"Yeah, Mary and I both live there during the semester."

For a moment, Mary looked sad.

"I used to go to a private girls' school near Plymouth, but our chauffeur took me every day. I was lucky then."

Mary perked up. "A chauffeur? Do you have one now?"

"No. We have a house on the beach, and everything is so close. My mom drives now. We like it better. More freedom."

Both girls looked genuinely impressed. Though it didn't matter to me, it might have to Adam. I shared so much on his account. The boys returned with punch and said a server would bring us a plate of cookies in a minute.

Adam sat next to me as close as he dared without alerting the chaperones, and we laughed about it.

"I see you are getting to know the girls. Chris and Dan had already asked them to this dance before we went to the movies that day. They really like your friends. They're easy to talk to you, like you." Then he leaned in to my ear. "Not stuck up like some girls from the private school." He shot a glance at Mary and Sandy.

"I'm glad to hear it. Can I tell Susan and Nina?"

"Sure thing. The guys and I are thinking about maybe going to the roller rink the day after Thanksgiving. Think you and your friends would want to go?" He leaned back against his chair and I noticed one chaperone coming our way, but he passed us by.

"That sounds like a fine plan. I'll ask." I said low, so Mary and Sandy couldn't hear.

They were playing the theme from *A Summer Place* and all of us crammed onto the dance floor and we danced the rest of the evening away.

When it was time to leave, I felt sad. Being with Adam was unbelievable. Mr. and Mrs. Greenberg were all smiles on the drive back to my house and asked me a lot of questions. Adam was more relaxed, too.

Mr. Greenberg parked the car at the end of our driveway and let Adam walk me up to the front door. I turned around and pulled Adam into the alcove out of his parents' vision.

Adam held me close, his arms around me. "I had a blast with you tonight, Ellie."

"I did too, Adam."

"May I kiss you?" His voice soft and gentle.

"Uh-huh." I wasn't sure what I was supposed to do. I'd never kissed a boy before.

Adam leaned in and pressed his lips to mine. It was nice and sweet. He stepped back. "I gotta go or they'll think something terrible," he laughed.

I hated to leave his warm arms, but he was right. Mom and Aunt Sylvi were probably standing in the foyer waiting for me. He walked away, glancing back every couple of steps until I was inside and I waved to him. Adam waved one last time before getting in the car and they drove away.

As I expected, the moment I shut the front door Aunt Sylvi and Mom came running down the hall, with Mrs. C right behind. Their voices clamored over each other.

"Wait, one at a time." I giggled with glee, missing Daddy even more.

We all went into the living room and I told them all about it. Every. Single. Thing.

CHAPTER TWENTY-FIVE
DEE

I was dreaming about a ringing sound that wouldn't stop until I realized it was the phone and picked it up. Mrs. Chambers had just picked up, too. "Hello? This is Mrs. Roth."

"I'll hang up," Mrs. Chambers said.

"No, stay on the line. Who is calling at this hour? It's nearly 4 a.m." I reached for my robe from the foot of the bed.

"Mrs. Roth. I'm calling from the Airlines Mr. Roth was traveling on to Seattle."

"Is something wrong?" My body tensed.

"I'm terribly sorry to report to you that Mr. Roth was in an accident at the airport."

I gulped, gripping the receiver with both hands. "What? How?"

"The plane had landing gear problems, and the landing was a rough one. Several passengers were injured. They took Mr. Roth to the nearest hospital. I have some information for you and . . ."

I couldn't breathe. The woman's voice sounded far away. "Just a moment." I held the receiver to my chest as I took deep breaths. "Mrs. Chambers please . . . take the information . . . from this woman." I stumbled from the bed and hurried into the hallway forgetting my slippers. Confused, I'd momentarily forgotten where I was then turned toward the foyer. Mrs. Chambers was standing there, her face stricken, holding a piece of paper.

"Mrs. Roth, the airlines are handling everything for you, travel, ground transportation to pick you up at the airport and take you to a hotel they've arranged. I told them it would be you and Ellen. They will cover the costs as well. I assumed you wouldn't want to fly the same airline, and they said no problem."

"Good. As usual, you read my mind." The thought of flying unnerved me, but the train would take way too long. I needed to be with Hugh. My hands shook and my knees about gave way as I slumped against the wall. "Help me to the sofa."

Her hand touched my shoulder, and I looked into Mrs. Chambers' concerned eyes. "Do you want to make the call to the hospital, or shall I?"

I sat down. "I'll call." Mrs. Chambers brought the phone to me and placed the receiver in my hand. She dialed the number written on the notepad.

My conversation with the hospital was short. "Hugh is in intensive care. He's stable."

"What a relief," Mrs. Chambers said.

"Coffee, I need coffee to steady myself before I wake Ellen. I'd rather let her sleep as long as possible. What a horrible way to end her perfectly wonderful evening." Tears filled my eyes.

Like a zombie, I walked stiff-legged to the breakfast nook and waited until Mrs. Chambers made coffee. My body wasn't responding correctly, my mind was spinning, and a headache threatened.

Sylvi must have heard us. She came into the nook rubbing her eyes, her hair all crazy. "What's going on?" she said in a throaty voice.

I filled her in with the vague news. The hospital didn't give much to go on. Sylvi scooted across the bench seats and wrapped her loving arms around me.

"Everything is going to be okay. We'll get through this together. When are you going?" Her voice was soft and soothing.

"The next flight out is 10 a.m.," Mrs. Chambers said as she entered the kitchen and started making coffee. "The airline is arranging everything."

"I can drive you to the airport. But I want to go too." Sylvi turned to Mrs. Chambers, telling her to get a seat on the same flight and a room at the hotel.

Mrs. Chambers finished getting the coffee started and rushed to the phone to update the arrangements for Sylvi.

"Oh Sylvi, thank you! I'm so glad you're here. Would you mind pouring me some coffee? I can't seem to function right."

Sylvi poured three cups. "I'll call Jack as soon as Mrs. Chambers is off the phone. He'll need to get in touch with the clients Hugh was to meet with on Monday." She handed me my coffee.

Two cups of coffee later, and moving a little better, I went into Ellen's closet using the adjoining door in my suite. I packed a suitcase for her, making more noise than intended.

Ellen stood at the closet entrance. "Mom? What are you doing? You look upset."

After I told her what I knew, we huddled together in each other's arms.

"Go on and shower and change into traveling clothes. I have everything you'll need in this suitcase." I hugged her again and wiped a flood of tears from both her cheeks.

Sylvi came in and hugged Ellen tight. What a blessing this happened on a weekend she was visiting.

"Mrs. Chambers got a seat for me in the row behind you. And I talked to Jack. He's stunned and said he would try to get a hold of someone at Bauer Cargo. He wants to fly up tomorrow after he lets the office know and wraps up some paperwork. Bauer might want Jack to make the presentation alone if they won't reschedule." She frowned. "Either way, he'll be in Seattle as soon as he can."

"I'd expect the meeting to be postponed. Isn't it important that Hugh be present?"

"My thoughts too. It's not Hugh's fault the plane crashed."

That was the least of my worries, but it was a huge potential client and I know Hugh would want to know things were under control.

By the time we had packed, despite needing sleep, we decided to just go.

Mrs. Chambers dabbed her eyes with a hanky. "I'll be here waiting on any news. Be sure to call when you get to the hospital. I'll have everything ready for Mr. Hugh's return home whenever that is."

"We'll be in touch." I pulled the luggage dolly to the trunk of the car, followed by Ellen and Sylvi. With everything loaded, we got into the car.

Mrs. Chambers stood in the driveway waving and crying.

Ellen dozed off as soon as Sylvi pulled my Continental out of the drive. My hand still shook as I lit a rare cigarette with the lighter from the dash.

"Hope the smoke doesn't bother you, since you stopped smoking during your pregnancy." I rolled the window down just a tad.

Sylvi gawked. "Sorry, but I've never seen you smoke. I may have stopped, but Jack hasn't." She tried to laugh.

"Just a cigarette now and then during stressful times. This situation definitely qualifies."

"I'm worried about Hugh too. They said he's stable. That means a lot. Did they tell you anything about his condition?"

"No. They said it would be best to tell me when I was present. It's probably best, cause if I know now, I might not make it there in one piece myself."

Sylvi reached over and patted my hand. She must have a lead foot since we got to the airport in record time and parked in the long-term lot. Groggy-headed, Ellen dragged behind us while we picked up the tickets and checked our luggage at the ticket counter. The flight departed on time and I relaxed in the first-class seats with Ellen next to me and Sylvi behind us.

I fell into a fitful sleep dreaming that Hugh had died and I was all alone floating in a dark foggy ether. I woke to someone gently moving my shoulder.

"Mom, are you okay?"

"Y-yes, dear. Just a bad dream."

"I think we're all having one, only we are awake." Ellen rested her head on my shoulder. "What about my school? I brought my homework with me that's due this week."

"I'll call the school when we get to Seattle."

"You mean tomorrow, Monday?"

"Right. Don't worry about it. Everything will be fine." Oh, how I hoped I was right. Please don't leave me Hugh.

Someone from the airline met us at the gate and took us to the hotel and we checked in. In the suite, I immediately called the hospital to tell them I had landed and to get any updates on Hugh.

Sylvi and Ellen were unpacking. I nodded when Sylvi asked if she could unpack my suitcase. I jotted some notes from the call.

"Hugh is in surgery, but they wouldn't tell me what kind. My God, I hope it's not serious."

I went to Ellen and held her for a few minutes. She had started crying again. "Lie down for a little while, honey. Sylvi and I will go to the hospital. When you are rested, have the concierge call you a taxi and then ask the information desk where the surgery waiting room is."

"I don't want to be alone. Please let me come with you?" Ellen begged.

I gave a side-long glance at Sylvi.

"Tell you what, Ellen," Sylvi said. "You get some more sleep and I'll come back in a few hours to get you. How does that sound?"

"Okay, I tried to sleep on the plane. Too worried about Daddy." Ellen retrieved her silk pajamas from the dresser and changed.

I tucked the covers around my darling girl and kissed her forehead. She was asleep within minutes.

Waiting was the worst. I paced like Hugh, wringing my hands. Sylvi had gone back to the hotel and brought Ellen with her, like she had promised. Ellen spent time writing a letter to Adam, then fell asleep again on the bench against the wall.

"Sit down Dee. The doctor will come out at some point and give us updates. There's nothing you can do until Hugh is out of surgery." She patted the chair next to her.

"You would know, being a nurse. I'm so worried though."

Hugh was in surgery for three hours, which seemed like days to me. When a man in white came through the double doors, my heart stopped. But he kept walking past us. I checked my watch again for the umpteenth time in the past hour.

Another man entered the waiting lounge.

"Mrs. Roth?" he said.

Sylvi and I jumped up, and I nodded.

The man removed his mask. "Surgery went well. Your husband is in recovery. He suffered internal injuries sustained from his seat belt not securely fastened. Apparently, he was thrown from his seat and must have slammed into something. He has a hairline fracture in his left ankle. It's swollen and painful and he'll need to stay off it for a while. He also suffered a concussion and may have trouble sleeping or sleeping too much, some irritability and nausea. The nurse will give you a full list of possible symptoms. It should resolve in about a week. The rest we got under control and expect a full recovery with plenty of rest. We'll need to keep him until he is cleared for travel again. I take it you aren't from Seattle."

I breathed again. "We live in the San Francisco area. When can I see him?"

"Another couple of hours. Someone will come get you once he's taken to his hospital room. He won't need ICU."

"Thank you so much." I felt lighter, though it wasn't over yet.

Sylvi's arm gave me a tight squeeze. "This is great news, Dee. He'll be fine."

"Mom? What's happened?" Ellen sat up yawning.

"Your father is out of the surgery and he will be fine." I took a seat beside her and we embraced, tears running down my face in relief.

The morning newspaper had already printed a story about the accident stating the landing gear hadn't dropped. The plane skidded across the tarmac until it finally crashed into the barriers. There were a few other injuries, but none required surgery like Hugh. Mostly bruises and whiplash. An investigation had begun to determine the base cause.

As soon as they took Hugh to the room, they notified us. The duty nurse said only one at a time. I went in first, not knowing what to expect, and found him lying peacefully, covered in white sheets.

"Hugh?" I stood at his bedside and ran my fingers through his hair.

He opened his eyes and his eyebrows knitted together, like he didn't know who I was.

"It's me, honey, Dee."

He blinked a few times. "Dee? Where are we?"

"You just had surgery. Don't try to talk much. You need plenty of rest."

"Surgery? Where are we?" He lifted his hand and I took it in both of mine, kissing his fingers.

"Seattle. I've been so worried. Sylvi, Ellen and I flew up this morning after the airport called."

"You flew?"

"It was strange, but I needed to be here as soon as possible. The flight was fine. I wore my seat belt, just in case. You were tossed around quite a bit I'm told."

He didn't look like Hugh. There were bruises and swelling on his face, probably from objects flying around in the cabin.

"I'm trying to remember," he sighed.

"It will come back to you. You're on pain meds. I'm just so glad you are alive. Ellen wants to come in. Only one of us at a time tonight. I'll be back later." I let go of his hand and waved Ellen in from the hall.

The nurse, an expressionless woman who said nothing, went in after several minutes to take Hugh's vitals.

"I'll wait to visit Hugh tomorrow," Sylvi said. "He's been through enough, and seeing the two of you will speed his recovery."

Tired and hungry, we called for a taxi to take us to the hotel and had dinner at the Howard Johnson Restaurant next door. Ellen had been begging for a hamburger. We slid into the circular booth and removed our gloves.

"What time is Jack getting here tomorrow?" I asked Sylvi after the waitress brought a pot of coffee and took our orders.

"Around three, I think. He'll meet us at the hospital, so I want to be there around that time." Sylvi lit a cigarette.

"You said you quit."

"All of this was too much stress for me, too! Just a couple will help." She blew the smoke away from the table. She offered me one.

I shook my head and pointed to Ellen, mouthing she didn't know about my smokes. Sylvi put the cigarette case away.

"Ellen, dear, you're awfully quiet." I said. "Your father will be fine."

"I know," she twiddled her thumbs on the table, her forehead crinkled in a frown.

The waitress brought Ellen her Coke and left again.

"Hands off the table," I reminded her.

"Sorry." She dropped her hands to her lap and continued to twiddle. "It was awful seeing Daddy in that hospital bed. This is the first time, ever." Her mouth turned downwards.

I stroked her arm. "Yes, it's upsetting." To say the least. I wanted to sleep for a week.

The food was served, and we ate quietly then headed back to the hotel. Ellen went to the adjoining room and closed the door. Sylvi and I each took a double bed and talked for a couple more hours before turning out the lights. Sylvi conked out right away.

I tossed and turned until finding only a fitful sleep. I woke with puffy under eyes, much like Hugh's. I felt as if I'd been hit by a truck.

CHAPTER TWENTY-SIX
HUGH

On Friday, almost a week had passed in the hospital and Hugh was climbing the walls. The doctor said when he could walk a short distance without guidance, he'd be discharged. When Dee asked how he felt about flying home, Hugh hyperventilated.

"No, not a plane. Too soon!" He stood at the window, leaning on crutches. "And I hate these damn things!"

Dee gave him a concerned look. "Okay, honey." She moved beside him and stroked his arm.

"Sorry, I raised my voice, darling. I'm feeling anxious."

"That's not unusual after what you've been through," said the nurse, who entered to take his vitals. "Take the train, if you aren't in a hurry."

No, Hugh wasn't in a hurry, though he worried about the missed presentation to Bauer Cargo. When Jack arrived at the hospital earlier that week, he said he was making a preliminary presentation on Thursday. Bauer said if they had questions, they'd wait until Hugh was up and around. He was grateful to Jack for keeping that project rolling, but the way his brain was not functioning correctly irritated him.

"Let's all take the train unless Sylvi and Ellen want to fly back together." Hugh looked around the room.

"No, I want to go with you on the train," Ellen said, ready to take her usual pouting stance.

Dee held up a hand to Ellen. "Even though Ellen's been out of the school all week, if we travel this weekend, she would be back in school Monday."

Hugh agreed.

Sylvi and Jack looked at each other and nodded. They must communicate telepathically. "Jack and I will fly back tonight. I have an early shift Monday," Sylvi said.

"I understand," Hugh said and Dee nodded her head. "Then it's all settled."

Everyone looked pleased with the plan.

Hugh had never felt the kind of fear he had during the plane accident. Even when he was in the Navy during the war. It was humiliating, and he was grateful his family didn't make a big deal over his not wanting to fly.

Later that night, when he was alone in his hospital bed, it happened again. Just as he would drift toward sleep, flashes of memory came to him.

The voice of the pilot warning the passengers . . . the sounds of the landing gear straining to release, but didn't . . . desperately trying to fasten his seat belt after the plane squealed across the tarmac without wheels until . . .

And he would awaken in a cold sweat, breathing heavily.

The only thing Hugh hated about the travel is that his doctor demanded they transport him in a wheelchair, particularly at the train stations. Hugh wasn't ready for that amount of walking with crutches, and the doctor didn't want him to overstress his body before the stitches were removed.

Hugh's ankle was double-wrapped with an ACE bandage and was told not to put weight on that foot for a couple of weeks. Then he could transition to a cane.

Using the crutches on the train was difficult because of the narrow aisles. But he managed, as long as he took it slow. They had two berths, one for Ellen and a large one for Hugh and Dee. Some meals were delivered to the berth.

Hugh discovered the less he moved around, the less he wanted the pain medication, which made his mind fuzzy and body uncoordinated.

Ellen kept busy writing letters to Adam and to her girlfriends, plus her friend Kathy in Plymouth. Sometimes she would sit in the observation car watching the landscape and ocean pass by while Hugh and Dee spent alone time together.

❧

By Sunday night, they were home again, and Hugh settled in their big bed.

"Oh, Mr. Hugh, I've been so worried about you." Mrs. Chambers fluffed his pillows and plugged in the electric blanket, handing him the control. "Here you go Mr. Hugh."

"Thanks, Mrs. Chambers. No need to worry anymore. I'm home now. You get some rest." Hugh adjusted the blanket control and set it on the nightstand.

"Good night, Mrs. Chambers," Dee said and closed the bedroom door. "Hope you don't mind if I snuggle up to you a little."

"You betcha I don't mind. Snuggle right up." He winced, then laughed. "It's nothing."

Dee turned out the lights and, in the comfort of her husband's arms, she slipped right off to sleep. Hugh relaxed and just as he did in the hospital, the same flashes of memory and fear pervaded him. His body jerked and Dee woke up.

"Hugh, what's wrong?"

"Just a bad dream." He pulled her back against him.

"Dreams about the accident? Sylvi warned me you might have something like that. You're sweating. Let me turn off the blanket."

"I already did. Sorry to wake you up. I'll be fine. It's all so fresh. I try not to think about it during the day, so my dreams are picking up the slack. Go back to sleep."

Dee kissed his cheek and settled back into his arms.

Hugh stayed awake till the sun came up Monday morning.

Dee woke up, moving her arm across Hugh's empty side of the bed. She raised her head. "Hugh?"

He was sitting in the easy chair by the window, gazing at her. He had changed into a long-sleeved pullover sweater and a pair of casual slacks, forgoing the belt because of his surgical wound.

"Morning sleepyhead," he said.

She pushed her hair from her eyes. "You didn't sleep, did you?"

He shrugged. "A little."

"Do you want the radio news station turned on while I get us some coffee?"

"No, I want to walk, er, I mean with the crutches, to the breakfast nook myself. I was waiting for you." He gave her his most loving and genuine smile, not wanting her to worry about him.

Dee complied and after breakfast, they spent the day together sitting on the terrace, talking about Ellen and her new boyfriend, carefully avoiding the accident. He knew Dee had questions, but he wasn't ready. The dreams were enough for him to deal with. He needed distance from the event in his mind.

Ellen came home from school telling how everyone wanted to know what happened with Hugh. She kept the details to what was in the newspaper like Hugh and Dee had told her. After dinner, they settled on the sofa in front of the TV and watched *The Shirley Temple Show.* Eventually, Hugh had to admit he was utterly exhausted. He even let Dee help him to their bedroom. The moment Hugh lay on the bed, he dozed off.

Someone was calling him from his dream. It was Ellen.

"Daddy? Wake up." She shook his shoulder.

Hugh opened his eyes into the frightened face of his daughter, Ellen.

"Something wrong? What time is it?" He looked around the room. "Where's your mom?"

"It's ten o'clock. I heard loud voices while on my way to the kitchen to get a glass of milk. When I reached the hallway near the living room, Mom and Mr. Stevens were outside at the steps to the beach. They were arguing."

"What is he doing here?"

"No idea. I once thought Mom was having an affair with Mr. Stevens but realized it was just on his end."

"I know all about that. Don't worry."

"What should I do? I don't want to go out there."

"No, stay in here. Is Mrs. Chambers awake?"

"She can't hear them from her suite. She's been saying her hearing isn't so great lately."

Hugh raised himself off the bed and put on his robe and slippers. "Ellen, go to your room and stay there. You hear me?"

"Yes, Daddy." She left.

Ignoring the doctor's order to stay off the bad ankle, Hugh limped without the crutches to his closet and pulled a box from the top shelf and set it on the bed. He retrieved the gun he had purchased years before, right after the incident with Becky Slade. Intended for protection, he never expected to use it. He put a couple of bullets in the revolver and made sure the safety lock was on, then dropped it in the pocket of his robe.

The hospital had provided him with a cane, which he knew he wasn't ready to use. He used it anyway while leaning against the wall to get to the end of the hallway.

When he reached the entrance to the living room, Dee and Patrick had moved to the terrace in clear view. Dee still wore her day clothes. She talked so loudly, he could hear her through the thick glass.

"There's nothing between us," Dee shouted at Patrick. "This is all your imagination. You need to stop bothering me and move on with your life."

Patrick was waving his arms in the air like a wild man. Dee listened to him, then turned her head toward the window and her eyes grew wide. Hugh put his finger to his lips not to tell Patrick he was there.

Hugh could feel the vein at his temple pulsing with anger and tried to force it down as he limped toward the sliding glass doors. Each step was excruciating as the pain shot up from his ankle. He ignored it the best he could.

Patrick's back was to the glass. Dee attempted to calm him down, but it didn't matter what she said or how she said it, Patrick continued to rant.

When Hugh slid the door open, Patrick turned around. The second he saw Hugh, he reached for Dee, pulling her against him.

The memory of the night Becky Slade held a knife to Dee's throat, rushed back to Hugh. The rage in him against Becky, now Patrick, and that damn airplane was about to burst from him. He touched the gun in the pocket of his robe. He didn't want to use the gun . . . unless it was absolutely necessary.

Hugh stepped out the door, dropping the cane inside behind him. He refused to look weak to the likes of him.

"Patrick," Hugh said lightly, leaning back against the glass, his temple still pulsing. "Whatever are you doing here?" He gave a forced smile to Dee. "Honey, why haven't you invited our guest inside?"

Dee first looked confused at Hugh, then her head nodded subtly signaling him she understood his intent.

"Forget it, Hugh. This is between Dee and me." He had both hands holding Dee's arms so she couldn't move.

It was clear Patrick was not in his right mind.

"I don't think you understand, Patrick." Hugh spoke slow and determined. "You need to take your *hands off my wife* and leave now or our housekeeper will call the police. I've already given her instructions."

Patrick froze. "You're bluffing."

"Now, why would I be bluffing? You are obviously on my property uninvited." He looked at Dee. "Did you invite Mr. Stevens here for a visit tonight?"

"N-No, I most certainly did not." She yanked one arm free and grabbed Patrick's other hand, pulling it off then stepped toward Hugh.

Patrick was left standing alone. If he wasn't worried before, he looked that way now.

"Okay, okay. No need to call the police. I just had some things I needed to say to Dee. I'll leave now."

Patrick turned and walked around the side of the house on the stone walkway to the street. Dee and Hugh went back into the house.

"I'll go out the front to make sure he drives away," Dee said.

Hugh picked up the cane and followed her as fast as he could, which wasn't fast at all. He balanced himself on the walls with his free hand, taking small steps down the foyer. He put as little pressure on his bad ankle as possible but his side ached.

Dee was looking through the window in the front door. After a few moments, she unlocked and opened it just enough to let out a long exhale. "He's getting into his car. He's just sitting there."

"I'm going to call the police."

"No, Hugh, wait another minute."

A minute passed. When they heard Patrick's car starting and driving away, Hugh put the receiver down. He was ready just in case that idiot was still sitting out there.

Dee shut and locked the door, turned and leaned heavily against it, breathing hard.

Hugh whispered, "Now, would you please explain to me how you ended up out on the terrace with that maniac?"

Ellen came out of her bedroom. "Is he gone?"

Dee was aghast. "Honey, have you been awake all this time?"

"Yes. I woke Daddy because you and Mr. Stevens were arguing. I was scared for you." She first ran into Hugh's arms and Dee wrapped herself around both.

Hugh stood at his daughter's door while Dee tucked Ellen into bed. "Now you try to sleep. Everything is fine now. Okay?"

"Promise?"

Dee nodded with a smile, shut Ellen's door and helped Hugh back to their suite.

"Please, darling, can we not have anything like this happen again?" Dee said.

"I can only make that promise when I find a way to get Patrick Stevens out of our lives. Tell me why he was here."

"I was in the kitchen when I saw someone looking in the window. I almost screamed until I realized it was Patrick. At first, I was going to wake you. Then I thought I could handle him."

Hugh rolled his eyes.

"I know it was stupid. I went out and told him he had to leave. He had come around the side of the house. The gate was unlocked. I guess the construction men left it that way. It was the same things he told me at the non-lunch that day. How he was in love with me, et cetera. Even crazier, he wanted me to leave you and Ellen and run away with him. I really think he's lost his marbles."

"That does sound crazy. I need to get the wall and security gate finished right away. There isn't any other way to keep him off this property." Hugh pulled the gun from his robe pocket, removed the bullets, and placed back in the box.

"What in the hell? Hugh!" Dee's hands had shot to her face. "Would you have actually used that?"

"Only if there was no other recourse. Gladly, it didn't come to that." He placed the box on the closet shelf and shut the door.

"When did you get it?"

"I felt responsible when I hadn't protected you properly, back when Becky Slade was causing so much trouble. It's a safeguard. I wasn't planning on using it."

Dee collapsed on her side of the bed. "I just don't know how much we can take with everything. Dana, Patrick, your accident."

Hugh hobbled over. "Hopefully, soon I will have the leverage we need."

"What do you mean?"

"I hired a private investigator. He called the office and left a message. He would have a full report for me on Wednesday."

"I'm flabbergasted. When did you do that?"

"Soon after the Harvest Dance."

Dee leaned into Hugh. "My knight in shining armor, with a cane." She giggled.

"Oh, and did you know Mrs. Chambers thinks her hearing is going?" Hugh said.

"She's mentioned it lately. Is that why she's still asleep? I thought it was because her suite is on the front side of the house and she couldn't hear us on the terrace."

"Hm, we should send her to an ear doctor." Hugh caressed his wife's back. "I'm really tired now."

"I noticed you were holding your side earlier. Let me check the incision?" Satisfied the stitches were intact, Dee tucked Hugh in and kissed his cheek.

"Let me tuck you in."

The next morning, when the contractor arrived early to work on the wall, Hugh used the crutches to get around outside to speak to him.

"Ramon, I need you to expedite completion of the wall and the security gate. Whatever the cost."

"Yes, Sir. When do you want it done?"

"Last week!"

Ramon laughed.

"I'm serious."

He straightened his face. "I will get it done right away."

As soon as Hugh went back in the house, he called the installer for the intercom system, telling them to get the system installed this week.

"I don't care what the expedite fees are. I want it in, now!" Hugh shouted into the receiver.

Dee came around the corner. "What is all this yelling about?"

Hugh smiled. "Just following through with some projects that needed my attention. By the end of the week, we will have the wall around the property completed and the security gate working. Plus, the new intercom system will be installed too."

She put her hands on her hips. "It's about time. I'll feel much safer. Breakfast is ready and Ellen should be up by now."

CHAPTER TWENTY-SEVEN
ELLEN

The horrible incident with Mr. Stevens the night before kept me awake. I woke after a couple of hours with red eyes and lethargy. A new word I'd learned. I didn't want to go to school. Mr. Stevens scared me. Mom and Dad didn't know I had peeked out from the hallway, watching what happened between the three of them. After Mr. Stevens left, Dad still seemed furious about the whole situation and I wondered what he would do.

The sun hadn't come up yet. I smelled breakfast and coffee wafting down the hall, so I put on my robe and slippers and went to the breakfast nook. Mom and Dad were sitting there, and Mrs. C was busy in the kitchen.

"Honey, you don't look so good," Mom said, scooting over on the bench to let me in. "Are you sick?"

"No," I looked down at my lap. "May I have a cup of coffee?"

"Coffee?" Mom looked at Dad.

"Maybe half a cup with plenty of cream," Dad said.

"Thanks. I couldn't sleep and I want to stay home today." I looked at them.

"Because you're tired?"

"Not because I'm so tired. I'm afraid of Mr. Stevens. He really frightened me last night. I was watching from the hallway and he had a strange look on his face and you looked scared too," I said, fidgeting with the belt on my robe.

Mom opened her mouth to speak, but nothing came out. She looked sad.

"Your mother was scared, sweetheart, but it didn't have anything to do with you," Dad said.

"It doesn't matter. I'm not going and you can't make me." Those words just fell out of my mouth. I'd never spoken to my parents that way, ever. Crossing my arms, I stared at the plate of eggs and toast Mrs. C put in front of me. When I looked up at her, she looked stricken. "I'm sorry, Mrs. C, if you had been awake, you'd feel the same way."

"Ellen, dearest, I had no idea you witnessed so much," Mom said. She put her hand on my cheek. "That never should have happened, and I feel to blame."

"It's not your fault, darling," Dad said to Mom.

"Certainly not, dearie," Mrs. C chimed in, her hands on her hips. "I wish I'd been awake. I would have called the police straight away." She sat on the chair opposite me.

"Thanks, Mrs. Chambers," Dad said. "I actually threatened Patrick you were in the house waiting for my signal to call the police. That's all it took, and he finally left."

"Good for you, Mr. Hugh," Mrs. C said. "Can I get you more coffee?"

Mom and Dad shook their heads.

"I'd like a cup of coffee, please?" I asked.

Mrs. C raised an eyebrow and shot a glance at Dad, who said it was okay. She poured a cup, added about an inch of cream, placing it in front of me.

I smiled at her and sipped it. "Oh, it's bitter."

Everyone laughed. "Add a little sugar like I do," Mom said.

She was right, it tasted much better and I could actually feel my brain waking up. But I was still physically tired.

"So, can I stay home today?" They hadn't given me a definite answer.

Mom said, "You've missed so much school your first semester." She looked at Dad. "I think that would be wise for today. Don't you think, honey?"

Dad agreed.

"I'll call the school to say you are staying home today, and should get some sleep too." She petted my curls and added cream and sugar to her coffee.

"I have some calls to make too. Let me know when you need the phone." He slid around the curved bench, getting up and walked past us using the cane.

"Gee, Dad, you are walking better this morning than last night," I said.

"A solid night's sleep helped a lot, plus pain meds. I think I'll use the crutches today." He went into the foyer and down the hall.

"That's my cue to get dressed," Mom said. "Take your time with your breakfast and go back to bed. I'll wake you for lunch. Okay?"

I had a mouthful of toast and jam and nodded.

I felt more relaxed and safer right where I was. Later, when the mail came, there was a letter from Adam. Ecstatic, I rushed to my room to read it in private. His handwriting was surprisingly neat for a boy. It showed me one more thing I liked about him.

Dear Ellie,

Hope everything went well in Seattle. I've been worried after receiving your letter explaining why you hadn't returned my calls. I understand and am very sorry about your dad. We saw the newspaper article about the crash in Seattle. Big news on the coast. My parents were shocked to learn your dad was on the plane. I'm sure he will make a speedy recovery with you and your mom by his side. I think about you all the time and missed you.

Don't forget about the roller-skating date the day after Thanksgiving, if your dad is doing okay. Send me Susan and Nina's phone numbers so Dan and Chris can call them to ask personally.

Adam

As much as I wanted to go skating, I would wait to ask my parents until things calmed down before mentioning it. This weird thing with Mr. Stevens took all the fun out of my life right now. I jotted down a note to Adam with my friends' phone numbers and told him I'd be in touch soon and thanked him for his letter.

On Wednesday, I went to school. My parents told me not to talk to Mr. Stevens except relating to class. I promised, but was still afraid of Mr. Stevens.

Susan and Nina, even Dana, said they missed me from class. Dana told me on Monday how sorry she was about my dad getting hurt in the accident. I think that was the first time she'd talked to me since they put her on detention. Maybe we could at least be friendly, if not friends.

When class was over, Mr. Stevens held me back until all the others were out of the room.

"Ellen, I wanted to tell you not to worry about the misunderstandings with your parents. It won't affect your grades or anything. If you have problems catching up on homework from when you were in Seattle with your father, just let me know and I'll give you more time. Okay?" His smile looked sort of cartoonish. Like he didn't really mean it, but was putting on a front.

It wasn't clear to me what he meant. Maybe he wasn't sure if I had seen or heard anything Monday night. I pretended not to know what happened.

"Uh, not sure what you're talking about, but I could use more time to get all my past homework in to you." My mouth formed what I thought was a sincere smile.

He seemed to relax and sent me on my way.

When I got home, Dad said they would finish the wall and security gate by the end of the week. He handed me a key to unlock the small pedestrian gate, just like at the mansion.

"That's great Dad, he'll be really surprised if he ever shows up here again. He believed me when I said I didn't know what he was talking about, when he said there were *'misunderstandings'* with the two of you." I felt a little smug that Mr. Stevens was in the dark.

CHAPTER TWENTY-EIGHT
HUGH

The private investigator brought his report to Hugh's house at 10 a.m. on Wednesday, which Hugh appreciated, since the man's office was north of San Francisco. They went into his den to discuss the contents.

Darius Andreas was a stocky man, in an average brown suit, with shined shoes and manicured hands. Hugh guessed he did most of his work in the office or on the phone. He certainly didn't look like one of those "gum shoes" you see in the movies or the classy-looking Paul Dake from the *Perry Mason* TV show. He was somewhere in between.

"Can I get you anything to drink, Mr. Andreas? Coffee, tea? That's a Greek name, right?"

"No thanks, Mr. Roth. Call me Darius and yeah, my folks came from Greece." He narrowed his eyes at Hugh.

"Oh, no offense. I'm just interested." Hugh took a seat at his desk.

Darius handed the report to Hugh. "You'll see the section on past incidents similar to what he's doin' to your wife. She's a beautiful woman, Mrs. Roth. You're a lucky man, if you don't mind my sayin' so." He pointed to the large framed photo of Dee on Hugh's desk.

"I don't mind, because I am lucky." He scanned through the pages while Darius looked around the room.

All of Hugh's personal framed photos from the library at Rothmorton Hall now hung in his home office. Darius nodded his head as if in approval of Hugh's accomplishments and connections.

"So, the incident at San Bernardino College was a hushed-up situation, just like we heard," Hugh said. "He'd been harassing one of his students? Tsk, tsk, the school hushed it up?"

"You know, they didn't want no scandal about their teachers. Happens a lot with professionals. I see in the medical field too."

"That was a few months prior to him taking the job at the high school. Is this all?"

"Look on the last page. I questioned some people where he came from originally. San Diego. I just came back from there. Not a lot, but sounds like he had a bad thing for a married woman down there when he was a teaching assistant. Years ago, but the woman's husband tried to report him, but there wasn't no reason to arrest him. If you want me to pursue that more, just let me know." Darius clasped his hands in his lap and gave Hugh a satisfied look.

"My God, and these are only formal complaints. I wonder how many other similar incidents people didn't report." Hugh closed the file and downed his drink. He opened the desk drawer, retrieving a checkbook and filled out a check.

"This should cover your work up to today and an added retainer should I need you to follow-up on this." Hugh stood and shook Darius' hand and gave him the check.

"Great doin' business with you, Mr. Roth."

Hugh walked him to the front door and Darius left. Dee was standing in the living room watching.

"Well?" She ran her hands down the sides of her skirt. "Tell me."

"It's just as we thought. Do you have the phone numbers for the school board members?" Hugh handed her the file. "Read it."

Dee took the file and went to the phone in the foyer where she kept her address book. "Here," she handed him a folded piece of paper, then sat on the sofa to review the report.

Hugh called the name at the top of the list and gave the man a brief on his complaint against Patrick Stevens. He didn't make any other calls.

"Dee, I have a meeting with the board next Thursday, which is good. I'll have the stitches out by then. The head of the school board said he'd call the other members and get back to me with a definite time. Where's that camera? I want to take photos of this report. I'll probably give the original file to them."

"This report boggles my mind and gives me the creeps." Dee shivered with disgust.

"Don't worry, darling. I'm sure the board will can this guy and he'll leave town."

"Hope you're right." He kissed the top of her head and then photographed the pages of the report.

∾

When Thursday morning came around, they sent Ellen to school, Mrs. Chambers had left for the grocery store, and Dee and Hugh waited by the phone in his office. Hugh was already in his best business suit, his hair combed perfectly, and his shoes shined.

"I'll drive you. You shouldn't be driving with your right foot," Dee said.

"Good point, though I hate to put you through that. This is my complaint, and I ordered the investigative report. Hopefully, that's all they'll need."

The phone rang, and Hugh answered. The call was brief, and he hung up.

"Eleven o'clock. You aren't needed at this time, as I'd hoped. He said it sounded like you've been humiliated enough, and he apologized for Mr. Stevens' behavior." Hugh took her hands and kissed her lips.

"How kind of him. He doesn't even know the half of it." Dee rested her head on Hugh's chest with her arms about his waist. Hugh rubbed her back.

"This will be over soon and hopefully he will be out on his ass."

"Hugh!" But she laughed. "I hate laughing at a time like this, but the tension is too great."

"Agreed."

Dee dropped Hugh off at the entrance to the Town Hall. His ankle felt better, but he used the cane just in case, and was glad he did since the meeting room was on the far side of the building. Hugh's meeting with the school board didn't last long. After they had read the report, they asked for time to discuss in private. Hugh sat in the hall on a wood bench, leaning the cane against the seat.

He crossed his legs, lit a cigarette and took a long drag, exhaling in circular puffs that floated up to the high ceiling. He felt confident about the outcome.

About thirty minutes later, Hugh was called back in the room and the board informed him they had unanimously agreed to remove Mr. Stevens as a teacher from the school. The board apologized to Hugh for what his wife had endured and they hoped the Roths continued to live in their community and Ellen attended the school.

Hugh called Dee and waited outside for her to pick him up. He was elated. As soon as he got into Dee's car, he told her the results.

"I'm so relieved," Dee said as she turned the car around heading home.

"We should celebrate," Hugh said.

"Let's wait until it's happened, then we can tell Ellen together."

"Better idea. I can't wait for him to get out of town."

The next day, Ellen came running into the living room after school.

"Guess what?" she said to Hugh and Dee. "When I got to English class this morning, we had a substitute teacher. Everyone wanted to know where Mr. Stevens was, but the teachers wouldn't say. What happened?" She jumped up and down with excitement.

"Calm down Ellen, don't get yourself all worked up," said Dee.

Ellen stopped and sat on the sofa and took some deep breaths. "Okay. Now tell me what happened to him?"

"The school board has removed from his teaching position," Hugh said.

Ellen's hand shot to her mouth and her eyes grew large. "Wow."

"You are not to say a word to any of the classmates that you know why. This is not to be spread around the school. Do you understand?" Hugh waved a finger at her. "We don't want the connection between his departure and our family known."

"Yes, Daddy, I understand. I'm so relieved. It was really hard to sit there in the same room as him. Where will he go?"

"We don't know where or when. Just as long as he leaves town." Dee poured herself a drink from behind the mirrored bar. "Okay, that's enough talk about that idiot. I'm going to help Mrs. Chambers with dinner. Ellen, go do your homework and after dinner we'll watch some TV together to wind down. Sound good?"

"Can we watch the *Ozzie and Harriet Show*? I just love Ricky Nelson." Ellen begged.

"Sure, sweetheart." Hugh was still a little worried that Patrick wouldn't leave town. There was the chance he might want revenge.

CHAPTER TWENTY-NINE
ELLEN

Thanksgiving felt very strange this time, not living in Plymouth. I missed the Pilgrim's Progress we did in costume every year. Here, it was just us and Aunt Sylvi and Uncle Jack for dinner. They set the table with all the best China, crystal, and silver. The house smelled of roast turkey and sage dressing. Mrs. C and Mom had been up early working in the kitchen preparing a huge turkey with all the trimmings, like our former chef would do. Well, sort of.

My excitement was the anticipation of seeing Adam tomorrow. Mom and Dad had given permission for me to go with them. Susan and Nina would be there too. It would be a blast and I could barely contain myself.

"Now Ellen," Dad said. "Don't get yourself all worked up over tomorrow. We want you and your friends to have fun, but just be careful and if you have any problem, you are to have someone call us. Understand?"

"Sure, Dad." I smiled and scooped out a lump of mashed potatoes from the serving dish and plopped it on my plate. "Pass the gravy, please?"

"You sure are hungry," Mom said.

"It's Thanksgiving!" I laughed and so did everyone else. "And we have plenty to be thankful for, right?"

"Right!" Everyone shouted together.

Life seemed back to normal since the school fired Mr. Stevens and a substitute teacher took over his classes. No one had seen him anywhere.

On Friday, Chris was again our driver in his family's car. He said when he graduated, he would get a brand-new car and he was having a hard time deciding what make and model. The Buick was nice enough and had plenty of room for the six of us. Three in front and three in back. Though Nina and Dan were separated, neither looked disappointed. I wondered if they didn't like each other as much as the rest of us, but we all had fun together.

I wore a pair of dungarees rolled up to just below my knees. So did Susan, but Nina wore a pair of capris. Even though it was an indoor rink, it was still chilly. We all brought cardigans to go over our long-sleeved blouses. Winters on the coast of California were mild compared to Plymouth.

The boys wore dungarees and collared shirts with sweaters. Adam's pants look pressed. Must be the private school thing. These boys were the first preppy types I'd hung out with.

The rink was called Skateland, in San Francisco, and my first time in the city without either of my parents. We paired up right away once inside and we all went to put on the skates we'd brought with us. My friends and I resisted squealing and my mouth hurt from smiling so much.

"Let me help you, Ellen." Adam was on his knees in front of me, slipping off my penny loafers and sliding my skates on and lacing them. "Is that too tight?"

I shook my head. My heart was beating fast when his hands touched my feet. I glanced over at Susan and Nina and they were having the same experience.

The boys had their skates on super-fast and we all joined the crowd on the rink. Adam held my hand while we skated.

"Ellie, do you know how to skate dance?"

"I've seen people do it, but I haven't. You're the first boy I've ever skated with," I said, feeling the warmth of embarrassment rising to my face.

"Do you trust me?"

"Yes." I did, and he was so patient with me until I caught the rhythm and it was glorious skating in circles just like we did on the dance floor. If a thirteen-year-old girl could fall in love, then I was falling, and it felt great.

Someone skated into us, sending Adam to the floor and me, right on top of him. We looked up, and Chris was pointing and laughing.

Susan glared at Chris. "That wasn't very funny," she said.

Dan and Nina skated up behind us. Dan was laughing and Nina covered her mouth with her hand. Was she laughing too and trying to hide it?

Suddenly aware I was still on top of Adam, my face went hot. "I'm sorry," I pushed myself up.

"I didn't mind," Adam winked. Then he scowled at Chris as he stood. "You could have hurt Ellie. It's not like the ice. This floor hurts more."

"Oh man, don't be sore." Chris held his sides, laughing. "Get it?"

"Ha, ha." Adam tossed his head then helped me up.

I couldn't help but chuckle. "I guess it was sort of funny."

We all laughed good-naturedly and resumed skating. When Adam purposely rammed into Chris, sending him flat on his behind, Chris wasn't laughing.

"What? Can't take your own gag, can you?" Adam taunted.

I laughed along with the others. Served him right.

The rest of the morning, we had fun teasing each other, and no one took offense. We ate hot dogs and drank Cokes from the snack bar. Before heading home, Chris drove down Lombard Street, the crookedest street in America. It was a gas.

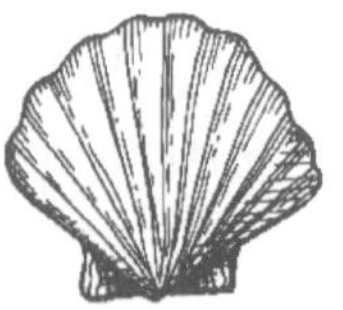

CHAPTER THIRTY
DEE

It had been two weeks since Patrick was fired. Ellen and I hadn't seen or heard anything about him. We assumed he'd left town. Feeling relatively safe, I scheduled appointments at the local hair salon for my hair and a manicure.

"Mrs. Roth, I was so happy to hear from you when you scheduled your appointment. We haven't seen you in weeks," Carole, the hairdresser said. Her pale, bleached-blonde hair was cut short in a teased bob, and she wore the cat-eyed shaped glasses with rhinestones, and bright pink lipstick.

She looked a bit odd to me, but she did my hair to my liking.

"It's been a while since our country club dance. Did the best I could myself. Do I look awful?" I wasn't a regular at hair salons, even in Plymouth, saving the service for special events. I removed my gray tweed swing jacket and Carole hung it on the coat rack. My gloves I put in my black leather handbag.

"It looks good. You have many talents, Mrs. Roth. We are glad to have your patronage. What do you need today? Wash and set? Day style?" Carole had me sit in her chair and she handed me a magazine. "Some new styles have come out. Flip through this and point to anything that interests you. Your hair is getting long. Do you want a trim too?"

I was in a marvelous mood and needed some pampering. "Let's do everything and . . ." I pointed to a page that caught my eye. "This style would suit me, do you think?"

"Excellent choice. That's the flipped bob, just like our new First Lady Jackie Kennedy wears, too. I'll have to cut three inches. Is that okay?" With the flare of a toreador, she whipped the nylon cape around me and fastened it at the neck.

"I've never worn it that short." I hesitated and looked at the picture again and at myself in the mirror. "You know, I'm due for a big change. Let's cut it."

"Sounds like a great idea, Mrs. Roth."

"I never met Mrs. Kennedy, but my husband knew both of them when we lived in Massachusetts." Why I divulged that piece of information to Carole eluded me. She was a gossip. But I was relaxed, and talked more.

"No kidding, really? I'm impressed, though I've already been impressed by you and your husband. The two of you have brightened up our little town."

While she washed and scrubbed my scalp, I closed my eyes, clearing my mind of all the stressful events since we moved to Starlight Bay. I was jarred alert when Carole turned quite chatty about a topic I had tried to forget.

"I bet you've been following the newspapers about that, Mr. Stevens. Terrible he was fired and all. You must have worked closely with him during the musical."

"Hm." I intended to remain neutral on the topic.

"That poor college student in San Berdue. Tsk, tsk." Carole wrapped a dry towel around my wet hair and guided me back to her station. There were two other hairdressers in the shop busy with customers.

I tensed. What was she talking about? "I haven't read the paper lately." I'd purposefully avoided the papers. Afraid to see something in print I didn't want to read.

"Oh yes," Carole continued. "Quite a story. At first, they were just rumors. You know how those spread fast. And then the newspaper printed it. What a scandal."

Good grief. Who leaked that story to the papers?

Next was the haircut. I touched my hair and where it would fall. "That really is short for me. You sure it will look like Jackie's?"

"Pretty darn close. Only the color will be different." With my hair cut and the curlers set, I sat under the hair dryer. Carole sure was a motor-mouth today. I couldn't relax like usual. Although I had brought a novel with me, I wanted to read that article she went on about and asked if I could read her copy of the newspaper. Carole handed it to me while I was under the dryer.

It read word-for-word like the investigator's report. Hugh told me he gave the original file to the board. Who did the board give it too? Or was someone on the board connected to the paper? I looked for the article byline. Sam Weston.

"Carole, is Sam Weston on the school board?"

"He sure is!"

I couldn't wait to tell Hugh. His foot had healed, and he was driving again to San Francisco daily and coming home every night. Just as he should and I loved it.

Life was feeling normal. The wall around the house was finished, and the security gate installed along with an intercom box on a post outside the gate. I had to remember to push the intercom button to let Mrs. Chambers know I was at the gate waiting to get through. It made me feel safer.

Hugh was happier ever since the insurance contract had come through with Bauer. His worries about the success of his company and cash flow issues were behind him, and me as well. We would never go broke. The sale of Rothmorton Hall secured all our futures for generations to come. That was never the problem. Hugh needed to feel successful on his own.

Back in Carole's chair, she removed the curlers and with her expert hands styled my hair into the most drastic of changes in my appearance. I placed the newspaper on her counter. The hairstyle really resembled the First Lady's. I thought it quite becoming and modern. The coast humidity usually wreaked havoc on my hair, but with enough teasing and hairspray it would stay that way for a week.

"Fabulous, Carole. I love it!" I stared at this new me in the mirror.

Everyone in the salon applauded the results, and I moved on to the manicurist. An hour later, I donned my jacket and headed down Main

Street toward the beach to the town's historic bakery to pick up some pastries for the next morning.

When I was ready to go home, I couldn't remember where I'd parked my car. I walked down the sidewalk, looking around. When I came to an alleyway, a car pulled right in front of me blocking my path. What in the world?

"Dee," a familiar voice said from inside the car. The passenger side window was rolled down. It was Patrick.

I couldn't move and almost dropped the bag of pastries.

"Patrick? What are you doing here?" I was completely unnerved. He was the last person I expected to see, or wanted to see, ever.

"I need to talk to you and apologize for everything. Would you please get in the car? People are looking." He reached over and pushed open the passenger door.

No one was looking, but I didn't want to get in his car. "I don't think I should. Hugh would be upset."

He frowned. "If you don't, I'll follow you until you let me say my peace." He had a pained expression and his voice was weak.

Still, I hesitated.

"Please, just get in the car, or I might have to use some unnecessary force." His voice turned shrill. He put his right hand in his coat pocket and turned it toward me. It looked as if he had a gun. First Hugh, and now Patrick? And threatening me?

"Patrick, please, don't."

"If you don't get in now . . ."

"Okay, okay, relax. Put that away and I'll get in."

Patrick's hand remained in the pocket but lowered it to the seat.

I kept close to the door with my handbag and pastries in my lap. The car had a strange odor, like garbage. I glanced behind me. Wadded up take out bags from local restaurants, paper napkins, and empty soda cups littered the back seat. Had Patrick been living in this car?

With one hand, Patrick made a U-turn and drove down Main Street to State Route 1, and turned right.

"Where are we going?"

"Nowhere in particular. I'll talk while we ride." He had a smug look on his face and took his hand out of his pocket. "I can't believe you thought I would use a gun on you. What do you take me for? I'm in love with you. I wouldn't hurt you." He let out a strange, guttural laugh.

An uneasy feeling came over me. I fell for the fake gun trick I'd seen in numerous movies.

"Yes, you've told me. But I don't understand how that happened."

"From the moment I met you at the Town Hall meeting. You are the most exquisite woman, intelligent, stylish, talented. How could I not fall in love?" He gazed at me adoringly.

"Patrick, the road!" The car swerved out of our lane, forcing a car coming toward us to ride on the shoulder.

"Sorry." He turned the steering wheel, and the car moved back into our lane. I grabbed the dashboard.

"Are you trying to get us killed?" My voice shook. "This isn't your car, is it?" This one was a black Chevy, not the white Fairlane.

"I borrowed from a friend. Mine is on the fritz." Beads of perspiration glistened on his forehead and slid down his temple, despite the cold in the car. The heater wasn't on.

Was that the truth? Or was he driving a different car to avoid being recognized? Oh dear, had I made the biggest mistake ever? I needed to get out of the car somehow.

"W-what did you want to tell me that you haven't already said?"

"You must have been scared of me that night on your terrace. I didn't mean to scare you." He glanced at me.

I tried to look calm, that I wasn't frightened half out of my mind. "Hugh was worried, is all. He didn't like you there."

"I understand." The look on his face told me he didn't. "But I needed you to understand how important you are to me. I've never felt this way about any woman before. Being near you is exciting." He had one hand on the steering wheel with his left hand on his left knee, his fingers tapped an uneven rhythm that must have been in his head. The radio was off.

"Thank you for your compliments." Not sure what to say, I kept my comments neutral.

He kept driving north past Pillar Point on the left. Where was he going?

There was little traffic and fog had begun to roll in off the ocean ahead. It worried me. What if the fog got too thick for Patrick to see? Hugh told me how winding this road could be and dangerous, especially if it rained. I recalled him telling me about a portion of the route with narrow lanes known for rock and mud slides. I shivered, and it wasn't because of the cold. There had been some fatal accidents along the pass too.

Patters of rain hit the windshield. I looked in my side view mirror. There was no one directly behind us, only a car way back. If I could get Patrick to slow down enough, maybe I could open the door and roll out without hurting myself too much. The thought terrified me. Which was worse? Getting hurt, or staying in the car with a man who was acting more and more unhinged?

"I'm concerned about the road, Patrick. Would you slow down a bit?"

Instead, he accelerated the gas, which worried me even more.

"I know your husband is rich and handsome and loves you. You know now how much I love you, too. I can make you happy. Really, I could. You are just in denial. Your actions all during the show and dancing with you at the cast party was sheer magic."

I bit my lip to keep from responding, not wanting to encourage or enrage him. Through Patrick's window, I could see the road was high above the cliffs and close to the edge.

"The fog is getting thicker. Maybe you should pull over and wait till it lifts."

Patrick didn't respond, keeping his eyes forward.

"We need to go elsewhere, so I can start over and get another job. Things didn't work out at the high school. I have a lead on a job up north, in Oregon. It's not that far. You'll love it there."

I tried to swallow, but my mouth had gone dry. He couldn't possibly be taking me with him. Now? I trembled with fear, not knowing what to do.

"But I can't go now. I need time to pack and tell Ellen goodbye."

"You can call her when we get there. We can send for your things." His hands gripped the steering wheel so tight his knuckles had turned white.

Now I knew he had completely lost his mind. He wasn't making any sense. I had to get out of the car soon. I pointed toward the windshield. "That must be the Devil's Slide area coming up. I've heard it's treacherous in bad weather. We should turn around."

Steep, rocky, and eroded slopes loomed ahead. I pressed my hand to my chest as my heartbeat pounded.

I turned to him. "Did you hear me?"

A strange smile spread across his face. His eyes turned glassy and unblinking, as if he was dreaming with his eyes open.

"Patrick, are you okay? Patrick?"

The car swerved . . .

CHAPTER THIRTY-ONE
HUGH

Hugh wanted to celebrate receiving the final signed policies with Bauer Cargo, at home with Dee. At the security gate, he pressed the intercom and noticed her car was gone. He waited a few minutes, but Mrs. Chambers didn't respond. He retrieved the remote from the glove compartment and opened the gate that way, parked and went in the house.

"Mrs. Chambers, I'm home." He removed his hat and coat, standing in the foyer.

"I'm coming, Mr. Hugh." She came puffing from the hallway. "Sorry, I was in my suite and barely heard you."

"No need to run, Mrs. Chambers. Didn't you hear the intercom?"

"I wasn't expecting you. I was napping. So sorry." She looked embarrassed.

"It's okay. I came home early to celebrate with Dee about the contracts. Where is she? Do we have any chilled champagne?"

"Mrs. Roth had appointments at the beauty salon this morning. She should have come home by now. I'll check the fridge in the garage for Champagne. I think there are a couple of bottles."

The phone rang. Hugh motioned to her he would answer. "Hello, Hugh Roth speaking."

"Oh hello, Mr. Roth. I'm so glad you are home. This is Carole at the beauty salon. Mrs. Roth was here, and she dropped one of her gloves."

"I'll have—"

"It isn't the only reason I called. I went outside to see if I could catch her on the sidewalk and I saw her getting into a car driven by a man. I could have sworn it was Mr. Stevens, though it didn't look like his car. This one is black. Mrs. Roth's car is parked up the street from my shop. I heard he was fired from the school and the rumors around town is that it had to do with Mrs. Roth. Please forgive—"

"Carole, just tell me what direction he went. Please! And when?"

"We aren't far from Route 1, so I saw him turn right. And that was about ten minutes ago. I should have called sooner but—"

Hugh hung up, wondering if she ever came up for air?

"Mrs. Chambers, call the police and tell them Patrick Stevens has abducted my wife. I'm going to catch up with them. He's driving north on State Route 1 in a black car."

Her hand shot to her throat as she let out a yelp. "Yes, Mr. Roth." She picked up the receiver and dialed.

Hugh grabbed his hat and coat, ran out the front door, and hopped into his car. The gate opened automatically as his car passed the sensor.

He pounded on the steering wheel. "Damn it, this gate moves too slow!"

The house was finally secured and Patrick captures Dee, anyway. "How in the hell did this happen?"

When he reached the main road, he turned left, driving straight through Main Street and up the coast. He'd have to speed to catch up with Patrick depending on how fast he was driving. Luckily, it was early afternoon with little traffic on the road.

With the ocean on his left, he passed Pillar Point pushing harder. The fog rolled in over the highway and light rain began. Driving fast would be risky as he neared the winding coastal pass. There were no cars ahead of him until an old truck pulled out from a road on the right and slowed down in front of him.

"Hell! Out of the way."

Hugh came up on the car hoping he would move over enough for Hugh to pass, but the lanes were too narrow. He gunned the accelerator, speeding around the truck when a car came at him from the other direction.

Quickly, he rolled the steering wheel to the right just as he cleared the truck. The car coming at him swerved to its right onto the shoulder, just missing Hugh.

"Damn!"

He took a deep breath to calm down and concentrate on the road and the fog.

How far ahead were they? If Patrick was still ahead and went any further, that would take him to the Devil's Slide area.

"Dear God," he muttered.

The fog thickened. He could only see a couple hundred feet ahead. Forced to slow down, Hugh hoped Patrick had to slow down too. Another several minutes, the fog lifted a little and up ahead he saw a car. Carole said it was black. That must be Patrick's car.

"Hang on, darling, I'm coming."

The road snaked around and was close to the cliffs that dropped to the crashing surf. Hugh strained to see who was sitting in the passenger seat. The woman turned her head toward the driver.

It was Dee! She had her hair cut short.

Not wanting to spook Patrick, Hugh slowed for more distance between them and checked his watch. He'd been on the road for almost twenty minutes and wondered where the damn police were?

Suddenly, Patrick's car swerved to the left, into the oncoming lane. The road curved to the right, but Patrick didn't turn.

The passenger door opened and Dee dropped out and rolled onto the narrow shoulder.

Patrick kept on driving . . . right over the edge and down the cliff.

Hugh gasped and increased his speed to stop where Dee lay, unmoving. He jumped out of his car and rushed to her side.

"Dee! Dee, darling? Wake up." He stroked her hair and kissed her face.

Dee moaned and tried to move. Her eyes opened. "Hugh?"

"I don't want to move you, in case you've broken something. Do you hurt anywhere?"

"Just winded." She tried to rise up and looked around. "Where's Patrick?"

Hugh ignored her question.

"Stay down. I think the police should be here soon. I had Mrs. Chambers call them after Carole called."

"Carole?" Dee's eyes were bouncing.

"Did you hit your head?"

"Maybe. I'm so glad you found me."

"I am too."

"Patrick was acting strangely. I was afraid."

Sirens wailed in the distance, and Hugh breathed a sigh of relief. "Stay here. I need to check on something."

She nodded and closed her eyes.

Hugh walked to the shoulder and looked down the steep cliffs. Pieces of the black car were scattered all the way down, and the car was on a strip of sandy beach as the surf crashed against the rocks. Patrick's body hung from the open door on the driver's side. Hugh shuddered.

What a way to go, he thought.

The sirens stopped, and Hugh turned. One man was at Dee's side. Hugh went to talk to the other police officer to give him a statement. The police must have radioed for an ambulance as soon as they'd arrived, for one showed up soon.

At the clinic, Hugh impatiently waited while Dee was examined. When the doctor came out of the examination room, Hugh raked his hand through his hair, tensing for the news.

"Mr. Roth," said the doctor. "Your wife is fine. Just a few bruises. I don't think she hit her head too hard. She can go home with you, but watch for these symptoms just in case." He handed Hugh a sheet of paper. "Oh, and the baby is fine, too. Your wife is a sturdy one."

"Baby? I didn't know."

The doctor shook Hugh's hand. "Congratulations!"

"Well, I guess so! Thank you, doctor." Hugh rushed into the examination room.

Dee was sitting up and buttoning her torn coat. "Did he tell you?" Her face beamed with happiness.

"My darling, this is wonderfully surprising news. Did he give you any special instructions? Did you explain your history? How far along?"

"Calm down, honey." She chuckled. "Yes, we had a solid discussion, and he suggested I make an appointment with an obstetrician he referred me to. I'll do that soon. I'm not exactly sure how far along. But we're guessing three to three and a half months. It's farther than I've carried before and I fell out of a moving car! That has to be a good sign."

"Did you have any idea you were pregnant?"

"I've been exhausted the past couple of months, literally dragging myself out of bed in the mornings. I thought it was all the stress from the show, and your accident, and then Patrick. You know my monthlies have been erratic. It's been years since the last pregnancy. This has to be a blessing. Don't you think?"

Hugh wrapped his arms around his wife and tears trickled down his cheek. Tears of relief and happiness. "It is a blessing, darling."

Dee stopped and her expression went dark. "What happened to Patrick?"

When Hugh told Dee that Patrick did not survive, she slumped against him and sobbed into his chest.

"Darling, why are you crying? He's gone now and will never hurt you." He petted her hair and held her close, never wanting to let her go.

"I can't help myself. It was all so strange. I thought he was such a wonderful person. He was, in a way. So talented, smart, and helpful and friendly to everyone." She pulled out her hanky and dabbed her eyes. "What a tragedy, you know? I don't understand what went wrong with him."

"You have a heart of gold, Dee, always seeing the good in people, even when they take advantage of you or try to hurt you. I admire you for that. But I won't shed a tear over Patrick. He caused a lot of grief for others, including you. Yes, it was a crazy way to go. I'm just so relieved he didn't take you off that cliff with him."

"He almost did."

Hugh felt her shudder. "You were very brave, what you did." He kissed her neck and inhaled her perfume. "I don't know what I would have done if—"

"But I didn't. I'm here and things will be just right again."

Hugh wanted to know what happened before she rolled out the car door.

"He seemed to disassociate and stopped responding to me. His mind had gone somewhere else. We'll never know why."

"No. I guess we won't."

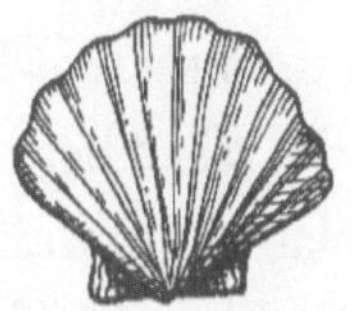

CHAPTER THIRTY-TWO
DEE

The holidays had passed when I attended my last day of bridge with Doris's crowd at her home in Burlingame. I had only been filling in for another lady who was recovering from major surgery. The bizarre tragedy with Patrick was behind me, too. Though the events had shaken me to my very depths. At the same time my life had suddenly become filled with joy after learning of my pregnancy. The doctor said the fact the baby survived my falling out of the car was a sign I would carry him or her to full term. I prayed every night before going to sleep and I wasn't the type to pray.

What a miracle, to have a baby that was created out of the love between Hugh and me. We truly felt blessed.

I was late arriving at Doris's house, and had expected her driveway would be full with the Club ladies' cars. But there were many cars parked along the street. I had trouble finding a spot. I figured there must have been another event at a neighbor's house. Walking up the drive, I could have sworn one was Mrs. Chambers' car. What would she be doing there? When I rang the doorbell, Doris answered and the moment I entered, a crowd of people greeted me with "SURPRISE!"

Doris slipped an arm about my waist and spoke low. "I hope you don't mind I turned this bridge meeting into a baby shower."

Overwhelmed with genuine surprise, all I could muster was a simple thank you.

Everyone in the bridge club was there, including the lady I had filled in for, who rushed to congratulate and thank me for sitting in for her. Behind her, several club members wanted to speak to me. I noticed Sylvi, waiting quite impatiently. I waved her to my side as I finished thanking everyone.

"How did you get invited?" I asked her.

"Invited? Heck, I helped plan this shindig." She laughed. "Doris called me and asked for names and addresses of anyone I thought should be included. Thank goodness for Mrs. Chambers, since she had your address book. She's in the kitchen directing the caterers, of course."

"Really? I'm stunned all this had been planned without my knowledge. Who's taking care of Nora?"

Sylvi gave birth on time the end of January. A baby girl they named Nora. Hugh was thrilled, and I thought it a touching tribute to Sylvi's late sister.

"It's not easy keeping secrets from you. I wanted to be here, though I hated to leave Nora with a stranger. Luckily, one of my nursing friends volunteered." Sylvi hugged me and kissed my cheek, my pregnant belly gently nudged her.

"I'm glad you have someone you trust. Did you have any trouble with your recovery after the C-section? I hope my baby's head isn't too big to pass through." I grimaced, recalling the hours Hugh, Ellen and I spent at the hospital with Jack, waiting for Sylvi to deliver.

"No trouble. I just need to be careful while healing. The doctor said to expect four to eight weeks, but I was just fine by last week. See?" Sylvi twirled around, showing off her balance. "I still have some baby weight on me."

"You look fabulous. Nora must be growing so fast."

"She sure is. I've been taking a lot of pictures, but they are at the photo lab.

"Great. So, when's the big move down my way?"

"Didn't Hugh tell you?"

I laughed and rolled my eyes. "Hugh isn't the best at sharing news. He gets so sidetracked at work."

"We are moving in two weeks. So much to do. The new house is twice the size of our apartment and close to you, Hugh, and Ellen."

"Let me know if there is anything I can do." A server walked by with a tray of canapes and I snuck a couple. The constant hunger during my pregnancy had me worried about unnecessary weight gain.

Sylvi took one, too. "By the way, a couple of your friends from the theater said they were coming. I don't think they made it, because they said they would introduce themselves." Sylvi looked over my shoulder. "I wonder if those two are them?" She motioned to the front door.

I turned around and Ethyl and Betty stood in the entryway holding wrapped packages and looking around. Then they saw me.

"Dee." Ethyl shouted and hurried over with Betty in tow. "I guess we missed the big 'Surprise'?"

"We got lost." Betty adjusted her flower-covered hat with one hand while balancing a large package on her hip.

"Thank you for coming. I'm so glad to see you."

Sylvi waived to an idle server to take the ladies' packages.

"Hi, I'm Sylvi, so happy you made it," she said to Ethyl and Betty. "Please help yourself to refreshments."

"Thank you, Sylvi." Ethyl said turning to me. "Look how big you're getting." She patted my tummy. "We're so excited for you. When's it due? It wasn't included in the invitation."

"First of May, and it can't come too soon. My back is killing me." I put my hand on my back and tried to stretch unsuccessfully.

"You should be sitting."

"Oh, I will in a bit," I said, too excited by all the people at a party just for me. Hugh had wanted to throw me parties for my birthdays, but I adamantly refused. He was the same. Something we had in common.

Betty gazed around Doris's home. "This is a splendid place to have your shower. I've missed spending time with you. I'm so happy you are expecting another child."

Hearing her say that made me relieved those nasty rumors about Ellen didn't do any harm. As far as I was concerned, Ellen was my daughter, and no one needed to know otherwise.

Catering staff continued rushing about with trays of drinks and hors d'oeuvres. After socializing with as many of the guests as possible, Doris ushered me to a much-needed armchair in a place of honor near a large table piled high with gifts. It reminded me of Ellen's birthday parties in Plymouth, where there was a similar table of gifts. I wished Ellen could have been here, but she was still in class.

"I've never had a surprise party," I said to Doris.

She glowed with pride that she was the first to give me one.

Mrs. Chambers finally came out of the kitchen, and I motioned for her to take the seat next to me. I leaned close to her. "Aren't you the sly one, keeping this big secret from me." I squeezed her hand, and she placed hers over mine.

"Oh, Dee, you know I would do anything for you."

My eyes might have popped out. "Mrs. Chambers, you just called me by my first name—for the first time!"

Mrs. Chambers blushed with embarrassment. "You deserve my familiarity after all we've been through together this past year. I hope you don't mind."

"Mind? I've been trying to get you to call me Dee for years." More tears of happiness threatened and Mrs. Chambers whisked out a clean hanky for me from her pocket.

"Always prepared." I smiled and dabbed my eyes.

Two ladies in the corner strongly resembled the ones who had spread rumors about me at the Harvest Dance. Surprisingly, they acted as if we were good friends. Doris had told me after the dance she'd heard a terrible rumor about me, which she claimed to have squelched. I soon learned Doris had a lot of clout at the country club. If a person belonged in her inner circle, she went above and beyond to protect that person. Apparently, she considered me a member of her circle the first night we met. That would explain how those two ladies were invited. I pretended not to recognize them and thanked them for coming.

I accepted a small glass of champagne, sipping it, thinking about Sylvi's abstinence from alcohol.

Those from the bridge group sat around me asking questions about the pregnancy. They were really sweet ladies, and I enjoyed playing cards with them. But I was secretly looking forward to joining Ethyl and Betty's bridge club in Starlight Bay.

I dreaded the possibility of the Patrick drama coming up during the party. Luckily, not a word was mentioned, at least not within earshot. It hadn't taken long for people to forget about poor Patrick and move on to the next topic of gossip, which I avoided listening to.

Despite the terror I felt that day in Patrick's car, I still felt sorry for him. Was he born that way? Or, did something happen to him early in life to make him so obsessive and delusional?

My thoughts of that day disappeared the moment two servers rolled a cart from the kitchen displaying a huge multi-layered cake. A little plastic baby in diapers sat on the top of three layers surrounded with lots of piped icing balloons in pink, yellow, and blue. They placed it right in front of me and I gasped with wonder. Everyone applauded while I cut the first piece. A server took over to cut the rest of the cake. They set aside the top layer for me to take home and share with Ellen and Hugh.

It took a couple of hours to open all the gifts while Doris sat next to me making a list of each item and who it was from. Some people I hadn't met until that day. Such a strange experience for me.

"Thank you, everyone," I said when the last gift was unwrapped. "Hugh and I hadn't even thought about all the things we would need. It appears all of you have done that for us. I love every item and so will Hugh. We will look forward to using them when our baby is born." I laughed and there was more applause.

Doris gave me a great big hug. "Don't worry about the gifts. I'll have them delivered to your house tomorrow."

"Bless you Doris. You have been a very special friend."

Moving to California had given me so much more than I had expected. I had everything I ever wanted, a devoted and loving husband, a beautiful daughter and another one on the way, and friends who supported me that I could trust.

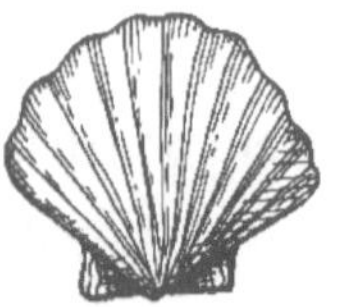

CHAPTER THIRTY-THREE
HUGH

The day Hugh thought he might lose the love of his life turned out to be a blessing in disguise. Patrick was out of their lives through his own madness, and Hugh found out that Dee was pregnant.

When April came around, Hugh's fortieth birthday was forced upon him with a party.

"You know how much I hate celebrating my birthday. Just like you," Hugh said, making a face at Dee.

"This is a milestone, honey. I refused to let it pass unacknowledged like all the others. Luckily, your birthday fell on a Saturday this year, so we could celebrate it today."

"I'll remember that when you turn thirty."

Dee laughed as she dragged him down the hallway into the living room, already filled with guests. Hugh looked around the room with a sheepish smile. A few of his golf buddies from the club stepped up and shook his hand.

Sylvi and Jack stood together smiling with drinks in hand raised. "Happy Birthday, Hugh." They must have found a sitter for baby Nora.

Ellen invited Adam, and they were sitting together on the sofa, a little too close, Hugh thought. But he ignored it, temporarily.

Mrs. Chambers' son raised his glass. When Hugh turned around, Doris and her husband had just arrived. He shook their hands heartily thanking them for attending, and motioned to a server to offer drinks. Dee slipped her arm through Doris's. "So glad you could make it, Doris."

Hugh was about to chime in when coming down the hall was Hugh's biggest client Thomas Bauer and his wife.

"Tom, what a surprise. You flew down just for this?" Hugh slapped his friend's back and greeted Tom's wife.

"I was planning to be in San Francisco when your lovely wife contacted me. Glad to be here to celebrate the big 4-0," he chuckled.

The party was going strong until Hugh noticed Dee clutching her belly and her face screwed up in pain. He rushed to her side.

"Darling, what's wrong? Is it the baby? It's too soon, right?"

"I'm fine. Just a twinge. I read the body can have early labor pains. That just means it's getting prepared. This is nothing. It's been going on all afternoon. Let me sit down, though."

Hugh helped her to one of the new overstuffed chairs he'd bought just for her. Jack was sitting in it, but when he saw Dee's face, he jumped right out.

"Are you okay, Dee?" Jack asked.

"Just dandy fine." Dee chuckled and plopped in the chair and Hugh put her feet up on the ottoman.

Sylvi sat next to Dee and took her pulse. "Elevated. How long have you been having contractions?"

"All day, but sporadically. Should I be worried?"

"No. But keep track of the time in between, starting with the next one."

Mrs. Chambers came out with a cup of hot tea.

"I'll take that," Hugh said, pulling up a chair next to Dee. "Here, this will help keep you calm."

Dee gave him one of her glorious smiles and urged him to enjoy his guests.

A couple hours later, after the cake was cut and served, Hugh stood with Tom and Jack deep in discussion. While Jack was talking, Hugh glanced over at Dee. Her face was flushed, and she strained, forcing a smile for him. He caught Sylvi's eye, and she shook her head. "Excuse me Tom, Jack, I need to check on my wife."

"Certainly, certainly. She looks a bit worn out," Tom said.

Jack's brow wrinkled. "Should I be standing by?"

"I'll let you know." Hugh went to Dee and took her hand. "Darling, do you think you are in labor?"

"Don't look so worried, honey." She reached over to stroke his cheek. "But, yes. We've been counting, and it's time to call the hospital. Tell them we are on our way."

Sylvi nodded her agreement. "Jack and I will follow you over." She waved Jack over.

Hugh hurried to his den to make the call to the hospital and also to the doctor's emergency number. When he returned to the living room Ellen and Sylvi had helped Dee to their bedroom to change. He signaled to Jack with his hand across his throat to cut the music playing through the stereo system.

"May I have everyone's attention?" The music stopped, and he waited until the voices died down and smiling faces turned toward him, probably expecting some kind of speech. Hugh cleared his throat, trying to remain calm, though his insides were like jelly with nervous excitement. "Thank you, everyone for coming tonight, but I'm afraid we must ask you to leave so that we can take Dee to the hospital."

Voices clamored over each other, wanting to be heard. Everyone offered to help. Mrs. Chambers' cheerful demeanor assured the guests the situation was under control as she ushered them out.

The caterers started packing things up and putting food into the extra refrigerator in the garage.

With the baby arriving a few weeks early, Hugh acted extra anxious. Behaving like a bumbling fool, he ran about the house, checking doors, gathering up the suitcase, and packing the car.

"Hugh, honey, calm down. I'm not going to have it this minute. For goodness' sake." She flashed her brilliant green eyes and gawked at him as she stood in the hallway. Ellen had helped her change from her fancy maternity dress into a comfortable day dress and slippers.

"I know, I know." He stopped and stared in awe at her. "How can you look this gorgeous and be about to bear our first child?"

"Give me a few hours and you won't be saying that." Dee gripped her belly and winced. "On second thought, maybe we should hurry it along."

"I sure wish there was a hospital closer. Hopefully, the roads will be clear and we can make the twenty-minute drive easy. I called the emergency number for your doctor and they said he will meet us there." Hugh put his arm around his wife as he helped her into the car. Ellen climbed into the back seat.

"I'm so excited, Mom. Soon I'll have a new brother or sister." She reached over the front seat and squeezed Dee's shoulder.

"We are all excited, pumpkin." Hugh slid into the driver's seat and shut the door. "Dee, are you comfortable?"

"As much as is possible. Let's go." She put her hand on his knee and gently pushed it.

Hours later, Hugh still held Dee's hand and wiped her wet brow for the umpteenth time. He hated seeing her in so much pain. With every contraction, he talked in a soothing voice. "Breathe darling, you are doing beautifully." Maintaining a constant smile.

"Sure," Dee sputtered. "That's easy for you to say." Her voice raised when another contraction hit her hard. "Why did I want this so much? I must have been mad!"

Hugh wanted to laugh, but knew that was not what Dee needed.

"Mr. Roth, she's nearing delivery. You will need to go out into the waiting room," the doctor said.

Reluctantly, Hugh kissed Dee's forehead. "Are you sure I can't stay?"

"There is the possibility of infection. It's best you leave. We'll call you in when it's safer."

Hugh found Mrs. Chambers, Ellen, and Jack in the waiting area. Ellen had fallen asleep with her head on Mrs. Chambers' shoulder.

"Where is Sylvi?" Hugh asked.

"She went home to relieve the babysitter. She'd been there all night. I wanted to stay."

"Thanks, pal," Hugh said.

"Is the baby here?" Ellen asked.

"Not yet, but the doctor says soon." Hugh collapsed in a chair, surprised at how tired he felt.

"I sure hope Dee won't go through what Aunt Sylvi did."

"You mean the C-section?"

"Yes. They say she would have to have a C-section the next time she has a baby."

He patted Ellen's hand. "Mom is having her baby a little early, so there are different risks for the baby's well-being." Hugh's brow knitted with worry.

Jack gave him a pat on the back. "Sylvi said the baby should be fine. I trust her judgment."

"That's what the doctor said, too."

"I hope the baby will be all right." Ellen said, clenching her hands.

Before Hugh could respond, a doctor came through the double doors. "Mr. Johnson?"

A man surrounded by three young children jumped up. "That's me." He crossed the room to speak with the doctor, talking in low voices. Then the doctor left.

Ellen grabbed Hugh's hand and squeezed. "I thought that doctor was for Mom."

"I did too. Hold tight, it's sure to be over soon. Mom will be fine."

Finally, Dee's doctor came out. "It's a boy, Mr. Roth, and you can come back in."

Behind Hugh, Ellen jumped up. "Can I go in too? I want to see my baby brother."

The doctor explained only Hugh, but once her mother was in her regular room, she could have visitors.

"He's not premature?" Hugh asked the doctor.

"No. His weight and size are normal."

Releasing a sigh of relief, Hugh followed the doctor in to the delivery room.

The nurse had just placed a little bundle in Dee's arms while Hugh waited, then leaned over Dee and gazed into the face of his first child. "He's so tiny, but perfect." Hugh kissed Dee.

"Do you want to hold him?" she said.

"Not just yet. Seeing the two of you together like this fills my heart so much I think it might burst."

"Are we sticking with the name we picked if it was a boy?" Dee said.

"Yes, Andrew. I love it."

"Me, too."

In a little while, the nurses took Andrew to the nursery while they moved Dee into a regular room so the rest of those waiting could visit her and the baby. It was morning, though no one had slept all night. Hugh and Ellen went to the gift shop as soon as it opened and bought a bouquet of roses before going to Dee's room.

Ellen rushed to Dee, and they embraced. "How are you? Where's baby Andrew?"

"I'm fine dear. They will bring him in a bit. Are you tired?"

"Oh Mom, you just had a baby and you're worried about me?" She laughed and kissed Dee's cheek.

"Mrs. Chambers, thank you for waiting with them. You're the best." Dee was glowing with joy.

"You couldn't keep me away. Sylvi and Jack brought me with them. I can't wait to see this little darling."

"Where's Jack and Sylvi?" Dee asked.

"Sylvi went home last night to relieve the sitter. Jack stayed with us, but he insists he wait outside, wanting us to visit first." Hugh said.

"That's nice of him. I wondered about Nora. Glad Sylvi is with her."

"She'll come tomorrow to visit." Hugh handed the roses to Dee.

"Good. Oh honey, these are beautiful. Thanks. Would you put them on the night stand for me?"

Just then, the nurse entered the room carrying baby Andrew. She started to place him in Dee's arms.

"Wait," Dee said. "Let his father hold him."

The nurse nodded and placed the baby in Hugh's arms showing how to hold him. Though he had plenty of experience with baby Nora, he graciously accepted her guidance. Hugh gazed at his son, rocking him gently, then sat on the edge of Dee's bed next to her.

Hugh leaned down and kissed Dee's forehead. "This is a dream come true. Thank you, darling."

Ellen and Mrs. Chambers stood on the other side of Dee's bed.

"Oh Mom, he's so tiny and red. Is that normal?"

Dee laughed. "I think so."

"He looks like a strong lad, dearie," Mrs. Chambers said.

The door opened. The doctor came in and asked everyone but Hugh to leave.

Ellen gave a worried look at Mrs. Chambers as they left the room.

"Is everything all right?" Dee said.

"I examined Andrew again, and I found an abnormality with his heartbeat."

Hugh and Dee inhaled sharply.

"I want to monitor him and we'll keep you posted daily. In most cases, it can clear up on its own. So, don't panic." He smiled and left.

"Oh, my God." Dee leaned into Hugh and stroked Andrew's wisps of dark hair.

"I'm concerned too, but let's not jump the gun. Like the doctor said, in most cases . . ."

"Right. I'll be optimistic." She forced a small smile. "Let's not tell anyone right now. Okay?"

"Agreed." Hugh gently transferred Andrew into Dee's arms.

Ellen and Mrs. Chambers returned to the room and were told everything was fine. They took turns holding baby Andrew until it was time for Dee to nurse him.

"I'll come back tomorrow, okay?" Ellen asked.

"After school, your father will pick you up and bring you. You need to go home and get some rest now. All of you. That's an order," Dee said with a fake stern look.

Hugh kissed Dee on her lips and herded Ellen and Mrs. Chambers out of the room. Just before closing the door, Hugh said, "I'll be back tomorrow morning, darling."

"You better be." Dee blew him a kiss and Hugh caught it in his hand and held it to his heart.

CHAPTER THIRTY-FOUR
DEE

The next day Sylvi arrived, wrapping me in her comforting arms. "Oh honey. I'm so sorry I wasn't here for the birthing."

"Hey, I understood. I was busy anyway." I laughed half-heartedly. "Did Hugh tell you?"

"About Andrew's condition? Yes, he asked me what I knew about it." She sat in the chair next to the bed, holding Dee's hand.

"And?"

"I know as much as the doctor. It's something that can correct on its own."

"What if it doesn't? What could it mean? I'm just so worried. After two miscarriages and years of trying. This is our miracle baby. We can't lose him."

"Now, now, no one says you will lose him. Stay optimistic. At this point, it's probably a murmur, the doctor heard through his stethoscope. If it doesn't go away, they would run tests."

My hand went to my throat, and I tensed. "Oh Sylvi. I'm so afraid."

"Let's take this one day at a time. Okay? I'll be here as much as I can, in between nursing."

"I appreciate you being here. Please don't put me ahead of your own child. I don't want that. Promise me. Use the phone." I gave her a wan smile and reached for the box of tissues.

The door opened and in came the nurse with Andrew for his feeding, and placed him in my arms. Andrew latched on right away. "That's a good boy, Andrew."

"He's mighty handsome," Sylvi said.

"He sure is." The moment I held him, my fears abated. I took Sylvi's advice and stayed calm, taking each day as it came.

Each day Hugh and I waited to hear from the doctor about Andrew's status. Each day, the doctor wanted to keep him another day.

By the sixth day, I had been getting up and walking around the halls. I wasn't sick, so being couped up in that hospital bed was about to drive me nuts. The nurses would bring Andrew in for his feeding, but this day, I went to the nursery.

I gazed at the other babies wrapped up and sleeping in their cribs. Like little cherubs.

All set up and Andrew in my arms, he latched on quickly.

"Will I see the doctor today?" I whispered to the nurse.

"Yes, though I'm not sure when."

"Is there anything you can tell me?"

"I'd rather you wait. He said he was planning to speak with you and your husband today."

"Is he here?"

"He's on his way."

I tensed and Andrew pulled off and cried, but I stroked his little face and rocked him till he latched back on. I needed to stay calm, especially while nursing. When the feeding was done, I walked back to my room and Hugh was there reading a magazine.

"There you are. No Andrew?" He asked.

"I just finished nursing, and he's asleep. We can go back and you can watch him."

"Let's wait. I took care of some business and I'm now all yours." He opened his arms and made that adorable crooked smile of his.

"Yes, you are." I sat in his lap and gave him a big kiss.

"Have you heard from the doctor?"

"The nurse said he's planning to talk to us today. I sure hope it's not bad news." I couldn't help but worry something was wrong with Andrew that would not go away.

"I try to not think that way. But it's hard." His lips turned downward, and I tried to turn them up with my fingers. He chuckled.

"I hope I'm not interrupting anything?" The doctor stood in the doorway grinning.

"Not at all." I began to get out of Hugh's lap.

"No need. You look comfortable there. I have some news about Andrew's condition."

I stopped breathing and Hugh's arms went rigid around me.

The doctor smiled. "It's good. Looks like Andrew's issue has resolved itself and we can release both of you. I've signed the release papers. But . . . I want to see him again in one week, then regular visits. Okay?"

"That's wonderful!" We both said in unison, then hugged each other and laughed with relief.

"See," Hugh winked. "Everything is fine."

I leaned into him and relaxed for the first time in six days. Life was getting better and better each day. My head shot up. "Oh, and just in time."

"In time for what?" Hugh tilted his head.

"Our seventh wedding anniversary is next weekend!"

CHAPTER THIRTY-FIVE
Hugh

Life sure had its twists and turns, and Hugh and Dee were ready for some smooth sailing.

After the birth of their son, Hugh bought a new sailboat docked in the San Francisco marina, less than half the size of the yacht he'd inherited from his father all those years ago. He hired a captain to take it out for him so he could focus all his attention on his growing family.

At one time, he had doubted whether moving to Starlight Bay was the right place for them. Now, with baby Andrew, and Sylvi and Jack living in their new house nearby with baby Nora, the home on the beach was the perfect place after all.

His company was on a steady course for financial success, and all the rumors and gossip had stopped about Dee and that miserable Patrick. Life was joyous and exciting, and he couldn't wait for tomorrow.

In May, Hugh and Dee rummaged through the storage building attached to the beach house. They were looking for the photos Sylvi had asked about months earlier, of her and her sister Nora. Puffs of dust scattered as they shoved boxes around.

"Where did you say it was?" Hugh stood and stretched his back.

"I vaguely remember directing the movers to put the boxes with belongings on this side. It should be near the wood trunk with your mother's name engraved on the top."

Dee shoved two cardboard boxes aside to make a narrow walkway.

"My mother's? I know nothing about that." He moved quickly climbing over boxes and pushing things around.

"I'm so sorry, honey. I just assumed you knew what the contents were in that room. Never thought to mention I saw these two boxes."

"No need to apologize. I dumped an enormous task on you to manage the packing and moving. I never even asked you about it. You did an amazing job. Did I tell you?"

Dee looked at Hugh as if he had two heads and threw her hands in the air. "Why thank you! I've been waiting a year to hear that." She hugged him and planted a big kiss on his full lips.

"My behavior was inconsiderate for a long time. I'm lucky you've forgiven me and stuck by my side."

"Honey, we are in this together, through thick and thin. And there has been a lot of the thin the last year or so. But that's all behind us now." Dee continued to shuffle through boxes. "I found your mother's." Dee lifted a moving box off the top of a wood trunk. "Oh, and right next to it is Nora's Stuff. It's marked that way. See?"

Hugh picked up Nora's box and set it on top of another set of boxes. He started to open it, then stopped. "You know what? Let's just give this box to Sylvi. I know most of what is probably in here. Didn't realize it was still in the mansion. I assumed my father had gotten rid of her things when I left to travel abroad. Where did you find these again?"

"In that locked room, up on the third floor by stairs to the attic." She moved Nora's box out of the way.

"Really? I went in there after my father died to store more boxes of his. I didn't bother to look around, thinking it had nothing to do with me. Do you still have the keys? The chest is locked."

"Here they are. I remembered some of the trunks and metal boxes were locked." Dee handed Hugh a large ring with dozens of different keys.

Hugh stared at the large wooden trunk. The lid was engraved in finely chiseled scrollwork and the name Eleanor. One after another, Hugh attempted to fit keys into the trunk lock, until one worked.

He took a deep breath. "Would you please turn on the rest of the lights in here?"

Dee flipped the switches on the wall and the whole room lit up. "That's much better." Dee brought over two folding chairs for them to sit on while going through the trunk.

Hugh shook his head. "This is strange. There are envelopes addressed to my mother. But the name is different."

"What do mean?" Dee stood next to Hugh.

"It's addressed to Eleanor Lambreth Roth. I thought my mother's maiden name was Smythe, not Lambreth."

"Did she use her maiden name after she married your father?

"I don't think so. Any documents I've seen with her name only showed as Roth."

"Maybe there is information inside that will tell you more."

"This one is dated 1925. I knew my mother was British. She had an accent. But . . ."

"But what?" Dee peered over his shoulder. "What's that crest mean?"

"I'm not sure. This letter must be from my great-grandmother, it's signed, your loving Granny. Odd that she addressed the letter using mother's full name and not simply Eleanor Roth. But the return address says, The Right Honorable Baron Worthing and Baroness Worthing. What the heck? She says mother's grandfather had passed away. She's begging Mother to attend the funeral."

"Your great-grandfather was a Baron? Holy moly." Dee shook her head in disbelief.

Hugh tapped his temple with a finger. "I remember going to England with Mother when I was five or so. That would have been 1925. I remember everyone wearing black, but don't have a memory of the funeral. We stayed in an enormous ancient castle much larger than Rothmorton Hall. I thought it was a hotel, not the family homestead. Good God."

"Maybe your mother didn't want you to see the funeral. Some people say it's bad for little children."

"Maybe or I blocked it out."

"What's in the other envelope? When was it dated?"

"Seven months after the first letter. It's another letter from Granny. Mostly day-to-day stuff and thanking her for bringing me to meet the family and that she missed her. She wished we had stayed longer than six months, and that my father should have been there. I don't remember that. She writes that my mother's Uncle Jonathan Lambreth Jr. officially became the 20th Baron of Worthing. A formal invitation should have been sent. Hmmm. There isn't one in the chest, so my father must have tossed it."

"Oh Hugh. This must be very upsetting for you." She rubbed his arm and leaned her head on his shoulder, trying to read the letter.

"She mentions a cousin, Edward Lambreth, Jr. and his family, blah, blah, blah. I don't recognize any of these names." He let out a frustrated sigh. "Why wasn't I told any of this?"

"I think you need to write to your great-uncle at this address and tell him you just found out about all this and ask if there is anything you need to do. I'm simply floored."

"Excellent idea. I'm sure my great-grandmother had passed away." Hugh's face fell. "I wish I could remember her."

"Does this mean you are nobility? Do I need to address you differently?" Dee sat up straight.

"It appears I am of a noble family in England, but of course, not in the U.S. I certainly wouldn't have a title. What little I know it's handed down from paternal oldest sons. I feel so strange about it. It's been forty years!" He placed the letters in the trunk.

"When they find out you never knew, they should understand it wasn't by choice."

"Did my father notify them that my mother had died? Did any of them come to the funeral and I not understand who they were? I was seven then and my memory is clearer, but not who the people were. There were hordes of them. Why didn't my father tell me about mother's family?"

"Must have been some kind of conflict between your mother and her family. For marrying an American and moving here?"

"That makes sense. But, why not tell me?" His eyes squeezed out a few rare tears. "You know how I hate being so emotional. It's overwhelming. All this time I believed there was no family of my mother's."

"This also sounds like classic Hugh Senior. I'm sure a lot of old feelings are resurfacing. It's perfectly understandable. You've told me how controlling your father was. Maybe it was between him and her family."

"I think you are right. It must have been my father. He was so possessive. That's why he pushed me so hard to be what he wanted me to be."

Dee lifted a few other items in the trunk and pulled out a square blue velvet hinged box. "This looks like a jewelry box. May I open it?"

"Of course."

When Dee opened the box, she gasped. "Oh, my!" Inside was a heavily ornate necklace of diamonds and rubies set in gold. "There's a card. It says, 'from Mother, for your coming out.'"

"Like the debutantes here?"

"I assume. I'm afraid the little I know of British nobility is what I've read in gothic romance novels." Dee laughed half-heartedly.

Hugh touched the necklace and sighed. "My father took all my mother's jewels and locked them in the family vault in Boston. Like the sapphire necklace I gave you. That was hers. I need to have those transferred here. But this necklace was mother's from before their marriage. I guess that's why he left it in her trunk."

"Probably. What else is in the trunk?"

"A few other pieces of jewelry. You might like to wear them. Lots of letters. I should read them. Later, I suppose. Here are more photos. But since I don't know who my family is, the names she's written on the backs mean nothing to me. Oh, this one is my mother with an older woman and man. Maybe they are my grandparents. I was told they died during an air raid in London the end of WWI. You know, let's take the whole trunk into the house. I'll look at them later, when I've collected myself and eventually, I can get some information to help identify them."

"When did your parents get married?"

"1919, after the war ended. Dad met her there. They got married and came to Rothmorton Hall. I was born in 1920, so . . ." He wiped away the tears and cleared his throat.

"Was your father in the service during WWI? He would have been, what, almost forty?

"He wasn't in the service. I don't know why he was in England. He would have been forty-three in 1920."

"Well, it looks like you have a lot of family history to get caught up on."

"No kidding. Is it odd I've not heard anything from the family?"

"I'm guessing again here, but if anything had changed since 1927, I'm sure they would have contacted you. We don't know what the situation was between your parents and them. Maybe your father severed all the ties after your mother passed away. Nothing for you to be worried about right now or feel guilty about. When you write and they get back to you, we'll know a lot more and maybe we could go visit the family castle and meet the relatives?"

"What you just said . . . sounds like some kind of fairytale." Hugh laughed and rolled his eyes.

"It does. Will you tell Ellen?" Dee wrapped the photos, the necklace case, and the other small box of jewelry in packing paper.

"No. Let's keep all of this under wraps until I hear from my uncle. Okay?"

"I agree. I'm excited though." She hugged Hugh and a broad smile stretched across her face.

"Me too. In the meantime, I'll have Darius investigate the family name in England and see what he can find out." Hugh took a last look around the storage. "I need to go through all of this . . . one day." He ran his hands through his hair. "Today has taken a toll on me. I need a drink. You?"

Dee nodded and placed the wrapped items back in the trunk and they each took one handle on the sides and carried it into Hugh's home office.

❧

Hugh sent a letter to his great-uncle the next day. It took a while before he received a response. Uncle Jonathan expressed his and the rest of the family's joy in connecting with Hugh and extended an open invitation for his family to visit.

Feeling complete with his nuclear family and now the connection to more family in England, Hugh and Dee shared the wonderful news with Ellen. They planned to travel to England to meet the rest of the family as soon as it could be arranged.

CHAPTER THIRTY-SIX
ELLEN

My freshman year ended, and the summer was upon me. I sat at my desk, pasting items into my scrapbook. All the memorable events from the past year. The letters and the Christmas card from Adam, the program to *Carousel*, and letters and cards from Kathy in Plymouth. Also, all the photos I'd taken since my last birthday. I had one enlarged of Adam standing next to his long board the day we first met. I put it in a mother-of-pearl frame and it sat on my desk next to the photo Mom took of Adam and me the night of our first dance. My first boyfriend and first love. So many firsts. Would we stand the test of time? Did it really matter? I was learning to enjoy what we had together as each day came. On the wall above my desk were photos of my late mother, Nora. One photo was of my mother with Aunt Sylvi, taken when they were teenagers. Another was a reproduction of a larger photo from Nora's box of stuff, the same as the tiny photo in Aunt Sylvi's locket. My treasures.

Right after Christmas, Dana disappeared. No one knew what happened, just that she and her mom, Connie, packed up and moved out of the apartment, and neither said goodbye to anyone. At least anyone I knew. Strange. I hoped they found some peace and happiness wherever they were.

Aunt Sylvi and Uncle Jack found a house with a yard closer to us to raise their baby girl, Nora. I thought it was cool to have a cousin named after my birth mother. Dad seemed very pleased. Our family was growing, and it's great having them nearby.

Mom and Dad had promised me a big birthday party this year, so I was already planning for it. This one would be all my classmates from school, of course Adam and my parents' friends too. It will be a blast with a live band to play my kind of music, too. I could hardly wait.

Mom came in holding the newest addition to our family. Two-month-old baby Andrew.

"What are you up to, sweetheart?" Mom sat on the bed and lay Andrew down while spreading out the lightweight blanket, careful not to wake him.

"Filling my scrapbook. He sure does sleep sound."

"Thankfully. But let's still keep our voices down."

Mom looked fabulous. Having a baby made her glow. However, she had become obsessed with the bathroom scale, watching for her pre-pregnancy weight to return. Even though her doctor said it could take up to a year.

"Mom, this baby is different, isn't he?"

"Different how?"

"You know, because he comes from you and Daddy. He's your *real* child." I tried not to appear sad, but Mom could always read me.

"Yes, he comes from your father and me. He bonds the two of us together, but it would never affect the relationship we have with you. You are our *real* child too. Our daughter, and nothing will ever change that. Andrew is the newest, but we don't love him more than we love you."

"Sure about that?" I furrowed my brow.

"I'm positive. And . . . he will look up to you as his older sister. You will play a very important part in Andrew's life."

"I like the sound of that." I grinned.

Andrew rustled. He awakened, and as soon as he saw Mom, he smiled.

"Would you like to hold him?"

"Sure." Mom placed Andrew in my arms. He wore a summer one-piece and held a little plastic rattle in his hand. I gently rocked him, touching his little fingers that gripped mine with surprising strength. The little wisps of dark hair had grown into a velvety covering. The same color as Dad's. After talking to Mom, I looked at him in a new way. Not my parents' baby, but my brother and it was crazy how fast I fell in love with him.

There was a tap at the door. "Is there room for one more in here?" Dad stood waiting.

Mom waved him in and together the four of us bonded as a thoroughly happy family.

ABOUT THE AUTHOR

An award-winning author, P. L. Jonas, has a creative spirit with a passion for literature, art, and music. She began writing fiction after a long career in marketing and technical writing and editing. A native Arizonan, she has traveled all over the U.S. and ten other countries. Drawing on her personal experience, a fascination with history, and a love of research, she weaves intricate stories of romance, sci-fi/fantasy, historical fiction, and suspense. When not writing, she is reading or painting while her beloved cat looks on.

In 2023, The Historical Fiction Company Highly Recommended 5-Star Award for *Hall of Deception*, Book 1 of *The Roth Saga*.

In 2021, she received First Place, Goethe category, Chanticleer Book Awards, late historical fiction.

". . . a well-written and compelling historical novel
that seamlessly weaves romance and suspense into a gripping tale. . ."
– The Historical Fiction Company, Highly Recommended 5-Star Award 2023

HALL
of
DECEPTION
A Post WWII Romantic Suspense

P. L. JONAS

NOTE FROM P.L. JONAS

Word-of-mouth is crucial for any author to succeed. If you enjoyed *Sea of Doubt*, please leave a review online—anywhere you are able. Even if it's just a sentence or two. It would make all the difference and would be very much appreciated.

Thanks!
P.L. Jonas

We hope you enjoyed reading this title from:

www.blackrosewriting.com

Subscribe to our mailing list – *The Rosevine* – and receive **FREE** books, daily deals, and stay current with news about upcoming releases and our hottest authors.
Scan the QR code below to sign up.

Already a subscriber? Please accept a sincere thank you for being a fan of Black Rose Writing authors.

View other Black Rose Writing titles at www.blackrosewriting.com/books and use promo code **PRINT** to receive a **20% discount** when purchasing.